Dr. One

a novel by

Peter Galarneau Jr.

ISBN: 978-0-9908653-4-6

Body text set in Times New Roman

This book is printed on acid-free paper.

Printed in the United States of America

Cover Design by: Peter Galarneau Jr.

Published by:

PTW

P.T. WILLIAM PUBLISHING CO.

PT William Publishing Co
8 First Street
Buckhannon, WV 26201

www.PTWilliam.com

also by Peter Galarneau Jr.

Short Stories

The Worms Within Us (1994)

The Edge of Hell (1994)

Blood Barters (1996)

Muldoon's Nursery (1997)

O-Time: PUSH* (2010)

Novels

The Cubit: The 2012 Trilogy I (2008)

The Djed: The 2012 Trilogy II (2009)

Journey of the Daggers:
The Complete 2012 Trilogy (2012)

Novellas

Crazy House (2014)

Thank You

To the artists, sound designers, videographers and other creatives who have made their works available on Pixabay, Freesound, and Videezy.

To Zappar for its incredible Augmented Reality web app that provided a unique and perfect accent to this novel.

To the great writers and researchers and editors who fill the pages with technology and business and foresight at three of my favorite publications: WIRED, Fast Company and Inc.

To my devoted fans who have supported me since my first novel "The Cubit."

For My
Wife

"...we receive as friendly that which agrees with, we resist with dislike that which opposes us; whereas the very reverse is required by every dictate of common sense."

— Michael Faraday

Thursday, May 23, 2041
Marlinton, WV

Shaun didn't know Dr. One had returned home until he almost tripped over the scientist's body. The emerald glow that had lured him into the riverside house so late at night filtered into the stark darkness from behind the shadow of a couch to his right, providing only enough light for him to realize that the green twinkle reflection from the old man's eyeball wasn't quite right.

He snapped on a penlight and moved it in a slow arc across the familiar living room darkness, looking for an intruder, crouching instinctively as he did so. Cicadas were out by the millions and had taken control of the Greenbrier Valley, their unified, background buzz adding to Shaun's anxiety. He pointed the penlight at the passage into the kitchen to his left and lit up a small corner just inside the doorway, but the light revealed no one. He then pointed the beam straight down and onto Dr. One's face. One eyeball bulged from the socket. The other was completely gone. Oddly, there was no blood, anywhere.

Shaun hiccupped some pizza sauce and tottered backward until his hands crashed against the back of the couch. The penlight dropped, bounced a couple of times on the hardwood floor, and rolled straight for the body. It stopped short of the doctor's outstretched right arm.

He pushed away from the couch and turned toward the source of the light behind him. A tube of glowing green liquid, about a foot long and an inch thick that reminded him of those emergency sticks you break and then throw into dark recesses, lay on the floor in front of the couch. Its invisible energy tickled the thin hairs on Shaun's arms and the more impressive swatches of black beard on his maturing adolescent face, and undulated with a slow rhythm that matched the cicadas' nocturnal hum.

"Dr. One?" he whispered while turning back around; he didn't expect an answer but the sound of his own voice helped alleviate the weight of death. "Should I call the cops?"

Wait! he thought. *Should he? Really?* He'd be the prime suspect! They'd make up some motive and then the data hoard would begin, his life sucked from every digital crevice available, sewing the Story of Shaun Winston as completely as the data-crunching brains of 2041 could render. They'd find something: perhaps his charge for peeing in public a year ago would be all they'd need to conjure up some behavioral trait for murder.

The glow stick behind him began to quickly fade and was completely out within seconds, making the penlight halo of the right side of Dr. One's body a main feature in the brash darkness and cicadas' million-voice orchestra.

Shaun stared at the shadowed face he could not see and was suddenly gripped with remorse. He'd known Dr. One for the past two years, but had built a relationship only to the extent that he collected his caretaking money and was told what his monthly tasks would be which, for the most part, included a once or twice check of the home's interior and lawn maintenance.

The penlight flickered and died, leaving Shaun in total darkness that the cicadas seemed to applaud as their voices rose in unison. Once Shaun's sight adjusted, he saw the darker outline of Dr. One on the floor and something else hovering right above him: tiny pinpoints of light so small only the complete darkness in the room revealed their presence. They moved in unison, about a dozen of them, as a mixed collection of red, green and blue specks. They floated like electric bugs and suddenly dropped toward Dr. One's shadow and disappeared.

Shaun stepped closer as if trying to sneak up on what he *thought* he'd just seen. It spooked him. It could not have been real. It made him feel as if he was losing the sanity he'd been able to maintain so far.

But there it was, still hovering, now situated just a couple of inches above the one remaining eyeball, a speck of colorful specks. They seemed curious of the dead eye and Shaun gasped when three, tiny green light beams that were thinner than the thinnest hair shot from the color speck and landed on the eyeball's gray iris. It was hard to see (the beams were so small) but it looked as if they were scanning it. This lasted a couple of seconds before the beams disappeared and the color speck flew quickly out of sight.

Shaun's head buzzed…all of those cicadas…all of this unreality. He opened his jaw wide to clear his popping ears and heard faint sirens that were getting closer. Perhaps, he thought, the doctor had called for help before he'd been killed. Maybe, he was just paranoid and the sirens weren't even headed to Dr. One's house. Regardless, he wasn't going to stick around to find out.

He ran from the house, sprinted up a short, grassy embankment and through a landscaping of maples and oaks, and crouched behind a shoulder-high bush about fifty yards away. The sirens remained distant as three black SUVs, that in no way looked like emergency vehicles, pulled into Dr. One's long, gravel driveway. Five of the local white suits got out of the three vehicles and quickly moved into the house. As far as Shaun could tell, none of them had guns drawn. The last person into the house carried a briefcase.

The cicadas' pitch was deafening. They were everywhere. A distant streetlight revealed dozens of them looking at him with red bulbous eyes from within the bush just a foot in front of his face.

It took about ten minutes before the group exited. They were in no hurry. The man with the briefcase was actually smiling. They eased into the SUVs, the man with the briefcase taking the last one alone, and all three backed out of the driveway and disappeared into the orchestra of the black night.

Shaun slowly stood and stared, perplexed, at the house.

What about Dr. One? he thought. *What about the murdered body he'd discovered? It was still in there. What did they do? Stash it somewhere? The house had an attic and some pretty deep closets. But why? Why didn't they just take it? Because they doctored it up! They changed it in some way. Investigators would come to the wrong conclusion. They'd pin it on the wrong person. They'd discover that a soon-to-be-eighteen-year-old who curiously remained off the Net was very capable of such a crime.*

Shaun ran from the bushes, thinking that his freedom was short, that someone would be coming for him and it wouldn't be long.

◎ ◎ ◎ ◎ ◎

In the dark, it was impossible to see Dr. One's house from his bedroom window but that didn't deter Shaun from sitting there, staring through the mucky screen and smeary glass for most of the night, calculating what might come next. The white suits would return but this time they'd be coming for him. At that point, Shaun would run from his mother's doublewide trailer. He'd move swiftly, taking the wooded back routes through parts of Marlinton that only teenagers who'd grown up in the town knew. There was a tree house that he and his two best friends had built about a mile beyond the west bank of the Greenbrier. There was a sinkhole with a shallow cave that they'd discovered when they were just kids another mile beyond that. An old sawmill provided a third option for getting away from cranky parents and boring school but it was located even farther up the western ridge. The white suits would never find him in any of these places. Then he'd use his wireless decader to send out the emergency code, one that he and Adam and Chris had agreed to use many years ago, back when they were six years old, back when the water terrorists and the Great Flood had changed everything. The code was a mix of old-school emoji and alpha numerals—one that, if intercepted, would make no sense to the interceptors. The last three characters of the code denoted one of the three locations where all of them were to meet—any time, any day. Sending the code meant that something was terribly wrong.

Like the day five years ago when Adam's father had gotten incredibly drunk once again, had slapped his mother through their porch door screen, had pulled out his 9mm, and had fired at Adam's bedroom door. Shaun and Chris had found him at the sawmill, terrified to immobility. The police had taken Adam's father away and had put him in one of the new virtual cells up in Huttonsville where, as far as Shaun knew, he still remained, a prisoner of the same technology by which everyone outside jails and prisons were allowing themselves to be reformed in *free* society. Adam's mother now had a boyfriend who was a really cool guy in comparison. They were waiting for the divorce courts to settle so they could get married.

The cicadas had not quieted in the least and their buzzing was a reminder of what Shaun had seen: the bulging eyeball, the green glow stick, the tiny, flying multicolored light speck. The cicadas were a reminder that everything eventually dies: high school, adolescence, Dr. One. In two days, he'd graduate and turn eighteen. Youth, by that account, would also die and the fear of being an adult without an apparent path into the future would jump all over him.

Like it was doing right now.

Mixing in with the fear of the white suits.

Taking his nerves to new extremes.

Causing him to cry.

Around three o'clock, Shaun did see headlights but they were from his mother's old pickup. When she entered the trailer, Shaun was tempted to run to her, to tell her all about it, to release the menagerie of emotions that were about to explode from within, but such a conversation would be useless. As a bartender at the Water Spout, she'd be tipsy and tired and unwilling to talk about anything until the next morning. She was a good person, had raised him all by herself since his father had disappeared, but she just didn't have a very good ear and her patience was never good at the end of a long shift.

Water flowed in the kitchen sink, the refrigerator door opened and closed, she said something that Shaun could not understand, then her bedroom door creaked in both directions as she entered the room to sleep away Friday morning.

The trailer again fell silent except for the cicadas. He grabbed the wooden chair from his small study desk, set the chair down in the opposite direction in front of the window, placed his arms across the chair's backrest, dropped his chin onto the back of his hands, and stared at the darkness that hid Dr. One's house.

Why did they murder him? What was that light speck? What has he going to do about it?

Suddenly, outside the dirty glass window, he thought he saw an orange and black monarch butterfly, which added to the nonsensical nature of the entire evening. It flapped against the window a couple of times then meandered into the darkness.

Shaun's eyelids fluttered like the monarch's wings and the song of the cicadas embraced him.

◎ ◎ ◎ ◎ ◎

All he'd needed was a little bit of sleep and a dream memory to tell him what to do.

When he woke, still in the chair, his fingers were numb and his neck felt as if it had been tied in knots. The morning sun blazed through the cruddy window and the cicada buzz had fallen in volume. It was around nine o'clock and he had an answer: the Great Big Thing. He would not send out the emergency code.

He would not take refuge in one of his juvenile hiding places. And he would not, still, tell his mother what had happened or what he had decided to do about it. Paramount in importance, right now, was to act like an adult, cool and levelheaded, with fear as baggage but not as his director. He had to find answers and they were waiting at the Great Big Thing.

Dr. One had a niece who worked with him up at the Great Big Thing, a fond term the locals gave to the enormous radio telescope in Green Bank. Shaun had met her twice, both times when she'd accompanied the doctor to his Marlinton home. Her name was Phoenix.

Back when Shaun was sixteen, when Dr. One had first purchased the house, she'd helped her uncle move in. Shaun had been mowing the lawn around the trailer and had noticed the moving van. New neighbors in Marlinton were always a big deal but Dr. One's entry into the community had taken on a special, gossipy appeal. That house was expensive and its proximity to the lower income properties and riverside cabins made it stand out not only because of its polarizing beauty but more so because of its history.

A real estate mogul had built it back in the mid-30s when his company had come into town in an attempt to revitalize the Great Flood's devastation. Before the flood, the west side of the river had been mostly commercial and industrial where shopping and eating and trucking had all lived together along Route 219.

But the high water had decimated those businesses. The mogul had wanted to turn the west bank into a residential paradise, particularly since there had been so much interest in land near fresh water sources after the water terrorists attacks in 2029. The mogul had assumed that city folks in search of nature's alternative would flock to his new development and the first house he'd built, as a showcase, was his own. For two years, the house had stuck out like a beautiful sore thumb as development of similar homes hit a snag. Apparently, there had been much less interest in high-priced real estate than the mogul had anticipated. Land had been cleared and new landscaping had been started, but no more homes had ever been built. When the mogul had finally given up and had left Marlinton, housing that was much more affordable to those around town had been developed instead, including the trailer park in which Shaun lived. The mogul mansion, as it had come to be known, had been empty since.

For Shaun, though, his curiosity of the new owner had been much less to do with gossipy appeal. Shaun's interest had been for the woman he'd seen helping the doctor move in and the fleeting fancy of having such a beautiful woman live so close to him. That was the reason why he'd walked over that day. That's the reason why he'd met Dr. One and had gotten the job of caretaker.

It had been in the fall and the day had been

very breezy. The many colored leaves had whipped through the woman's long blonde hair in a way that had reminded him of so many commercials where beautiful women sold with sex. She'd been wearing a red skirt that blew tantalizingly upward to reveal legs that had energized Shaun's dreams for many weeks. Knowing that she was in her mid-twenties had not helped either. An older, gorgeous woman was going to be his neighbor.

He'd spent the day helping them move in but had said very little to the woman beyond *My name is Shaun* and *Where do you want this?* and *Let me help you with that box*. When she'd told him her name was Phoenix, well…that had locked in his newfound crush: a beautiful name for a beautiful woman. And she was going to be living right next him, within eyesight, for every day to come.

But when the doctor had offered him the job of taking care of the lawn and looking after the house while he was gone, that the house would serve Dr. One as a second home in which he would visit just once a month, the Phoenix fantasy had been dashed.

He'd seen her just once since then and that had only been a month ago. She'd been on Dr. One's back porch, sitting on the bench swing, while Shaun had been pruning one of the doctor's young red apple trees. Her hair had been shorter and she'd been wearing jeans and a t-shirt that had a picture of the Green Bank Telescope with the words "Great Big Thing" printed in an arc above it. She'd waved and had said *Hello* but Shaun had not been brave enough to start a conversation.

Hello. Shaun?

She'd called him over and he'd moved in that direction.

Shaun, isn't it?

He'd nodded.

I want you to know that, if you need me, you know where I'll be.

This was the memory that woke him, still seated in front of his dirty window. A month ago, he'd thought that she was coming on to him. Now, her words took on a whole new meaning: a warning, perhaps. Phoenix had known something bad might happen to her uncle and she'd offered herself as a choice. He could stay in Marlinton and face an investigation that would certainly center on him, the neighbor lawn boy, or he could get the hell out of town and find comfort and safety away from misguided fault, and that's exactly what he was going to do.

He could tell no one, of course, of his intended destination—not his mom and, particularly, not his friends. Adam and Chris were incredible gossipers. One word to either of them and, through their digital connections, the world would know.

When he rose from the chair, his knees buckled for a moment and he bent over to stretch out the stiffness. He replaced his chair in front of his study desk and stood next to his mountain bike that leaned against the white wall to the left of the chair. Atop the desk stood a tall, wood-framed mirror. He took off his t-shirt and, in the reflection, saw the man he was about to become, one who was an inch over six feet but still growing. He'd been pushing more weights recently so his upper body looked lean and strong. He wished his beard had matured more but, for entry into adulthood, he'd have to go with patchy. On the desktop below was a scattered reminder of his current status in life:

A dog-eared and dirty piece of paper with the words "Application for U.S. Registry" that he'd had for many months but had yet to fill out because to do so would have meant giving up personal information to the Net.

Three spiral notebooks that he'd used in school instead of complying with the teachers' preferred method of digital memory because to do so would have meant giving up personal information to the Net.

The remainder of last week's pay from the bike shop, a folded wad of three ones, one five and one ten, instead of an eCash account that would have meant giving up personal information to the Net.

Shaun was as bad as all of the crony old retirees in town…at least that's what his mother always said. He needed to get registered, not only because it was the law, but because it would allow him to get a car and get the hell out of Marlinton to a place where he could be more successful.

Over the past four years she'd been constantly harassed by the high school to "make" Shaun conform, but he'd always known that no one could dismiss a good student like him for learning by his own preferred pencil and paper method.

As for the hard cash…that was a concern that she'd let slide, mostly because she, too, dealt with currency since tip jars in Marlinton had not yet fully converted to digital touch technology. She had agreed that having real money in hand was better than relying on a Net that was susceptible to hacking, and losing just one dollar in a household as poor as theirs would have meant too much uncertainty.

At least, that's what she always said. Truth was, they weren't as bad off as she wanted him to believe. They lived in a decent trailer that had many modern furnishings, including a VR-ready flat screen that could not be fully appreciated since they lacked the funds to buy the necessary VR-enabling hardware. They had a refrigerator with an intelligent monitoring sensor that had never been used because they had never been able to afford the connection fees. She'd even bought him an older smartphone, a decader they were called, one with a keyboard, so that he could broaden his social circles and not remain in such solitude, but its use was limited in a town so close to Green Bank.

She tried…she really did. She was a loving mother. She rarely raised her voice. And she was careful in choosing the men she dated, never once bringing any of them home because she still believed that Shaun had only one father, the one that had disappeared during the Great Flood.

He pulled on a pair of shorts that would hold up well for the thirty-mile bicycle trip he was about to take, slipped a white t-shirt over his head that promoted the Greenbrier River Trail, and shoved his cash and decader in one shorts pocket. He'd need some water and food but he didn't want to wake his mother, so he decided to fuel up at the bike shop. Slowly, he rolled his bike from his bedroom to the trailer's front door and his mother yelled out to him just before he could exit.

"Shaun? I thought you were off work today."

"I am. Just gonna get a little morning ride in."

"You going down to the Registry today?"

Uh-oh, he thought. He didn't want to start another argument—not now. "A little bit later," he said. It wasn't a complete lie. Even if he went next week, that would be a little bit later.

"Be careful," she said and he closed the trailer door.

◉ ◉ ◉ ◉ ◉

Shaun rode across the Great Flood Memorial Bridge and looked down over the railing. The Greenbrier was already bustling with activity with the Memorial Day weekend coming up. The crystal fresh river water had swelled from plentiful May showers and lifeguards stood on their towers, whistling at vacationers who wandered too far toward its deep center.

After the Great Flood of 2030, Marlinton officials had decided that part of the town's rebuilding efforts would include a reconstructed riverbank that resembled a wide sandy beach much like one you'd find at the ocean. There were umbrellas and beach chairs and lots of white-skinned sunbathers. Beach shop outfitters and restaurants and a few two-story motels stood in one long line from the bridge in both directions. It had taken a few years to catch on, the idea of a beach side riverfront, but it had paid off: Marlinton would nearly double in population for the majority of the months that extended from late May to early September.

Shaun worked at an outfitter two blocks from the riverfront in a location that provided a buffer for him from the crowds. Being in the midst of all those city folk was unnerving. His impatience with their ignorance tended to steer him away from the beach. Jennifer Outfitters was far enough away that the masses never really inundated the shop. As an additional plus, his job entailed staying inside for most of the workday. He'd sign up cabin rentals and bike rentals and occasionally escort diners to the shop's attached restaurant appropriately named The Greenhouse, but the majority of his responsibilities was in bicycle repair. Vacationers tended to treat their rentals rather badly. It seemed that most didn't even know how to ride, let alone know how to take care of their rides.

He wove his bike through pedestrian traffic, remaining as polite as he could be, remembering what Jennifer had told him: that he was an extension to the business—that even outside the shop he was representing. Jennifer Collins was a great boss. She'd moved to Marlinton back in the mid-30s after she and her family had finally given up on Tucson's efforts to reclaim the desert after the terrorists attacks. Tucson had become a ghost city, she'd told him. Water was so scarce there that much of the population that had remained resembled third world poverty. *You should be lucky to have lived in such a prosperous town as Marlinton*, she'd often remind him. In Jennifer's vocabulary, prosperous seemed to infer easy access to fresh water.

He parked his bike behind the shop and entered through the back door that led into the repair room. Jennifer's youngest son was busy fixing a flat tire when he entered. Bobby reminded him a lot of himself when he'd started working at the shop three years back. Still a little green at the edges (not only as it applied to bicycle repairs but also to life itself), Shaun often thought of Bobby as a younger brother, one who needed the guidance that only a sibling could offer.

Bobby looked up from the tire. "Shauner," he said. "I thought you were off this week."

Shaun walked over and looked at Bobby's work. "That tube has already seen too many repairs." He pointed at four other patches. "It's a gonner. It needs a new one. I'd hate to see you hauling off down the trail to rescue some stranded kid a few miles away."

Bobby stared at the patch, scowled for a moment, then tossed the tube onto a small pile of unwanted bike parts. A smile crept onto his lips. "You're right." He walked over to a bookcase where boxes of new tubes were stacked in categorized sizes. "You can't always rely on what the Net tells you. Sometimes you gotta go with instinct." He repeated aloud this common "Shaunerish," as he called it, which he used to describe Shaun's frequent reminders about relying too much on information found in the digital world. Bobby respected Shaun's Shaunerisms unlike so many others, including Shaun's mother. Most people thought that Shaun was just too paranoid. Bobby unraveled the tube from the box. "So, what gives?"

"Taking a ride up the trail," Shaun said. "Stopped in to grab some energy for the trek."

Bobby laid the limp tube across the back of the bike's frame. "Mom got some new squirts in this morning," he said. "They're from the Cheat. Pure energy. West Virginia wildwater."

"Flavored?" Shaun asked, knowing what the answer might be.

Bobby huffed as if the word was toxic. "Yeah, right. Orange and purple-flavored. Colors to appease the outsiders. West Virginia lake-flavored of course."

His words mimicked Jennifer's reminder that Appalachian fresh water was the reason many people came to Marlinton. "Color sells…" Shaun began.

"But our water provides," Bobby finished. Shaun offered a high-five that Bobby immediately slapped. "Front side's got a lot of people today. Most we've seen this early in the season. The Greenhouse has seen a lot of traffic, too. Mom mentioned more than once that she wishes you were here. She…" he paused for a moment, "…we understand, though. Graduating is the bigger deal."

Graduation, Shaun thought. He doubted that he'd be in Marlinton tomorrow. He wondered what might happen before he even got to Green Bank. He wondered what would happen once he found Phoenix.

"You good, Shauner?" Bobby asked.

Shaun blinked. "Just thinkin'."

"I wish I was graduating."

Shaun forced a smile. "Say that now but take your time. Trust me."

"Times all we got," he replied with another Shaunerism and turned his attention to the bike repair.

Shaun left Bobby to his work, happier for a moment because, just perhaps, he'd lent some wisdom to the boy's mind. As he neared the wooden door that led to the front of the shop, he paused. A small window in the door at face height allowed him to see beyond several new bicycles sitting in the sales racks in the middle of the floor to a white suit who stood at the front counter next to Jennifer. Shaun pushed the door open just a bit so that he could hear a conversation that was muffled by the shop's low volume internal sound system. Bluegrass mixed with Jennifer's voice.

"...not here," she said. "Probably at home."

...I've got those Blue Ridge Mountain blues...

"No." said the white suit. He didn't smile. They rarely smiled. "Just came from there."

"Well, I can't help you any more than that."

...Every day I'm counting 'til I find that mountain...

The white suit glanced over at the door window and Shaun quickly ducked. He held the door ajar with one finger. "When you see him, let him know that we'd like to talk to him."

Jennifer remained rigid in her response. "You'll probably see him before I do."

...On that Blue Ridge far away...

The white suit didn't answer, turned away, walked to the shop's entrance, peered once more toward the repair room, then exited.

Shaun waited a couple of minutes before entering

the front of the shop. Jennifer stood staring beyond the glass, storefront door as he approached. "What was that about?" he asked before Jennifer turned around. When she did, a curt smile grabbed her lips.

"I hate those guys," she said. "Always suspicious. Always making everyone else suspicious. Makes you wonder what this country is coming to." Short dark hair touched the shoulders of a t-shirt that was exactly like Shaun's except hers was forest green in color. The small diamond stud in her right nostril sparkled in the light coming through the glass door and it reminded Shaun of the light speck he'd seen hovering over Dr. One's dead body. "He asked about you. Is everything copacetic?"

"Copa…?" Shaun replied as his mind searched for the word's meaning. "Yeah. Copacetic. It's just that…"

Her smile faltered.

"It's just the same old thing," Shaun continued. "The suits are always curious about those who aren't squarely on their Net."

Jennifer knew something more was going on; he could tell by her stern, motherly look. "You still haven't gotten your card, have you? They can't stand it when citizens don't do what they expect them to do. You go on being who you want to be. You're not required to register…at least not yet. You still have another day."

A moment of uncertain silence between them left nothing but the low volume bluegrass banjos that suddenly skipped in harmony. Jennifer walked past him to a turntable where a vinyl disc revolved and popped under the needle. She tapped the turntable's arm and the banjos regained fluid revolutions across the vinyl's grooves.

"You can't do that with digital recordings," she said. "So, what brings you in on your day off? I'd think you'd be preparing for your big eighteen and graduation."

"I'm gonna take a ride north. Just stopped in for some fuel for the trail. Bobby said you got some new Cheat Lake squirts."

"Uh-huh." Jennifer bent down then stood with a cardboard box in both hands. She reached inside and pulled out a handful of small, flexible bottles. A colorful orange and purple emblem of the Cheat Lake brand labeled each. "Three? Four?"

"Four. Thanks. And a couple of nut bars would help, too."

"No breakfast yet?" She handed him four bottles and plucked a couple of nut bars from the shelf behind her. She added a small backpack with which he could carry everything. "Why don't you get a quick bite in the Greenhouse? Egg protein would do you some good."

"Not enough time. Gotta get going." He looked out the storefront door where pedestrian traffic had not yet reached its holiday morning peak. Jennifer followed his gaze.

"I don't know what's up, Shaun, but I figure it has something more to do than a worry about registering with the government. You've never steered me wrong and I appreciate that."

It could have been an attempt to get him to tell but Shaun believed she was truly concerned. He felt bad for not telling her the complete truth but he didn't want to pull her into all of it, especially since he didn't know all of it himself. "Yes. Got it covered."

"See you at graduation tomorrow?"

Shaun forced a smile. "Thanks," he said and tried to walk less quickly than he really wanted to. He went through the repair room, waved at Bobby and exited the back of the shop.

◎ ◎ ◎ ◎ ◎

The river trail crossed through Marlinton just a few dozen yards from Jennifer Outfitters but Shaun decided to ride a few blocks north and catch the trail where it was more likely to be less crowded. Though he felt pressured by them after last night, men in white suits walking the streets was not unique or even particularly odd in Marlinton, and had not been since the federal government had decided to label the popular mountain vacation spot a "watch town," as in one to be watched, as in one that bordered precious fresh water, as in one that could succumb to violent attacks...as in one that needed protecting. The white suits, as the townies called them, didn't really wear white suits—they were more like white uniforms with unobtrusive gold braiding at the shoulders and cuffs. They wore gold badges, carried holstered guns, and were equipped with the very latest in personal digital surveillance, though in a town so close to the Great Big Thing, connections to the Net were limited—at least they were for the civilians. These men (and at least one female that Shaun had seen within the last month) were security-for-hire from one of the three big private companies in the U.S., groups sent to monitor and patrol and survey and thus promote suspicion. He'd seen how the community had responded. Friends didn't trust friends. Families didn't trust each other. On the surface, you would have never guessed. Familiar "Hellos" and cordial greetings had survived but Shaun knew this was all cover talk for paranoia. The white suits were a metaphor of the world as it had become.

He hopped his bike from the curb and cruised carefully on the asphalt. Traffic wasn't much of a problem in the winter and early spring months but that always changed after Memorial Day. He was more concerned about the mindset of the vacationing drivers. So many would come from the New Cities where automated navigation of electric vehicles never required operators to pay much attention. Accidents in Marlinton always rose in direct proportion to the number of visiting outsiders.

Riding north from the center of town was like moving back in history. After the Great Flood, many of the buildings from the town's hub in a four-block radius had been totally rebuilt. Leaders had done a pretty good job of maintaining the face of his rural homestead, using brick and stone and wood instead of the new, fancy compounds found all over the New Cities, but they'd cared less about saving the residential houses beyond a radius where most businesses prospered. Much of the "crony old retirees," as his mother called them, lived in these homes. They'd used their own savings and the sweat of family bonds to rebuild instead of accepting government funds that had been offered in limited portions. Shaun's heart and soul remained anchored to this heritage, where the past unparalleled the present, regardless of the incessant pressures by peers and his mother to move out and explore what they said the world had to offer.

It was close to ten o'clock and lots of people were wandering the sidewalks, looking for deals on items they couldn't find in the places from which they came. Artisan water was a favorite. Marlinton sold a ton of it. There were at least a dozen bottlers within and around the town. The Greenbrier River and several of its attached tributaries and springs were their sources. Greenbrier Tea, Knapp's Pure, Stony Creek Fresh and Lost Spring were the biggest sellers. Each had their own special taste, their own secret ingredients, their own choice of colors, and their own personality much like the wide variety of craft beers that were also purchased and transported back to the New Cities by the cases.

He rode along the final block of the residential outskirts where Greenbrier Tea had its central office. A few years back, around the same time that Jennifer Collins had opened The Greenhouse, the bottling company had built its own adjoining restaurant. Several people sat under its outside veranda, eating breakfast that included fresh water fish and wild game. How anyone could eat fish for breakfast, Shaun could never understand. That taste so early in the morning… yuck! Those poor outsiders, he thought. Scarfing down the delicacies that they just couldn't get back home, food staples that, for the locals, were as plentiful as the water and mountainous tree lines they'd grown up around for generations. If this is what the world had to offer, an incessant drive to leave the New Cities just for a week of fish breakfasts and bottles of Greenbrier River water, then, really, what was the point in leaving? He already had what they all wanted. Why couldn't his mother understand?

And as a reminder of her opinion, the last building on the block was the U.S. Registry Office, a two-story brick structure that had decorated its exterior with several U.S. and assorted memorial flags, one of which was a reminder of the Aquifer Attacks of 2029, the event that had led to the law that everyone had to register with the government, regardless of birth place. Sooner or later, he'd have to do it. Without registration, he couldn't drive or, for that matter, move around the country with much ease. Today's Suspicious Society had made sure of that. The Suspicious Society wanted everyone over eighteen logged in their data systems because, as they'd often promoted on the Net: Who wants another attack like the one we suffered in 29, like the one that had created the national water crisis, like one that, without registration, could destroy the nation?

"Bullshit," he said to the building as he slowly passed. "You got bigger things to think about when it comes to Shaun Winston."

Inside, a white suit stood with his back to the window and Shaun quickly pedaled away.

◎ ◎ ◎ ◎ ◎

Old man Smith was rocking on his porch when Shaun rode by. Most people considered him to be one of the longest living homesteaders. He had to have been ninety, Shaun figured, but the old cronies in West Virginia wore their age well so who knew? To the left of his white, wooden, single story house was a rather large garden. Smith, like so many homesteaders around town, supplied fresh produce to local businesses.

Smith's garden was quite young but the rows of tomatoes and corn and peppers and cucumbers were apparent.

The old man waved and Shaun was tempted to stop and soak in a bit more of the special sauce that made Marlinton home. Smith would tell him another great story from the town's past, or he'd offer some great tips for the perfectly landscaped backyard. Most of all, he'd provide an unbiased ear. Shaun needed that right now. He needed someone to listen and not judge. Old man Smith had perfected that virtue.

Shaun stopped and set one foot on the pavement. Smith still waved and smiled and rocked. "I'll come by later," Shaun yelled. "You'll be here, won't you?"

Smith's deep baritone was as strong as ever. "Depends," he hollered, "but should be."

He stopped rocking and placed one open hand on either side of his mouth and added, "Got a great new story for you. Happened just last night. Come back around and we'll talk."

Shaun swallowed, hard. The word about Dr. One was already out and circulating. "Sounds good," he yelled. "See you later."

Old man Smith resumed rocking and Shaun took off, quickly accelerating all the way to the trail.

◉ ◉ ◉ ◉ ◉

North from Marlinton, the Greenbrier River Trail started as fully paved asphalt but within a few hundred yards turned into a two-lane, wheel-rutted road of crushed stone with a foot wide dash of green grass and weeds separating the ruts. It hadn't changed much in the many years since it had been converted from a centuries-old C&O railroad. Even the Great Flood hadn't worn away what engineers had cleared back in the logging days before West Virginia was a state.

At the trailhead, a few families that lined the end of Marlinton's manufactured beachhead seemed to relish more in the simplicity of lying and baking under the sun, than exploring what nature had to offer. Those swimming in the river looked as if they were being baptized for the first time. Those few that rode the trail had adorned their bicycles and bodywear with mini-cameras and other kinds of tech. Some stood in the middle of the trail, posing in front of their bikes for pictures, turning their cameras toward the river and the trees and the birds and the multitude of cicadas and other insects that buzzed around them. It was if they'd never seen these real creatures before and, by the quizzical expressions on the faces of the children, probably hadn't. Shaun wondered if Nature, in their mixed reality worlds, even looked the same.

A couple of hundred yards beyond the beach, at the first right-hand bend in the trail, Shaun stopped his bike because he saw several police cars parked next to

Dr. One's house on the other side of the river. Officers roamed around Dr. One's back porch and could be seen only in shadowed sun patches through a thick line of trees. They were far enough away that they wouldn't recognize him, but Shaun thought about binoculars and rolled his bike to stand next to a thick tree line by the river twenty yards ahead.

He watched the investigators sweep the backyard, ducking in between bottlebrush bushes and young apple trees that Shaun had trimmed well over a dozen times, searching the four-shelf rattan bookcase on the back porch that Shaun kept free of nature's wind blown foliage, looking around and under three large potted plants that Shaun kept watered and alive outside in the summer and inside in the winter. It was if they were invading his own personal property.

Beyond keeping Dr. One's backyard in shape, Shaun had used it for himself on many occasions, especially the back porch. Easing into one of the rattan high back chairs, or better yet the bench swing, often provided him needed solitude. He often completed homework on the bench swing. More than a few times, he'd eaten some meal while pushing his feet across the dark wood floor as his knees and the swing gently moved with the rhythm of the river.

One blue-coated officer probed the bench swing, pushing aside yellow, green and blue throw pillows and lifting the matching three-color striped bench cushion before sitting down.

And Shaun thought: that's exactly where Phoenix had been sitting the last day he saw her. She'd looked straight at him, had leaned forward, had urged him closer with the wave of one index finger, and had said:

If you need me, you know where I'll be.

She'd known something was going to happen. She'd known that her uncle might be murdered. And if Shaun, the innocent lawn boy caretaker ever came across such a murder, well…

If you need me, you know where I'll be.

She said it to him again through those same pink lips while gently swaying back and forth on the bench swing. The Great Big Thing t-shirt stretched forward and the picture of the telescope collapsed within her cleavage.

If you need me…

His decader suddenly vibrated in his pocket. He pulled it out and read the pictographic text that only he and his two friends understood. Chris had sent the emergency code and Shaun peeked through thick leaves at the police. Had they gotten to him? he wondered. Was Chris over there sending him the code right now? Was he warning him to hide?

A hand grabbed his bare knee. Chris Wallace rose from the trees, laughing. "Jumpy, ain't ya?"

"Crap, Chris! What are you doing?" Shaun turned to his friend. Chris was wearing a pair of new tech called ClearGlasses.

"Wanted you to know we have an emergency."

Shaun didn't look across the river. "What are you talking about?"

"It's an emergency for the rest of the population that we are graduating and that you are turning eighteen…though I don't know which is more frightening." Chris giggled and rose from the tree line with his own mountain bike clasped in one hand. "You know what's going on over by your place?" He pointed at Dr. One's house.

"No," Shaun said.

"You think someone murdered him and left him in the house to rot?"

Shaun rolled his eyes. "Guaranteed no. I would have smelled it." He giggled nervously. "I told you. He's just a quiet guy that likes a little time away from work every now and then."

"He's stirred up a lot of people. You never know who might be pissed off enough to whack a guy like that."

Shaun looked straight at Chris' baby smooth face. The ClearGlasses sat as a thin, transparent strip across the bridge of his nose. A rainbow halo captured one of its edges. "It's crap gossip like that that's got this whole country suspicious of everything and everybody. You don't know squat about Dr. One. Stop with the rumors."

Chris smirked. "Don't get 'em in such a bunch. Didn't know you and the doc had such a thing going."

"Kiss my ass…and what the hell are you doing with those things on? You can't even get a good enough signal for them to do what they're supposed to do."

"They're limited outside the New City Net but with a VR flat screen you can get quite an experience at home. And they automatically translate a thousand foreign languages. Come on. Say something foreign."

"Chris Wallace."

"Funny."

"Worth the bucks?"

Chris smiled. "A gift don't cost nothin'. Got them for graduation. Mom thought CGs would be helpful in the city."

"I still don't know what you think you are going to do in Cleveland. You really don't have much work experience."

Chris took off the glasses. "Yee of little faith. They got training programs and then I'll get all the experience I could want. Besides, anything is better than sticking around here. Aren't you sick of it? Don't all these visitors make you want the city? Besides, the government is taking over this town anyway."

They were growing up and growing apart. It had been accelerating over the last year. Chris had visions of grandeur in some big New City. Adam had decided on the military. And both of their allegiances to these projected futures had grown very rigid—about as rigid as Shaun was for not leaving home. "You know better. Our town still has West Virginia in it. The Feds don't have it yet."

"Oh no? Well, I found out a curious thing today while wearing my CGs." Chris fondled them in the palm of his hand. "These might not be able to take full advantage of the Net around here, but they sure do a great job of revealing the Feds' new technology."

Shaun scowled. "What are you talking about?"

"Come here."

They dropped their bikes and Shaun followed Chris into the tree line from which Chris had emerged. They stooped within thick branches and Chris pointed across the river to where Stony Run emptied its narrow stream into the Greenbrier a hundred yards to the right of Dr. One's house. Along the river bank stood a ten foot square, green metal shed. These federally-owned "maintenance buildings" had been appearing along the river for the last year. Most were spread about a mile apart with longer distances between those that were more rural. Tons of speculation had surfaced with their arrival. Surveillance was the most worrisome. But the Greenbrier belonged to the Feds. Occasionally, you'd see someone moving around one of the sheds but, for the most part, they were unmanned, guarded only by the sensors and cameras mounted in the surrounding trees.

Chris handed Shaun the CGs and pulled out his CELL to adjust a setting. "What do you see?" he asked. Shaun started to put on the glasses but Chris stopped him. "No. Now. What do you see?"

Shaun peered at the building. "A green shed."

"You mean you don't see the guy standing right behind it?"

Shaun squinted. He'd been able to see the cops at Dr. One's house but he didn't see anyone near the shed.

"Put them on."

Shaun hesitantly placed the thin glasses across his nose and ears and they comfortably snuggled his eyebrows so that his periphery was totally covered. They were incredibly light. It was hard to believe they contained any real glass. "These things aren't gonna read my mind are they?"

Chris smiled. "Not yet."

Shaun turned his attention to the shed and gasped. There *was* a man standing behind it. He wore casual camouflage and didn't appear to be armed. He smoked a cigarette while he looked off into the trees. Shaun removed the glasses and the man disappeared.

"Neat trick, eh?" Chris said. "Looks like we have a new flavor of stealth. You set the CGs to a certain frequency and voila!: invisible people revealed." Shaun put the glasses back on to verify Chris' truth. "They must have some kind of new tech either around them or on them or both. Like I said, the government is taking over the town and we can't even see it."

"What do we do?"

"Nothing, really."

"You're not going to tell anyone? That ain't like you."

"I tell someone then they'll know I know…that we know. And then you know what they'll do?"

"Throw us a graduation party with ropes for lynching?"

"Too much baggage. They'll just discredit us. All they have to do is change the frequency, which I'm sure they do on a daily basis anyway. Hell, I can't believe I got lucky enough to happen on it today."

Shaun returned the glasses to Chris and they both moved out of the trees. "I guess it's all a part of our new society. People wanting to do harm."

"You see." Chris grabbed his bike, straddled it and put on the glasses. "The New City is the place to be. A safe, controlled environment where all young Mountaineers can be successful."

Shaun reached out and grasped Chris' shoulder. "That's your future, not mine."

"Yeah," Chris whispered. "Gotta get outta here." He quickly stiffened. "So where you headed?"

Shaun paused, wondering how much truth he should reveal, hoping that Chris would not invite himself to tag along. "I'm thinking, Cass."

Chris smiled. "Sounds like a winner but I'm

gonna have to say no."

Typical Chris, Shaun thought. Thankfully, a ride to Cass could not squeeze into his plans that seemed more centered on finding hidden people with his brand new grad gift. "Ok, then. See you tomorrow."

Chris stepped up onto his bike pedals and slowly rode in a half circle. "Graduation brother," he said, smiling. "Watch out for the invisible Feds." He spun his rear tire then took off toward town.

◎ ◎ ◎ ◎ ◎

Shaun stood straddling his bike for several minutes. A wave of upset careened through his body as cool mountain air, moisturized by the Greenbrier, whipped across his chin whiskers. He took deep breaths as if trying to capture the entire essence of this single moment, as if trying to inhale all of the Greenbrier Valley right down into his lungs, into his blood, into his soul. More federals using secret camo tech was a clear sign that the government was beefing up its surveillance and control, and that they were probably not doing it so covertly as Chris had insinuated. Some community leaders had to know. The mayor? The police chief? Wealthy business owners? A collusion of the Suspicious Society intent on changing Marlinton from its rural roots to some New City, wannabe police state?

Shaun took another deep breath to quell growing anger. He looked across the river to his left as one of the police cruisers over at Dr. One's house drove off, then turned his attention to the shed and concentrated on the spot where the invisible sentry stood. He saw nothing more than the birds that flew above it and the insects that buzzed around it. Three butterflies tangled in a playful display in front of the shed above the river's edge and this caused Shaun to smile for a brief moment before the reality of impending change flooded back through him. Anger mounted.

And then Shaun had a revelation, one usually kept in check by young adolescents until life as an adult forced new realities. If he was going to stay in Marlinton then he'd have to save Marlinton and the only way to do that was to become involved—become a part of the decision-making so he'd know what was really going on. He'd have to come out of the shadows, get on the Net and maintain a clean Story so that others would respect him, accept him and follow him. A young mayor wasn't out of the question. Then he could control…

Shaun laughed once very loudly then said to no one, "Right!" He looked back over at Dr. One's house, thinking that he was probably already their number one suspect and how a suspected murderer could be mayor. How could someone who loathed the Net be in public office? How was he going to change anything?

He sucked in another large helping of Greenbrier air.

The three frolicking butterflies broke ranks and one of them headed across the river in his direction. It flopped up and around and side-to-side just a few inches above the water and Shaun waited for the brook trout that would certainly, at any moment, fling itself into the air for a quick morning snack. But the butterfly avoided such calamity, floated over a large rock right in the middle of the river and continued toward Shaun. As it neared the bank, he saw that it was a large monarch, bright orange with black stripes, just like the one he thought he'd seen outside his bedroom window. It steered directly for him as if he'd called it by name and it was responding. From habit, Shaun reached one hand out. In almost eighteen years, no butterfly had ever landed on it but this one did. It flopped around his extended fingers, its wings lightly grazing the thin hairs, before landing in the center of the back of his hand. Tiny feet tickled two knuckles. Its black antennae probed the skin near his wrist. Two eyes within its white-spotted black body stared right at him. Slowly, Shaun bent his arm to bring the monarch closer.

"What do you say?" he whispered. "Do you see them?"

Shaun marveled at the butterfly's markings. They were unlike any he'd ever seen on a monarch: not just black lines filled with orange patches. This monarch had stripes…like a tiger.

"Tony!" he said to the butterfly. "That sounds like a perfect name for you."

The butterfly winked at him…or, at least that's what it looked like. At the center of each of its black eyes was a red dot that glowed. One of them quickly blinked off and on, giving the impression of a wink and Shaun winked back.

"I'm gonna miss you and all of your kin," he said and the monarch took flight. It flapped around his bike for a good thirty seconds before flying off along the trail in the direction he was heading. Shaun took the cue, stepped up onto his bike and followed Tony.

⊙ ⊙ ⊙ ⊙ ⊙

Whoever it was wore a black shirt with a big yellow dot right in the middle of it and had been keeping identical pace with Shaun since he'd left Chris almost thirty minutes ago. Whenever he accelerated, so did the person riding ahead of him. When he slowed, they slowed. And every time the big yellow dot came into view for more than a few seconds, it disappeared around a turn or thick patch of trees.

Shaun decided to let the other biker move on ahead of him and he stopped next to a river-view wooden bench, removed his backpack and sat down. He drank a bottle of Cheat Lake while he nibbled through half a nut bar, and stared at another green shed across the river. Cicadas buzzed around it at the water's edge. He wondered if someone sat there, hidden.

The butterfly he'd named Tony had kept pace and now flapped in front of his face. Shaun smiled as he offered the back of his right hand, and the butterfly quickly flew over and landed, its tiny legs and antennae, again, tickling his skin.

"No one there, is there?" he asked the monarch. It winked both tiny red irises at him. "What was that? One wink for Yes and two for No?"

A tiny crumb of nut bar rested atop one of the hairs on his hand and the monarch played with it for a few seconds before taking flight. It drunkenly flapped to the riverbank where it landed on an orange honeysuckle bush. As if being summoned, Shaun walked over to stand next to the bush and to look up the river. None of the honeysuckle blossoms had yet opened but the orange bulbs provided good camouflage for Tony's stripes. A couple of cicadas took refuge in the bush's shade near the ground. He looked over at the green shed, wondering how they did it. The butterfly used color. What were the Feds using?

The butterfly took off again and flew along the riverbank, dodging tree limbs and bush branches to a point where the river turned a bit to the left. Through some of the trees, he could see the trail ahead. Fifty yards off, in line with where the butterfly floated, stood the person with the black shirt and yellow dot. Whoever it was straddled a bike and looked right at him. Shaun waved but the cyclist just stood there.

"Strange way for a person to follow someone," he said to the river. "Staying ahead in plain sight?"

Then he thought, just perhaps, someone was trying to punk him. It was a popular high school antic and with graduation just around the corner…well…not Chris, but perhaps Adam. While his other friend wasn't as juvenile as was Chris, Adam was known to pull off some pretty good gags when he put his mind to it. Maybe he, too, had heard that there had been a murder near Shaun's home and now he was acting the "suspicious character" role that all good murder mysteries have in them. Adam, or whoever it was, would keep at it until they got to Sharp's Tunnel and then he'd pop the big reveal, the big scare, the big laugh. He might even have an accomplice. Inside the tunnel's dark shadows and on either side of the bridge were several well-placed ambush locations and Shaun would be ready.

He put his empty water bottle and half-eaten nut bar in the backpack, slung the pack on his shoulders and took off on his bike, pedaling as fast as he could around the left turn ahead, but no one was there.

◎ ◎ ◎ ◎ ◎

About a year ago, when Shaun, Chris and Adam had still been very tight, Chris had gotten the grand idea that hanging someone from Sharp's Bridge would be a real hoot. Though the gag had not been meant for them, many of the vacationing bystanders witnessed what they thought was Chris pushing a young boy, whose neck was in a noose-knotted rope, from the middle of the bridge. There had been lots of screams and an off-duty police officer from Marlinton had even showed up. The officer had come running out of Sharp's Tunnel before Shaun could zip up.

"What the hell are you doing?" the officer had asked him while staring at the bush leaves Shaun had just peed on.

"Sorry," Shaun had said. "Had to go."

"No, dammit! You and the Wallace kid. He didn't really just hang someone did he?"

Of course, Chris hadn't but it had looked real enough to sufficiently punk more than just his friends. Chris and twelve-year-old Ben Jackson had performed the illusion to perfection. The trick's success had been partly due to their distance out on the middle of the bridge. You really couldn't see that Chris had both Ben and a dummy double standing on the bridge railing, both dressed in black with a black hood covering the faces, and both with ropes around their necks. And because the evening October sun had already dropped below the western ridge, limited light had caused everyone who had been fooled to miss the fact that as soon as Chris had pushed the dummy over, Ben had quickly stepped down and had squatted against the bridge deck.

It must have taken Adam a month to get over that one and Shaun suspected that the other innocent witnesses were still in therapy today. The police officer had not been amused one bit. He'd ticketed Chris and Ben for creating a public nuisance, and he'd written Shaun up for pissing in public. They were only juvenile misdemeanor offenses that the three of them had worked off by picking up trash around town for twenty hours each, but it had been worth it. Even the five bucks Shaun had surrendered to Chris on a failed bet that the gag would really work had been a small price to pay to see all of those people so bent out of shape. It was the kind of entertainment you couldn't get in the big city.

The memory of the mannequin swinging from a rope a few feet above the river accompanied Shaun for the final mile before Sharp's Bridge and Tunnel. He'd not seen the yellow dot rider since he'd last stopped and he figured that it had just been a coincidence that the two had paced each other for a couple of miles. Still, he rode the last part of the trail before the bridge with his head on a pivot. Something was up! He felt it. He was about to get punked.

He rode across the wood-planked bridge toward an arched opening in the rock on the other side that had been carved to create Sharp's Tunnel and was only tall enough and wide enough to get a nineteenth century locomotive engine through it. A couple of low intensity solar cells provided just enough light to see the path at ground level. Other than that, the tunnel was very dark because a right hand turn at its center hid its sun brightened exit.

Shaun slowed as he approached. Should he ride fast? he thought. Should he zip through to throw off any would be gagmaker's timing? Or should he take the more cautious approach…maybe even punk the punker?

Slowly, he entered. Attached at ground level to the right side tunnel rock wall was the first of the internal light cells. This provided enough illumination to see the centuries old scratches made by centuries old machines in the rock walls about six feet up. The ceiling of the tunnel remained mostly dark and, of course, that's from where Shaun imagined the gag would come.

He rolled forward, his attention consumed by the shadows above. As the tunnel turned right, he reached a point where he could see the arched exit ahead and squinted because of its bright haze.

"I know you're there!" he yelled and the tunnel echoed his pronouncement. "Not gonna work on me today!"

Something moved behind him and he stopped pedaling, set one foot down, and turned. At the center of the tunnel entrance's arched white glare was the gray shadow of a person, and smack dab in the middle of that shadow was a hazy yellow circle. "That you, Adam?" he said, thinking that he'd never seen Adam wear a black t-shirt with a big yellow dot on the chest. "Who is that?"

Shaun rolled his bike a few feet closer to reveal what looked like tiny beams of green light shooting from the shadow figure to points outside the tunnel that he couldn't see. It reminded him of the night before, of the color speck that had used similar green beams to check out Dr. One's dead eyeball. In the hazy white archway, they glowed at mixed angles, three to either side of the figure.

"Who?..." he said and walked his bike a few more feet until the white haze and tiny beams disappeared, and the yellow dot on the figure's chest became readable.

Have A Nice Day, was written in yellow under a big smiley face. When Shaun looked up to see who was wearing the shirt, his first thought was *Why?*

Why had Dr. One faked his own death?

◉ ◉ ◉ ◉ ◉

Phoenix Messenger didn't hear that her uncle had died until Friday morning. She had been sitting in the break room sipping coffee from a cup emblazoned with the Green Bank Telescope logo when Carol's head had appeared in the open doorway. She hadn't entered; she'd just popped her brunette head in to say, in her very special monotonic way, "Your uncle died last night," and then she had left.

In the hour since, three fellow scientists had stopped in to give her more heartfelt condolences. Even the GBT director, a short man with short hair and short patience, visited and urged Phoenix to go home. But she couldn't. No scientist could leave behind the data they were starting to piece together, especially *this* data: evidence that her uncle had helped them acquire.

"No thanks, Dr. Carpenter," she said, staring at the full coffee cup that had long gone cold.

"We're all going to miss him. Perhaps you need some grief time."

Phoenix looked up too abruptly, not meaning to startle Dr. Carpenter. "No. I've got much work to catch up on." Dr. Carpenter waved goodbye and left.

She really didn't have much grief for the loss of her uncle. She was only a distant niece even when they were away from the telescope. And at work, it was always all work with no time for family pleasantries. Dr. One had been a highly introverted individual. Relationships had never been his strong points.

But she did feel an immense loss for his mind. As one of the top RF scientists in the country, he'd been brilliant and quite controversial. A little more than a year ago, he'd found God, the beginning of the universe, the beginning of everything. He'd detected a radio signature in the cosmos so many multiples of light years away that it could have been nothing less than this holy grail of science. Religious leaders had balked, of course, but a greater abundance of researchers from around the world had argued the validity of his discovery, making it the top story of conversation in the new decade.

It was easy to imagine that Dr. One had been killed because of this. There were enough religious fanatics out there that such a threat to their own beliefs could have inspired a thousand torturous endings to her uncle's life, and that's exactly what Phoenix had been contemplating for the past hour. Was he dead because he'd found the so-called God Light or was he dead because of a new threat to an insular world that he and the rest of the Green Bank scientists had found in just the past two months—a world in which God really didn't matter anymore because of the terrestrial powers that wanted to control all reality.

They'd collected tons of data and were just beginning to piece it all together. Dr. One had configured observatory technology to detect not what was up there in the cosmos but what was going on right here on earth: the electromagnetic radiation emitted from all of the technology that he'd called "the vibrations of interconnectivity," particularly those vibrations that were en masse in the United States that seemed to be growing exponentially.

How do we really understand our own existence? he had often contemplated aloud. *Human experience is no longer explored through the laborious interactions with nature but is, instead, dictated via all the devices that have come to enslave a lazy, fear-filled population.*

She left her coffee and the break room and slowly walked the short distance down a hallway to the laboratory's control room. None of the other software engineers and analysts were at any one of the six monitoring stations. Plenty of morning sunshine illuminated the space that would have been overly sterile with its white walls and floors had it not been for the colorful prints of the most dramatic objects the GBT had collected over the years. Above her own computer screen was her favorite, the Horesehead Nebula, the brightest and most recognizable object in Orion's Belt, the one that pointed in the direction in which her uncle had found God. She stared it as she sat down, thinking about death and religion and mankind's manipulation of the two.

Her uncle was dead, now what? How would the research continue? Could she do it herself? Maybe, he'd already collected enough for the proof they needed.

And then Phoenix caught herself and gasped at the Orion print. How could she be so insensitive? She cared more about the research than she did for the life of her own uncle. Where was the remorse? Where was the grief? And if he *had* been murdered, she had to feel something for that possibility. But she didn't. They'd used each other and that's all there was to it. The only important thing to both of them was the research and, sometimes, sacrifices had to be made.

◎ ◎ ◎ ◎ ◎

He'd heard that if you just blink, imaginary visions would go away. Shaun blinked a dozen times but Dr. One just stood there, not making a sound, a strange, stern grin planted in the middle of his frosty white mustache and beard, his eyes planted back in place where they should be.

"Dr. One?" Shaun's dry throat cracked out the two words. Suddenly, gravel crunched and someone giggled behind him. When he turned his head, a man and two young girls no older than ten came into view within the tunnel's timid light.

"Oh. Hello," the man said, a bit startled. "This is really great stuff…right, girls?"

"Yes," the red-haired twins said in unison.

Shaun thought of asking them if they saw the man at the end of the tunnel, but when he peered back over his shoulder, Dr. One was gone. "Hi," he said, instead.

"You from 'round these parts?" The man apparently wasn't. His fake accent just didn't cut it.

"I am," Shaun said and got off his bike to push it toward the spot where he'd seen the doctor standing. The man and his girls followed.

"What's the story with Sharp's?" the man said. This wasn't the first time someone had asked Shaun about the tunnel or the trail. Storytelling was part of working at Jenn's.

Shaun walked with the family out of the tunnel and onto the bridge while telling them a short history of the Chesapeake and Ohio Railroad. The twins stopped at the very spot where Chris had performed his punk on Adam and leaned on the railing to point toward Marlinton. "Beautiful," one of them said. "Not like the VR back home, Daddy."

The father and twins stood together in what appeared to be awe at what they were seeing. "In many ways, you're lucky," the father said. "I'm sorry, I didn't get your name."

"Shaun."

The man reached forward with an open hand and Shaun shook it. "Charles. And this is Rachel and Rebecca." He tapped each of their heads. "There's too much fakery from where we're from. Sometimes I wonder if they really want anyone to leave."

"Fakery?" Shaun asked.

"Yeah. We can get river bridge experiences that you'd think would make this look boring. But there's something about actually being here that can't be equaled. You have that privilege every day. And all that mountain water."

Shaun looked out over the Greenbrier. "If you're staying for awhile, I know where you can get a great cabin. No better way to experience my home's reality."

"They're right," Charles said to the river. "Country folk are very friendly and hospitable." Charles looked at Shaun. "I hope you don't mind me calling you country folk."

Shaun waved an open hand. "That's what I am. And, thank you."

"We're only here for the day, then we're headed up to see the Great Big Thing."

"Great Big Thing!" the twins yelled.

Shaun didn't reveal that Green Bank was also his destination. "You'll have a good time there," he said. "They love taking kids through that huge telescope. It's educational."

Charles and his daughters continued across the bridge and Shaun turned around, looked for Dr. One at the mouth of the tunnel, then raced his bike through it as he headed north, still twenty miles away from Phoenix.

◎ ◎ ◎ ◎ ◎

It was more than a full minute before Phoenix realized that her computer screen was active and animated. A blue status revealed that data was being downloaded from the server on which she and her uncle had stored their collected "vibrations of interconnectivity." She tapped the cancel button with her right index finger and the screen should have immediately recognized and confirmed her fingerprint but it didn't. Immediately, she launched a program that would allow her into the server's backdoor, but after a few desperate attempts at entering command codes, she realized that she'd been locked out.

She pushed away from the desk, her chair easily rolling across the hard floor, and watched helplessly as the download status bar reached its end and a short message read *Download Complete*.

Three men entered the control room and Phoenix swiveled in the chair to face them. All three wore matching blue suits. The only thing that individualized their wardrobes was their tie colors. The last one in closed the door.

"Phoenix Messenger?" the man closest to Phoenix asked. He wore a red tie.

"I am." Phoenix started to stand.

"Please remain seated," Red Tie said and grabbed a chair that he rolled over next to Phoenix and sat down. "Just wanted to ask you a couple of questions. The man with the black tie stood next to the closed door. The man with the white tie stood next to Red Tie. "What are you working on there?" He pointed at Phoenix's computer screen where the words *Download Complete* still remained.

"You have something to do with that?" She thumbed over her shoulder toward the screen.

"Why would you think that?"

"Oh, I don't know. You guys look like the type that would steal scientific research."

"Type? What type would that be?"

"G-type."

Red Tie scooted to within two feet of Phoenix. "If you mean government…well, you're almost right."

"Are you stealing our data or not? It's encrypted, you know." Red Tie's face was way too close. His thick, black eyebrows and thick black mustache unnerved her.

"Trust me." He smiled a set of big white teeth. "I am not doing anything to any data. Besides, it belongs to me anyway. If I wanted it, I'd take it. But that's not why we've come here today. We've come here because of your uncle. Have you heard?"

"He's dead," Phoenix said and rolled her chair another two feet away from Red Tie who turned to White Tie and looked up.

"You hear that? The doctor is dead." He swiveled back toward Phoenix. "Sure would like to know where the dead doctor is."

Phoenix shrugged. "Just found out an hour ago. I wouldn't have a clue."

"Police tell you?"

"No. Carol."

"You mean that dumb bitch who works the front lobby? I wouldn't exactly call that a trustworthy source."

"You hear different?

"Dr. One came up missing last night. No body has been found. I suppose he could be dead but for now we're treating the case as a missing person and we wanted to know if you had any information. Apparently, you don't."

"Is that all, then?"

Red Tie looked at Phoenix's computer screen again. "You make any backups?"

"I thought you weren't interested in our research."

Red Tie rolled closer. "I'm not, but I represent those that are…backups?"

"Of course we do. It's on a second server."

"No." Red Tie inched even closer. One of his thick eyebrow hairs had fallen onto the bridge of his nose. "I mean, personal backups. Ones you could take with you. Did you or he ever make one of those?"

Phoenix couldn't take his proximity anymore and she stood. Her chair rolled backward and crashed into the desktop. "Not to my knowledge."

"That's good," Red Tie said while slowly standing.

"Because you know, it's against the law. We prosecute to the fullest extent, and that's a guarantee."

"Now that I've had my legal lesson for the day, is that all?"

Red Tie and White Tie walked together to stand next to Black Tie. "If you hear anything about your uncle other than from Carol, get a hold of us. Dr. Carpenter has the number."

Black Tie opened the door and the three of them walked out, leaving Phoenix standing there wondering, again, not of her uncle's demise but of the research they'd collected and the personal backup of it that Dr. One kept in a secret hiding place at his Marlinton home.

⊙ ⊙ ⊙ ⊙ ⊙

Shaun was no longer interested in stopping for a rest or sightseeing the trail. When one young woman asked him for directions, he continued on without responding. At that pace, he arrived in Cass an hour after the encounter at Sharp's Tunnel.

He had to find Phoenix. He had to find out what the hell was going on. Was her uncle dead or what? He'd sure looked it, all sprawled out on his living room floor with one eye gone and the other bulging over his cheek. But he wasn't dead. He'd been standing in the tunnel's arched light. And if he wasn't dead, who'd been lying on the floor? If Dr. One wasn't dead, why did Shaun still feel like a prime suspect in something he'd witnessed that no one else saw? Someone had been dead on the doctor's floor and he'd looked just like the doctor. Or had he? Eyes sockets had been mutilated. It could have been a really good double—maybe some poor sap they'd found wandering a New City street, looking for the training and jobs that had been promised but never fulfilled. Perhaps the white suits had offered the sap some cash to do a simple job in a small West Virginia town where he could pose as a double for them. Then they'd killed him and had stashed his body in the house; then Shaun had found it; then they'd returned; but they'd never left with a body.

And the thing that *really* didn't make any sense was that Dr. One had been shadowing him all the way to Sharp's Tunnel but no farther. Shaun hadn't seen him since. Why had he started then stopped following…on a bicycle? The guy must have been sixty-five years old, easy. Maybe he'd keeled over from trying to keep up with Shaun's accelerated pace and really was dead in a ditch somewhere along the riverbank.

A train whistle startled him from thought. The Cass Scenic Railroad Tour was about to leave the station. Four cars behind the steaming engine were filled to capacity. Again, steam blasted from the whistle to bellow out one last warning before departure.

He'd have to leave the trail now and ride northeast along Routes 66 and 92 for about six more miles to Green Bank and those roads didn't' have much shoulder. He'd ridden them a couple of times but the traffic beyond the trail was such that bicycles were usually absent.

A small, black pickup truck with door signage that read Valleyside Outfitters rolled up and parked at the curb beside him. Jenn's and Valleyside competed for vacationers, but Valleyside was located in Watoga, one town down the trail south of Marlinton. Valerie was driving.

"Need a lift?" she said through the driver's side window. "I'm heading south."

Valerie was a year older than Shaun and had short, black hair and a big rose tattoo on her left shoulder. She usually wore purple lipstick but had chosen bright pink today. They'd ridden the trail together many times and Shaun had a bit of a crush on her, but their limited friendship was more important to him than getting involved. "Not going home," he said and rolled his bike next to the truck.

"Yeah?" Valerie smiled and her pink lips pursed. "You being adventurous?"

"Going to Green Bank for the day," he said.

Valerie squirmed behind the steering wheel and her black top's shoulder strap slipped down over the tattoo to hide one rose petal. "What a shitty ride. It's Memorial Day Friday. You sure you want to do that?"

Shaun caught himself staring at her and blinked.

"No. I guess not."

"I could make a quick detour." Before Shaun answered, she added, "Go on. Put it in the back. We haven't talked in awhile. Should be fun."

He locked his bike into one of the truck bed's bike racks and got in the cab. Valerie's pink shorts matched her lips and she smiled at him before putting the truck in gear.

◎ ◎ ◎ ◎ ◎

It is said that the Great Big Thing is so sensitive, it can detect the energy of a snowflake as it hits the ground. That's why very few electromagnetic radiation-emitting devices were allowed in Green Bank, population one thousand, a number that had grown considerably over the last two decades because of this "Quiet Zone" ordinance. It was home to not only the GBT but also to a heavy handful of what they called electromagnetic hypersensitives: people who claim to get sick when exposed to EMR, even in small quantities. In Green Bank, you couldn't have microwaves or gas-powered cars, and anything that needed wireless access to be functional was useless. If you wanted to call out to the big world, you used one of the pay phones located in town.

And that's where Valerie stopped her truck to let Shaun out. He grabbed his bike and rolled it over to stand next to the phone booth. It looked just like one from the early days, a kind of phone booth Clark Kent could change in. Stainless steel metal had deterred most of the rust and the glass was free of cracks and looked as if it had been kept clean. "Public Telephone" was emblazoned on a green plastic plaque above the booth.

"Now there's a picture," Valerie said and leaned over to snatch a small camera from the glove box. She pointed it at him and Shaun gave her a casual pose and smile. She took three pictures. "Enjoyed our little conversation and I'm taking you up on your lunch date offer. Don't forget."

"I'll ride down to Watoga next week after graduation."

Valerie's pink lips spread wide in a big smile. "Graduation. How exciting!"

Shaun was not as enthusiastic but he didn't want her to know it, so he didn't respond.

"Well…catch up with you later," Valerie added, waved goodbye by twiddling the fingers of one hand, then drove off.

There wasn't much in town beyond the phone booth. He passed a gas station with no one filling up, an antique store with no one parked outside, and one Quickie convenience store where "Two for a Dollar" hot dogs were available, according to the sign in its window, but he saw no one other than the clerk inside. Within minutes, he rode beyond the limited businesses to a stretch of farmland where some strikingly beautiful homes sat away from the main road. These were big, white two-story farmhouses that had been a part of Green Banks' culture for well over a century. Each was surrounded by a uniquely constructed white picket fence. One looked like a fence that Tom Sawyer might have convinced him to paint. Another had wood-carved busts of horse heads attached to each post. A third had a 1860s-styled split-rail fence that soldiers commonly scaled during battle in the Civil War. All of the fences trekked for miles across each home's acreage where horses and cattle roamed in numbers.

The appropriately named Observatory Road came up on his left and he turned onto the two-lane, unmarked, asphalt. He passed a relatively full parking lot in front of the Welcome Center to his left. A sign in one window read: *Carnegie Science Students Rock!* The lab, where Shaun suspected Phoenix worked, was the next two-story building on the left and he rode to it.

He stepped off the bike and rolled it toward tinted double glass doors as three men, wearing blue suits, exited. The one with the red tie glanced over at him and Shaun bent over to look down at his bike's gears, pretending that they needed his attention. He remained in that pose until he heard three car doors slam, then he rose and quickly moved from the parking lot to the entry doors. He opened one door and rolled his bike inside as he looked over his shoulder to see the red taillights of a car with three men in it. They'd stopped in the middle of the parking lot and Shaun quickly stepped behind the shelter of the door's tinted glass. He stood there, holding the door open, until the car drove off a full minute later.

Feds, Shaun thought. Had to be. He'd missed running smack dab into them by just seconds.

"Can I help you, young man?" A woman in a green dress walked up to him. She pushed the horn-rimmed glasses further up the bridge of her nose. A name badge above her left breast labeled her as Carol Walkerman. "You should leave your bicycle outside."

"Yes. Well, I forgot my lock," Shaun replied and released the door so that it closed behind him.

"We don't steal bikes around these parts. Where are you from?"

Shaun knew that insinuating tone very well. It's how disgruntled small town folk reacted when a suspected outsider annoyed them. "Marlinton. And we don't steal bikes there, either."

Carol's attitude shifted. She smiled but the act of doing so seemed labored. "Didn't mean to…"

"That's okay. Do you have a scientist by the name of Phoenix working here?"

Carol's smile disappeared. "Phoenix Messenger?" she asked. Shaun had not known Phoenix's last name until now.

"Yes. I need to talk to her on some urgent matters."

"And who are you?"

"I worked for Dr. One at his Marlinton home. My name is Shaun."

"So, your urgent matters include the news that Dr. One is dead? We've heard. So has Ms. Messenger."

"I'd still like to see her. Is she here?"

Carol considered the request with a frown. "You can leave your bicycle leaning against the wall next to the door over there. I'll show you where she is."

Shaun followed Carol around a reception desk and into a very white hallway where she stopped and pointed. "Second door on the right," she said. "Someone's in there with her right now so you'll want to knock."

Carol replaced her frown with a false smile as he stepped around her and continued down the hall. Behind the second door to his right, he heard two women talking about cicadas.

◎ ◎ ◎ ◎ ◎

The last person Phoenix thought she would see after the G-men left was Bethany Higginbotham. Certainly, Dr. Carpenter and her fellow researchers would want to know why the Feds had stopped by, but none of them showed up—just Bethany.

Bethany closed the door after entering. "I must talk to you," she implored. She was in her fifties and had been living in Green Bank for much of the past decade. She was one of those that were highly "allergic" to electromagnetic radiation. She was also one of those that habituated embellishment. Something covert was always in the making, spies were everywhere and her life was always in jeopardy, at least that's what she'd claimed in the many sporadic meetings they'd shared since Phoenix had arrived at the GBT two years ago.

"Hi Bethany," Phoenix said. "You know it's not a good idea to meet here."

Bethany's expression turned into one of a caged animal. She squatted a bit while looking through long bangs of salt and pepper hair at the walls and ceiling. "Doesn't matter," she offered. "They know. Of course they know."

"Who? What do they know?"

"They're trying to silence me by driving me mad."

"Didn't they try to silence you three months ago with microwave ovens?"

Bethany huffed. "It's all a part of the same thing, but now they've taken it too far."

"What have they done now?"

"Bugs," Bethany said and her wrinkled nose wrinkled just a bit more in disgust. "They have bugs that emit radiation."

"Bugs?"

"Mostly cicadas right now."

"Radiation-emitting cicadas?"

A gentle tapping on the control room's closed door drew their attention. The door inched open and the young man who maintained her uncle's Marlinton home entered.

◎ ◎ ◎ ◎ ◎

When Shaun knocked, the door, which was not completely closed, eased open. He stepped in and saw Phoenix standing next to an older woman who looked to be in some dismay. "Excuse me…Phoenix," he said. "I don't know if you remember me…"

"Shaun, the lawn boy," Phoenix quickly responded.

Shaun forced a small grin. He was happy that Phoenix had recognized him though the attached moniker of lawn boy didn't particularly sit well. "Sorry to bother you but we need to talk."

"Seems more than a few people need to talk to me today. It has to do with my uncle, doesn't it?"

"Yes. I found him in his house dead last night." Phoenix's reaction was not one he expected. She showed no remorse.

"Excuse me," Bethany interjected. "Are you Phoenix's boyfriend?"

Shaun and Phoenix looked quizzically at each other. "Boyfriend?" Shaun said.

"Phoenix's boyfriend from Marlinton. Are you he?"

"I'm from Marlinton, but…"

"Dr. One said you'd be here today and he left something in my house to give you. Now, don't argue with me. Both of you need to come over to my house tonight, I insist…Dr. One insisted…so's I can prove the bugs, and to give your boyfriend his band." Bethany quickly covered her mouth with one hand and gazed around the room. "Oops…how about six o'clock? You know where I live."

"You okay with that?" Phoenix asked Shaun but he just shrugged. "Yes, Bethany. We'll see you this evening."

A fraction of hope etched its way into Bethany's overall expression of dread and she left.

"So, where are we going and why?" Shaun asked. "And who was that?"

"Sorry," Phoenix said, a bit flustered. "She can get on a person's last nerve."

Shaun remained silent.

"Bethany," Phoenix continued. "Bethany Higgenbotham hates electromagnetic radiation. She says she's allergic to it."

"And I'm your boyfriend?" A touch of red embarrassment colored his cheeks as Phoenix walked over to him. A white lab coat covered most of her body and her blonde hair cascaded over the left shoulder.

"Not really sure what my uncle was thinking. I don't have any boyfriends…not from Marlinton…not from anywhere." She paused and then added, "Is my uncle dead?"

"Bethany seemed a bit paranoid. Is it safe to talk?"

Phoenix looked at her computer screen where the words *Download Complete* were displayed. She walked to it and pressed one finger against the words to make them disappear then turned the monitor off. "Probably not," she said.

"I'm on my bike…the pedal kind."

"You ride all the way from Marlinton?"

"Mostly. The trail makes it pretty easy."

Phoenix moved to the open door that Bethany had not closed when she exited. "If you're hungry, I know a place where we can eat and talk in a fairly safe environment. Gotta use the bathroom first. If you need it, it's just down the hall."

"No. Thanks."

While he waited for her in the hall, Shaun took a bottle of water from his backpack, consumed it in four big swallows and tossed the empty back in the pack. When Phoenix returned, she was dressed in jeans and her Great Big Thing t-shirt, the exact clothes that she'd been wearing while swinging on Dr. One's porch the last time he'd seen her, and it immediately reminded him of what she'd said.

If you need me, you know where I'll be.

"You knew something was going to happen to him, didn't you?" Shaun whispered and Phoenix responded by placing a finger to her lips.

Carol stood at the far end of the hallway. "Hey," she yelled. "What are you going to do with this bicycle?"

Phoenix ignored her. "Roll it into the control room," she said to Shaun. "You can get it when we return."

⊙ ⊙ ⊙ ⊙ ⊙

Phoenix hadn't had a boyfriend since she'd started working at the GBT—her uncle knew that. Frankly, he was part of the reason why she didn't date. There was always a good bit of work to complete just for the observatory and her uncle's added side projects often left her with no time.

"Did you tell my uncle that you were my boyfriend?" she asked Shaun who sat across from her at a table in Sandy's Restaurant. It was a small mom and pop establishment about a mile from the observatory. Sandy, the owner, served great homestyle dishes and made what many said were the best pepperoni rolls this side of the Alleghenies.

Shaun peeked from above his menu and he looked confused. "That wouldn't make any sense," he said. "We really don't know each other that well."

"I guess not. But why would he say so?"

"You know him better than I do."

Phoenix sipped the rest of her iced tea and Sandy came over to refill her glass. "What'll ya have?" Sandy asked Shaun.

"I'd really like some cornbread," he told her and gave Sandy his menu.

"That all?" Sandy asked. "No beans? No bacon? If you don't eat meat, we can put you something else together."

"Thanks, but cornbread and extra butter…maybe some tomato soup if you have it."

"We do. That actually sounds like a pretty good combo."

Phoenix raised her hand. "Make that two Shaun combos," she said.

Sandy left and Shaun waited a moment before he said, "You knew, didn't you? You knew he might be killed and you knew I might see something."

Phoenix used her straw to play with her ice cubes, and she stared at the glass for too long without saying anything as she thought about the day on the swing when Shaun had been pruning the apple trees. She and her uncle had driven to Marlinton because Dr. One had been threatened to have the funding pulled from his EMR project. She remembered her uncle's enraged obscenities that he'd screamed into the phone before leaving. She remembered him telling her on the way down that he had a backup drive full of some older data, and he wanted to stash it…just in case.

Just in case he came up missing.

Just in case he was murdered.

"Yes," she finally said and looked up. "As you probably know, he's not liked very much. Is he really dead?"

Shaun remained patient. "Your receptionist said that all of you had heard that he was."

"Carol." The word tasted bad. "She's a gossiper. I don't know how she heard but some G-men I ran into said that he's only missing."

"You mean those guys that were here when I arrived?"

"The three ties." Phoenix grinned. "But you said he was dead."

Sandy set their food down and both of them began dipping spoonfuls of buttered cornbread into the tomato soup. Now, Shaun took an uncomfortably long pause in the conversation. He ate a bite, sipped some tea and said, "I'm pretty confused. It might be nothing more than a high school prank." He leaned forward and looked around the small, dimly lit room to where one other couple sat. They were elderly and were busy with their meals. He lowered his voice to just above a whisper. "I saw him last night. I was in my backyard and looked over in the direction of his house. Something inside was glowing green so I went to check it out, you know, being the caretaker and all. When I got inside, your uncle was lying on the floor, dead. Someone had plucked one of his eyes out."

Hearing that her uncle had died and knowing how he'd died were two different things altogether. Phoenix reacted to the idea of torture and mutilation with watering eyes.

"No," Shaun said and reached out to pat one of her hands. "That's why I'm so confused because, even though I saw him dead, I don't think he is."

They ate slowly while Shaun told her about the men he'd seen go into Dr. One's house but leave with no body. He told her about the green glow stick and the energy he'd felt emitting from it. He told her about the encounter at Sharp's Tunnel and that he thought, since her uncle couldn't be both alive and dead, some of his friends might have punked him as a juvenile graduation gift.

"That would be a pretty elaborate punk," Phoenix said. She twirled a chunk of cornbread in the soup with a spoon.

"I suppose the body I saw in the house might not have been him, but I'm pretty sure…still, those men would have removed the evidence."

Phoenix was beginning to enjoy the conversation. Solving complex problems was right up her alley and this mystery seemed ripe with complexity. With the idea that her uncle might not be dead, her mind was able to move from remorse to curiosity quite easily. "I think I know what the green glow stick might have been," she said. "An EMR bomb. It emits an electromagnetic radiation-blocking shield so that sophisticated surveillance can't penetrate a location. My uncle was up to something he didn't want anyone else to detect which is not unusual."

"Your uncle or whoever killed him, if he's dead."

"Was his place in a shambles?"

"Shambles?"

"Was it as if someone had tossed all of his stuff around?"

"No. Everything was as tidy and clean as always except for Dr. One, of course. Why? Is there a reason someone might?"

Phoenix wasn't ready to share her knowledge of the backup drive—at least, not yet. "My uncle had lots of secrets and lots of haters. Something was bound to happen to him sooner or later. Maybe we'll find out more tonight. Bethany seems to be a link of some kind. She thinks you're my boyfriend." She smiled at her own use of the word. Teenager Shaun wasn't quite her boyfriend type but he *was* now part of her life.

Shaun returned the smile. "Right," he said. "So, what are we..."

The front door to the restaurant jingled a new arrival and Phoenix turned to see Black Tie enter first. He stood with his hand on the open door as Red Tie and

White Tie walked in then remained by the door after it closed. Red Tie waited for a moment to analyze the elderly couple then abruptly spun on the back of one heel and sauntered over to stand a few feet from Shaun. He stared at Shaun but talked to Phoenix.

"New acquaintance, Ms. Messenger?" he said, his thick, black mustache stretching horizontally above his lip as he grinned.

"No," Phoenix said. "We are…friends."

"Really?" Red Tie shifted so that his shoulders were square with Shaun. "So, friend. Who might you be?"

Shaun opened his mouth but Phoenix raised her hand. "You don't have to say a thing. I'm surprised they don't have a complete work up on you already."

One of Red Tie's thick eyebrows raised and he peered with the one eye over at Phoenix. "We didn't get a good shot of him coming into the lab earlier but we can remedy that pretty quickly." From inside his blue suit coat breast pocket, Red Tie removed one of the newest CELLs and a pair of CGs, just like those Chris had shown Shaun earlier. He adjusted a few settings on the CELL with one thumb then placed the CGs on his face. Colorful lights flashed on the CELL screen as Red Tie grabbed an empty chair and sat down to stare at Shaun's face. "So, who are you?" he said and Shaun flinched as Red Tie suddenly raised both hands. He drew a box in the air with one index finger then used the index finger of the other hand to point at one of the invisible box corners he'd just created. With both fingers, he adjusted the marquee he'd made so that it framed Shaun's face then pressed one of the fingers against his invisible drawing.

"Those things aren't allowed around here," Phoenix offered.

"No," Red Tie said. "Not for you. Only for those that make the rules." He tapped the air and Shaun scooted his chair away from the encroaching finger waving. "Shaun Winston. Yes. I see. Connections to Phoenix Messenger? Uh-huh. Nothing social between you two on the Net. Seems like Mr. Winston doesn't even use the social nets. Hell, Mr. Winston. You don't have much of a Story at all." He tapped the air to continue his augmented reality session. "Wait…wait! Here we go. Yeah. Pissing in public. You do have a record. Now, what kind of man shows his pecker to innocent women and children?"

Red Tie's comments caused the elderly couple to look up. Sandy came from the backroom kitchen and stood next to the couple as she glared at the men in the suits.

"I don't know what that thing is telling you," Shaun said, "but that's not what happened."

"Yeah? Well, the reporting officer thought otherwise."

"I peed on a bush. I didn't show my peck…" He

glanced at Phoenix.

"And because you were a juvenile at the time," Red Tie continued as if Shaun had not spoken, "you served a sentence of community work…you, and it looks like a boy named Chris Wallace and one named Adam Sullivan. Creating a public nuisance. Running around in a pack are you? Three boys who can't keep their peckers in their pants."

Sandy walked over. "You are not welcome here. I told you that already. I'd like you to leave. Y'all are disturbing my customers."

Red Tie ignored her. "Oh…and look at that. Well, Mr. Winston friend of Phoenix Messenger, you don't have much of a Story with us yet but that's gonna be changing real soon, isn't it?" He looked at Phoenix. "You know what tomorrow is?" he asked her. Phoenix shrugged. Sandy asked him, again, to leave. "What kind of friend doesn't know of their friend's birthday?... and turning eighteen, too. So how *do* you know each other? No, wait! Here we go. Marlinton address for Dr. One." Red Tie lowered his hands, removed the CGs, and put them and his CELL back into his breast pocket. "Neighbors. And let me guess: I bet you're the kid that does the doctor's lawn, am I right?"

Shaun didn't respond.

"You see anything unusual over at the good doctor's place in the past day or two, Mr. Winston?"

Shaun remained silent.

"When was the last time you saw Dr. One?"

Still, Shaun revealed nothing.

"And of course the million dollar question is: Why are you here?" When Shaun still didn't respond, Red Tie added, "I suppose I could scan your facial nonverbals and eyeballs for trustworthiness."

Shaun had enough. He stood next to Sandy and Phoenix joined him. "I don't have to tell you a damn thing," he snarled. Shaun's raised voice caused White Tie to move another foot closer. "Figure it out for yourself. These are my friends. I'm having lunch with my friends."

"The sheriff hates you guys, too," Sandy interjected. "You want I should call him?"

Red Tie casually stood and eased his chair back to its spot at an empty table. "As you wish," he said. "But there really aren't a lot of places to hide in Green Bank. If Dr. One is here, we'll find him, and that's a guarantee." He winked at Sandy then exited the restaurant with White Tie and Black Tie right behind him.

Sandy rubbed Shaun's shoulder. "Sorry," she said. "Those goons have been coming around here way too often. Can't have privacy anywhere anymore." She looked at what little food there was left on the table. "At least they didn't spoil your appetites. And don't worry about the check. This one's on me." Phoenix started to protest but Sandy grabbed two empty plates full of cornbread crumbs and walked away. "See you soon, honey," she added.

Shaun was now firmly marked on the Feds' radar and Phoenix knew they needed to share knowledge. For some reason, her uncle had decided to involve his lawn boy and she had to find out why. Besides, they had a few hours to burn before their meeting with Bethany.

"She's right," Phoenix said to Shaun. "Privacy is hard to come by, even around here, but I know one place where it's guaranteed." She paused for a moment because she was struck by Shaun's bewildered, innocent expression. "We'll go to the top of the Great Big Thing."

◎ ◎ ◎ ◎ ◎

They could have been the men that had gone into the doctor's house right after he'd fled but Shaun just wasn't sure. They'd not been wearing blue suits and ties last night. Still, Shaun wondered. Had they followed him to Green Bank? Had they really not seen Dr. One's dead body? Did they really believe that Shaun was hiding it somewhere? Then, of course, it might all just be coincidence that he'd run into them in the first place. Maybe the Ties had nothing to do with last night. These were a separate bunch of "goons" who had only been interested in Phoenix's knowledge of her uncle's death until they'd met Shaun. Now, his Story, though limited, was a part of their investigation.

Phoenix's reaction to the whole thing told Shaun that she was hiding something painfully confidential. She wanted to go where no one could eavesdrop on them—so she could tell him what was begging for release. The restaurant, apparently, wasn't safe enough and this sparked Shaun's concern that the information about last night that he'd shared with Phoenix might have been intercepted.

"They were listening to us, weren't they?" Shaun asked as Phoenix turned onto Observatory Road. Her Chevy eco-Sedan was a 2038 model throwback to a 2020 Malibu in all of its physical accouterments. The steering wheel was even anchored in a forward position and didn't retract like all of the newer models with driver's assistance.

"I would trust less any conversation we have in this car than at Sandy's." Phoenix passed the lab on the left and continued straight along an asphalt road that curved around a short hill where the big telescope dish lived. Five much smaller radio dishes that were separated by several hundred yards paralleled the road on either side. "She constructed the restaurant using wire mesh to cut down on EMRs for those who are allergic. Still, it's not a place that can't be penetrated, even in Green Bank where the Quiet Zone rules don't seem to apply to everyone, equally."

At this point, nothing they could say to each other

would be absent some need for secrecy so Shaun sat quietly and studied the interior of the car. As someone who'd never driven anything before the 2030 models, he found the throwback 20s styling of the dashboard to be much more complex than the digital touch-enabled dashboards in today's cars. Phoenix's throwback model, though energy efficient to meet current standards, required too much mental engagement with dozens of buttons and knobs and sliders.

"What is it?" Phoenix asked. "You act like you've never been in a car before."

"Not like this one. It looks complicated."

"You a self-driving advocate?"

"I'm a bicycling advocate." He pointed at the console's controls. "Compared to today's cars…I mean, don't you just want to get safely from point A to point B?"

Phoenix shifted sideways in her seat to look at him, and the Great Big Thing on her t-shirt stretched against her chest as the real big thing came into full view in front of them. "Yes. But I want to do it with some style. We've sacrificed too much individuality for efficiency. A car is supposed to reflect its owner."

Shaun smiled. "Like I said."

Phoenix parked and got out then looked up at the GBT's five-hundred-foot-tall white dish. Shaun stepped from the car and followed her toward the monstrous structure, his head slowly pivoting toward the sky as he walked until his neck muscles could move it no farther. "Jesus," he said.

"Some call it God," Phoenix replied. "Isn't that right, Mr. Agey?"

Shaun refocused his attention at ground level and saw a middle-aged man standing near the base of the dish.

"God, hell, bitch, miracle…she's been called them all," Mr. Agey said and swung open a white metal gate to allow access. "Who do we have with us today? You look mighty young for a doctoral student, but that ain't peculiar around here. Ain't that right, Ms. Messenger?" Mr. Agey shook both of their hands.

"Teenage doctoral students we've had, but this isn't," Phoenix said. "He's doing some reporting for his high school newspaper and I wanted to give him the complete tour."

"Going up in the nest, are you?" Mr. Agey closed the gate and turned to leave. "Have a good time, young man. It's a neat experience."

Shaun nodded and waved, then followed Phoenix across a three-foot-wide, white metal walkway to a caged service elevator. They stepped inside and Phoenix pressed a green button labeled with the number 4 to get the elevator moving. Three folding chairs leaned against the back wall.

"It's taller than the Statue of Liberty," Phoenix said as the cage rode up the main structure toward the receiver, a bulbous mass of technology that pointed down into the dish to collect extraterrestrial data.

"Don't the electrical mechanics of this elevator mess with the telescope?"

"No one rides it while experiments are taking place. None are scheduled for this afternoon."

Acres of newly turned soil spread out toward the horizon in patchworks of evenly spaced rows. Some of the farmland was etched in perfect rectangles across the flatter valleys while other agricultural plots curved in wavy lines up and around short foothills. When the elevator stopped and they got out, Shaun's fascination shifted from the farm-covered landscape below to the cobalt blue sky, fluffy clouds, and mid-afternoon sun that seemed to suck him right up into its heaven.

Phoenix grabbed two folding chairs, walked out onto a metal platform, and unfolded the chairs next to the railing at the edge of the platform.

Shaun walked over to the railing, his senses filled with high altitude wonderment. Today, from up here, in a place where great discoveries had been made, West Virginia never looked more beautiful, more inviting, more like home. Phoenix pointed left and down and Shaun shifted his attention to the incredibly huge white bowl of the Green Bank Telescope that stared up at him. For a moment, he lost his balance and felt as if the dish might yank him right off the platform and into its gaping concave mouth. Phoenix grabbed his shoulder.

"The brain can't quite stitch it all together the first time," she said. "Vertigo is common. Here. Have a sit and we'll talk. I have the rest of the day. My co-workers will think I took time off to grieve for my uncle, which brings us to our first topic."

They sat and Shaun looked up at the enormous radio receiver above him, the component that collected whatever was bouncing up from the big dish below. "Quietest place on earth?" he asked.

"Ironically, this might be the quietest and noisiest place on earth simultaneously. Quiet of man-made radio waves; noisy with the radio waves from the cosmos. No terrestrial wireless can bathe your body up here, but the energy from a star a billion years old…" Phoenix sniffed the air as if she could smell the stellar reflections. "Once that gets a hold of your soul, you'll never look at the sky the same again."

Shaun *had* felt something—different. The moment he'd reached the top of the elevator, the breadth of the extraterrestrial above had dominated the farmland below. Is that what Phoenix was talking about? Had his soul actually been touched by the dense, invisible cosmic voices that coalesced right here, at the top of one of the biggest telescopes in the world? Shaun sucked in a deep breath and his lungs filled with fresh, cool electricity.

"What do you think?" Shaun said as he leaned into his chair. "Is he dead?"

"The Ties seem to think not. You saw him alive after you saw him dead. Some evidence leads to doubtful while…"

"While motive exists for someone to kill him," Shaun added.

Phoenix shifted in her chair so that when she extended her arm, her hand rested more naturally on his knee. The heat from her skin sent soothing vibrations into his groin. He couldn't help but to stare at her t-shirt's print of the GBT they now sat atop. "I was wearing this that day wasn't I?"

Shaun shifted his gaze to her face long enough to nod then looked up at the sky, feeling a little embarrassed.

"I was worried about you that day," Phoenix continued, a curt little smile snatching the corners of her lips. "If anything were to happen to him, I thought that you might see something and that you might need…me." She patted his knee and withdrew her hand. A sudden breeze whipped Phoenix's blonde hair and it slapped Shaun's shoulder. "There's something hidden in my uncle's house in Marlinton. At the time, we did it because we didn't trust who we were working for. As it turns out, we were right."

"Dr. One could have been killed for it?"

Phoenix nodded.

"And you?"

"And me what?"

"You two stashed it together. Are *you* worth killing for it, whatever *it* is?"

"I like the way you think." Phoenix's hand slapped his knee this time. "And by association, of course, your question becomes: Am I, Shaun Winston, worth killing for whatever this crazy woman and her equally crazy uncle has done to piss off the Feds?"

Whittled down to the basics, *Yes*, Shaun thought. He was about to become another eighteen-year-old graduate of a small high school in the middle of the Allegheny Mountains with a future in bike repair and he was worth killing just because he'd wanted to earn a couple of bucks a month by mowing some old man's lawn. If only he'd stayed in the damn trailer last night he would have never seen the green glow. He would have never gone to investigate. And, by association, he would have never been sitting atop the world with a woman who shared his jeopardy.

When Shaun didn't answer, Phoenix continued. "Thanks for caring. The good thing is, we don't think he is dead. Maybe the Feds, or whoever it was you say you saw go into the house, aren't interested in murder. Perhaps all they want is to create false truths and diversions. We're not gonna know until we analyze the data."

"Data?"

Phoenix stood so that Shaun could read the Levi's label on the back of her jeans. "That's what's hidden in the house. A storage drive copy of the data that the EMR project collected." She looked over her shoulder and saw him staring. It took a moment for her to smile and a moment longer for a red blush to color Shaun's cheeks. He blinked and stood and stared straight into Phoenix's eyes that were less than a foot away. For the first time, he realized how much hazel color veined its way through her mostly brown irises.

"Tell me about it," he said and scratched the beard stubble on his chin because he felt the flush in his face. "Why might it be worth killing for?"

Phoenix looked toward the horizon and the wind feverishly whipped her hair. A few grayer clouds hovered over the distant mountains. "I don't know. It must be or else why would my uncle make a copy? Why would someone want us to think he is dead? Why would they want to take the data from us?"

"Take it? Who?"

"Those three goons. Someone took the data off our servers and I'm guessing it's them. Those Ties must represent whatever government agency funded the project in the first place."

"Then that would make it theirs. And since Dr. One is gone, the project probably is, too."

Unexpectedly, Phoenix looked at him and scowled. It was a hateful look that made Shaun wish he hadn't said the obvious and that, thankfully, lasted just a second or two. She turned back toward the horizon.

"I guess you're right. It's pretty much over."

"But you do have some evidence you can use, right? I mean, is blackmail an option?"

"You like living dangerously, Mr. Winston."

"Come on." Shaun shuffled a half step closer. "Dr. One wouldn't have made a copy, probably not the most legal thing to do anyway, unless his purpose was to use it as proof for the just-in-case."

"Just-in-case?"

"Yeah. Just in case some goons tried to make the project go away, he'd have proof it existed. What's on the drive that we can we use?"

"We've got to get it and look at it first."

"There must be something that made you think we should talk about it, up here, where no one else can hear."

Phoenix looked around the heavens then down to the ground where Mr. Agey's balding head looked like a dot. "We were collecting EMR data, using highly sensitive satellites that our grant funded. You ever see one of those earth-from-space photographs that shows evidence of all the man made lights our world has created? The picture is taken at night so you can't see earth's actual landmasses but you can tell what they are by the light emissions that surround them. That's kind of what we were doing except our interest was in EMR emissions from the planet. Since the data is of something you can't see, I was hired to write the software that maps the data to a visual map, one that denotes locations and intensities and types. Ours was a longitudinal study so the info had been remapped several times over the last couple of years to show progressions in EMR emissions in that time frame."

"You use this ginormous telescope for that?"

Phoenix playfully slapped his forearm. "No silly. This thing is interested in billion-year-old data. We used the hundred and forty footer over there." She pointed out beyond the lip of the GBT's dish to the closest of the five telescopes along Observatory Road.

"And what did you find?"

"Over time, a lot of what we saw was expected. Lots of buildup of all kinds of EMR frequencies around large bodies of water like the Great Lakes, and around urban centers, particularly the New Cities."

"But..." Shaun knew it was coming and this made Phoenix smile.

"There's always a but, isn't there? But—we also found some unexpected results. Our equipment and my software are so sensitive to radiation emissions, we can get a pretty good indication of not only the density of emissions in a particular area, but what is actually causing them. Certain frequencies are associated with radio broadcast waves, others with cellulars and so on. I was mapping Dr. One's vibrations of interconnectivity. So, when we started seeing small pockets of very low frequencies pop up inside the Quiet Zone, we became curious for a few reasons. One, EMR is controlled in the Zone. Two, the frequency of the emissions is so low, we can't understand what might be causing them. And three, the low EMR signatures are appearing along rivers throughout the Alleghenies, beginning in western Virginia and traveling up and through West Virginia and into Maryland's arm. Along the Greenbrier, there are dozens of them that began appearing just six months ago."

"It's not a natural occurrence." Shaun said it as a statement of fact because he already knew the answer.

"No."

"And that's because the signatures are pretty much equally spaced."

Phoenix grabbed his forearm and squeezed. "How do you know that?"

They sat down and Shaun explained what Chris had shown him earlier in the day. Phoenix responded by saying that such a stealth technology could be possible but she wondered why anyone would use it along a rural river in the middle of the mountains.

"Another terrorist attack?" Shaun asked.

"That would be a first best guess."

"That would be awful. Everything changed so much in 2029. I don't know if the country could survive another."

Phoenix settled back in her chair and placed both hands on top of her head, clasping the fingers together and through her hair. "I was just beginning high school," she said. "It was because of that event that I decided to get into computers in the first place. The terrorists' use of drones sparked my curiosity about what made drones work and how they were controlled. Even in college, I pursued a degree that could get me into one of the top drone colony companies in the country, perhaps even with the Zon." She scratched her head with both hands and her hair tangled between her fingers. "But—and there's that but again—my uncle came along, pretty much out of the blue, with an offer for me to work at this prestigious research center beside him, a well-known scientist for good and bad, and to help create what my uncle said would be much more challenging and fulfilling than programming drone colonies." She dropped her hands to her lap leaving her hair in a mess. "Plus, the pay was twice what a starting job at the Zon would have been."

"So, 2029 made you want to work for a big corporation?" Shaun said. "It changed me in a completely different way. Slaving for a big corporation has become the last thing I want to do with my life."

"We're all slaves to some master."

Her statement silenced both of them for several minutes. They stared at the sky and Shaun started thinking about all of the *masters* in his life: those influences that controlled him. His mom was the obvious first thought but he deeply contemplated how much the Suspicious Society directed his actions. The laws that had been made since 2029—the requirement for registration and the use of Net tracking among others—were all attempts at controlling the masses. Worse, was the fact that so many people volunteered their private information, even if that information could be analyzed in ways that created inaccuracies and false Stories. Shaun's only real master, like every other U.S. citizen, was the Net or more directly, the software that ran it.

Shaun began a conversation with Phoenix about what he was thinking and they shared opinions about the Suspicious Society; she argued the pros and Shaun countered with the cons. They talked about the scarcity of water and broader concerns for environmental protection which, for the most part, they were in agreement. Then the conversation turned to more personal stories: what foods did they like and what was their favorite restaurant, what movies they thought were the best and which new releases, if any, had they seen at a VR Theatre; what hobbies beyond the obvious that they enjoyed and why.

Around five-thirty, as Phoenix was describing how working for the GBT had made her much more appreciative of the vastness of the universe, the elevator clicked on and the cage started to descend. A couple of minutes later, it returned and Mr. Agey stepped out.

"Pardon, Ms. Messenger," he said. "Dr. Carpenter

was looking for you earlier. He thought you might have gone home but wondered if I had seen you."

"You didn't tell him, did you?" Phoenix responded.

Mr. Agey grinned. "I know why you come up here. It's to get away. I told him nothing."

"I guess it's time for us to get going anyway. Thanks for watching my back, Mr. Agey."

Phoenix started to fold her chair and Mr. Agey waved his hand. "Don't worry about them. I'll take care of 'em." She and Shaun walked over and stepped into the elevator cage and Mr. Agey added, "Sorry to hear about your uncle, Ms. Messenger, and I hope your high school reporting goes well, young man."

He closed the cage door and Phoenix started the elevator. Once they were on the ground and walking toward Phoenix's car, she said, "You know we're going to have to go back after our visit with Bethany."

Shaun knew exactly what she meant and the thought of returning to the scene of the crime both frightened and excited him. Would the Ties or the white suits being waiting? And just what was on the secretive, to-be-murdered-over, backup drive? More so, what was going to happen once they recovered the drive?

Phoenix opened her car door. "If we go tonight, I can grab the drive and you can head home and get some sleep for your birthday and graduation tomorrow."

He stood next to the passenger's side door and

tapped the roof of the car with one finger. "I don't know. Nothing about any of this has gone in any predictable way. The last place I ever thought I'd be today would be on top of the big thing." The roof-tapping finger pointed at the telescope. "And who knows what it is that your uncle gave Bethany to give me."

"You would miss your own graduation?"

Shaun thought about the question for only a second. "I've graduated already. Maybe I'll have an excuse to miss the ceremony."

"The ceremony isn't for you. It's for all those that supported you getting the degree. What about your mother? Won't she be upset?"

"I'm not sure she is going to be able to make it anyway. Because it's Memorial Day weekend, the Water Spout wants her to work. She said she was going to try to get out of it."

Phoenix sat in the car and Shaun followed her inside. Once they'd closed their doors and Phoenix started the engine, she said, "If you get the chance, you should go. The opportunity will only be available one time."

Shaun leaned forward to look up through the windshield at the telescope. "I think I'm already headed for several first time opportunities."

⊙ ⊙ ⊙ ⊙ ⊙

Bethany Higgenbotham lived in a small, self-constructed home several miles away from the observatory. The last mile traversed a back road that reminded Shaun of the river trail; two dirt-rutted tracks snaked through tree lines that became less dense the closer to her house Phoenix slowly drove. Several potholes had been filled with gravel but the road's condition still preferred a truck to a car.

Phoenix parked in a grassy area next to an old Ford truck where felled trees lay like giant pickup sticks within the sparse wooded perimeter of the clearing. Shaun left his backpack and got out of the car. He paid no attention to Bethany who stood on a small wooden porch next to the home's front door. He was interested in the truck: a 2030 model, hunter green-colored F150, the last year the classic had been built. It was fully gas-combustible, probably didn't get more than twenty miles to the gallon, and was much more minimalist in its design than what Phoenix was driving. Most alluring to Shaun was that the model had been released right before the laws that required all new vehicles to be connected to the Net had gone into effect. It might not have been the smartest or environmentally cleanest vehicle, but it sure was cool. Shaun looked into the driver's side open window and found inside what he expected: simplicity.

Phoenix came around her car and stood next to Shaun. "If I was a car salesman right now, I'd have all your money," she said.

Bethany hollered from her porch, "Pretty ain't she? Nearly a dozen years old and going strong." Shaun and Phoenix walked over. "Bought her when I moved from the city. Pickups ain't particularly useful in New York." She craned her head to look down the access road. "Didn't bring anyone with you, did you?"

"Just the two of us," Phoenix said.

"And you ain't got your radiation devices on do you?"

"Left them in the car."

"Then please, come in."

The home wasn't old but it had been built in a way that resembled those from the frontier days. Inside, there were two rooms: a bedroom with a door for privacy and a large living space that included a small kitchen that had no appliances in it except a small refrigerator that sat atop a wooden stool at the end of a six-foot countertop. Other than the fridge, the home seemed vacant of any electrical device, which magnified its frontier feeling. Six windows, two in each of three walls, supplied all interior light. Built into the back wall to the right of the bedroom was a brick fireplace that held glowing orange wood coals. All of the walls had been constructed with what looked like ten-inch shelving boards. The knotted, six-foot-long planks had been nailed in a patchwork, caulked at the seams, and painted a dismal gray color.

Three green propane lamps sat dark in various locations within the room: one was on the kitchen counter next to a sink and faucet. Under the windows in the left wall, another lantern sat on a long, six-foot wooden table that looked handcrafted. Next to this lantern and strewn across the table was a collection of fabrics and zippers and buttons and thread spools. A red ball that had numerous sewing needles sticking out of it rested against the lantern. An incomplete blouse with marigold prints hung on a coat hanger from a hook in the ceiling to the right of the table; it was designed just like the sunflower-printed one she was wearing. The third lantern sat atop another handcrafted table (this one smaller, about four-feet squared) that was located between a couch and a rocking chair in front of the fireplace.

"Please, sit." Bethany offered them the couch with a wave of her hand and once they were seated, she dropped into the rocking chair as if she was exhausted. She pushed some of her frazzled salt and pepper hair away from her forehead. "I don't like those guys," she said with a scowl. "You just can't trust men in ties." And then, as if hospitality had been carelessly forgotten, she added, "Heavens. My manners. Would you two like something to drink?"

Shaun looked at the kitchen sink and faucet. "Some water would be fine," he said. "You have a well?"

"Damn straight," Bethany exclaimed. "Probably some of the best H2O around. Better than even your Greenbrier." She got up, walked to the sink, grabbed two coffee cups that hung from small hooks under one of two wall-mounted cabinets, and filled them with water that streamed slowly from the faucet. When she walked back over and handed one of the cups to Shaun, he sniffed it, saw that the water was crystal clear, sipped a mouthful that really did taste better than Greenbrier Tea, then chugged the rest. He set the cup on a flowery doily on the small table in front of him as Phoenix took one drink and placed her cup next to his.

"You're talking about the men that were at the lab today," Phoenix said. "Do you know who they are?"

Bethany cackled one laugh. "Don't you? Isn't it obvious? Those are the guys responsible for all of the bugs that are trying to drive me insane. They don't want to kill me; they want to discredit me. They want to make me out as an idiot for the world to see."

"Bugs," Phoenix said. "You mean they planted listening devices to drive you insane?"

Bethany leaned forward. "No. Not that kind of bug. I mean bugs—ones that emit radiation and have caused me to lose almost all sleep in the last three days."

"I don't think I've ever heard of such a…bug," Phoenix said.

"You wanna see?" Bethany's tired eyes sparkled

with exhausted excitement. Before either Phoenix or Shaun could answer, she jumped up, went to the kitchen, opened one cabinet door, and removed a glass jar like those used for canning. She looked into the jar and smiled before returning with it to the rocking chair.

"It's a cicada," Shaun said.

"Yes," Bethany agreed. "Just look at those radiation-emitting red eyeballs."

"I don't see…" Shaun began. "What? Is the radiation a feeling?"

"I don't feel anything," Phoenix said, "and I only see a locust."

"A cicada," Bethany corrected. "And you can't see the radiation until after dark."

Shaun thought he knew what Bethany was talking about since he'd seen something similar in Dr. One's house, but what had buzzed over the doctor's body had not been anything like what sat at the bottom of Bethany's jar. The cicada was many times larger.

"So we wait?" Phoenix said. "Shaun and I have to get going by then."

"You want to see, don't you? And not just what this little feller can do. I'm talkin' at least a half-dozen that's gonna show up once the sun is down. Besides, the time will give us a chance to eat and talk some more. As you can probably guess, I don't get a lot of visitors."

"Eat?" Shaun said.

"You should know better, being a Mountaineer and all. It's only polite to serve a meal to expected guests. We'll eat like off-gridders eat, my treat." Shaun looked over at the timid glowing coals in the fireplace and Bethany followed his gaze. "Not cooking on the fireplace tonight. The solar oven steams veggies and rice real nice like. Come on, I'll show you. It's about time to check on it anyway." She took the glass jar back to the kitchen. "Be seeing you in a little bit," she said to the cicada before closing it inside the cabinet, then she walked out the front door, leaving it open as an invitation to follow.

Around the back of the house, Shaun and Phoenix found Bethany standing next to what looked like any ordinary, medium-sized barbeque grill except for the closed lid which was made of glass and silver reflective metals, and the cooking base which looked to be ceramic. Little steam or smoke escaped the enclosure until she opened the lid. The aroma of butter mixed with garlic consumed Shaun and this caused his stomach to growl.

"It does make you hungry," Bethany said. "And not one drop of electricity is used to create such a wonderful smell."

Shaun peeked in to see a skillet full of long green beans and brown rice, and something else that was cooking within its own rectangular glass container. "You do have some electricity, though, don't you?" he said. "The fridge runs on…"

"Solar energy," Bethany said, lowered the oven lid, and nodded toward a large wooden shed that sat next to an outhouse a hundred feet farther away at the perimeter of the backyard. "Solar is captured at the top of the oak and runs down into the shed."

She pointed at the huge tree behind the shed then up toward the sky. The oak's trunk was at least two-feet thick and it held a wide canopy of branches that fanned out, beginning hallway up the hundred-foot behemoth. Within the branches and situated in a way that would gather most of the day's sunlight were four black solar panels. One black wire from each oval panel traced the branch on which it was fastened back to the tree trunk, and all four of these panel power feeds combined into one large cord that was nailed to the trunk and traveled all the way down to the shed.

Suddenly, a butterfly that flapped haphazardly near the house to his left distracted Shaun. He took a step in that direction which drew the attention of Phoenix and Bethany, and when he raised his arm and the butterfly landed on the back of his hand, both of their expressions turned, simultaneously, into astonishment.

Shaun couldn't believe it either. The monarch had the same, unique Bengal tiger look—but it couldn't have flown all the way from the river trail, he thought. It couldn't have followed him. "I never saw a butterfly with this pattern before today," he said.

Bethany smiled. "Beautiful. And very trusting. Now, you can say that you've seen one."

"No," Shaun responded. He gently leaned forward to get a better look. "I mean, this afternoon. Back on the trail. One just like this met me right after I left Marlinton. One like this landed on my hand, too."

Bethany shook her head. "That's not possible. She's been flying around my house for days now. Never landed on my hand, though."

Shaun bent his arm to bring the butterfly within a foot of his face. "How about it, Tony?" he whispered. "You got a twin?" The monarch's tiny red eyes seemed to stare right into his soul. Its feather-light legs rubbed his knuckles as if trying to comfort his confusion. "I guess you're right," he said to Bethany. "There's no way this one could be the same."

When a timer on the solar oven suddenly dinged, Shaun's arm jerked forward and the butterfly took flight, quickly disappearing around the left side of the house. "Where there's one," Bethany exclaimed, "there's always more than one of anything." She opened the oven and was enveloped by savory smoke. As she stirred the rice and green beans with a large wooden spoon, she asked Shaun, "Would you mind going inside to get some plates? Should be in the kitchen cabinet to the right."

Shaun walked around the house in the same direction as the monarch had flown but he didn't see it anywhere.

In the kitchen, Shaun opened both cabinet doors. The jar with the cicada sat to the left at just about eye level. The insect looked like any of the other million cicadas that had settled into the hills to offer their united, perpetual buzz. He grabbed three plates, closed the cabinets and turned to leave, but became curious of the items he saw in the far left corner of the room next to the long sewing table. He set the plates on the counter and walked over to a four-foot high, three shelf, handcrafted bookcase. The bottom shelf held a cardboard box full of green glow sticks that Phoenix had called EMR bombs. Three handheld EMR frequency meters occupied the center shelf. Several books stood upright across the top shelf and all of the titles had a common theme: Survival. He plucked a book with a title on the spine that read "How to Remove Yourself From the EMR World" and opened it to one of the first few pages. He read:

The presence of electromagnetic radiation was once very benign. Today, it is a warning that someone might be looking at us without our knowledge or consent. The Suspicious Society wants to know where we are at all times for reasons only it can comprehend.

A Bethany Higgenbotham kind of book for sure,

he thought, but, honestly, a Shaun Winston kind of book as well. He replaced it in its open slot on the shelf and when he turned, his shoulder brushed against a coat that hung on the back of the bedroom door, causing it to swing on its hook. He removed the coat to find a symbol that looked like it had been burned into the wood.

He'd never seen one like it. An F and an M, artistically styled with halos of energy wrapped around them. He quickly discarded the idea that the initials reflected Bethany's name but he wondered if the obvious was also true: FM, as in frequency modulation. He'd learned about radio broadcasts in school as part of a history class. Bethany said she was allergic to such waves so why burn such a reminder into her bedroom door? She was an odd sort for sure.

"Shaun!" Bethany yelled from beyond the bedroom wall. Her voice cracked. "Food is ruining. Plates please."

He returned the coat to its hook, grabbed the plates and headed outside.

☉ ☉ ☉ ☉ ☉

After Shaun left, Bethany continued telling Phoenix all about her resourceful, clean green energy.

"Too much shale in the ground to go geo-thermal so I improvised with solar," Bethany explained. "This oak is the best solar panel pole money never had to buy, but there was a bit of an installation cost. It's been a great investment with no utility bills. All thanks to your uncle."

"My uncle?" Phoenix said as confusion consumed her. "What does he have to do with solar energy?"

Bethany shook her head. "No. It's not that. He's been a good friend who has lots of resources, particularly for someone in my condition."

"Condition? You mean your EMR allergy."

"Yes, yes. The doctor knows about electromagnetic everything—how to live without generating it yourself. How to hide from those that would use it against you."

"How long have you known him?" Phoenix asked.

Bethany continued stirring the rice. "Well, we do go back a piece. 'Bout five years, I'd say. That's when he suggested that I use the big oak to get the solar panels up closer to the sun."

"He's been here, at your home?"

"Of course." Bethany looked up from the food and waved the big wooden spoon in front of her as she talked. "Lots of times. Made him lots of rice and lots of beans over the years. If it wasn't for him, I think I'd be dead already…or at least shackled to some psycho care center for those who imagine things that don't exist. In many ways, he helped me build the entire house. Mind you, he didn't actually hit any nails with any hammers, but he did direct me on how it should be built."

Phoenix was absolutely floored. She'd been working closely for the last two years with a man who was a workaholic. Her uncle had never had the time to go red-lighting with some woman who thought bugs were driving her crazy. Besides, he hated relationships—all of them: those with co-workers, bosses, government agents and nieces. And thinking about Dr. One being romantic? That really sent chills down her spine. Her thoughts must have shown because Bethany immediately reacted.

"I got good senses," Bethany said and pointed the spoon right at Phoenix's face. "You think we did the dirty, don't you?" Phoenix was about to say that her thoughts had not gone that far but Bethany waved the big spoon very quickly two times and continued. "My momma brought me up better than that. I may have worked in the city for a dozen years, but I was born and raised in Greenbrier County. The doctor is just a really good friend…maybe kind'a like you and Shaun. A boyfriend but not *that* kind of a boyfriend, which reminds me. Where are our plates? Shaun!" she yelled. "The food is ruining."

◉ ◉ ◉ ◉ ◉

Less than a minute later, Shaun came around the side of the house. "Sorry," he said and handed Bethany the plates.

"Hope you don't mind a little over-solar-cooked rice," Bethany said and scooped a heap of rice and green beans with her big spoon, dropped the serving on one plate, and handed it to Shaun. She did the same for Phoenix then dropped one final scoop on the remaining plate and asked Phoenix to hold it for her. Bethany used a hand mitt to remove the hot skillet from the oven rack then grabbed the glass container that was about the size of a small loaf of bread. When she opened it by lifting straight up, Phoenix was surprised to see a crispy, brown-topped loaf of bread. "We don't waste anything around here," Bethany said. "Cooked just enough for the three of us. No room inside for leftovers." With the mitted hand, she grabbed the loaf and pulled off an uneven third with her bare hand. "Hurry," she said. "Hot…hot…hot."

Shaun offered his plate and Bethany quickly dropped the chunk of bread onto it. She tore in two what remained of the bread and put them of the plates that Phoenix held.

"That should do it," Bethany said. "Now let's eat us some sun-baked goodness."

◎ ◎ ◎ ◎ ◎

Shaun and Phoenix sat together on the couch next to the fireplace. Their plates of food were on the table in front of them.

"This bread," Shaun said. "It cooks up just like real bread."

"That's because it is real bread," Bethany responded. She stood in the kitchen with her back to them as she searched through a cabinet drawer that she'd opened under the counter. "You all want some fresh market tomatoes? These things are ex…pen… sive in the city."

"Sure," Shaun said. "I'll have one." Phoenix nodded with a forkful of rice stuck between her lips. "Make that two, please."

"You are a proper West Virginia gentleman."

"Lived in Marlinton all my life."

"I wish I could say that." Bethany took three metallic silver bags from the drawer and closed it. "But no. I had to listen to everyone else. Get out of White Sulfur and move to the city, they said. I had too much brain to be wasting in a small West Virginia town." With the three silver bags in one hand, she opened the small fridge with the other. "Butter for your bread?"

"Yes. Thank you," Shaun said. "For both of us."

"Got a Coca-Cola in here, too. I use it mostly for recipes and for cleaning battery terminals but if either of you would like it…" Both Shaun and Phoenix said that they preferred her tasty well water.

Bethany juggled the bags, butter and cups of water to the table, adjusted the rocking chair's back cushion, and sat down. Shaun said, "You were saying that you moved to the city. Which one?"

"New York." Bethany ripped a chunk of bread from her share of the loaf and dipped it against a dollop of butter on the plate. "Mostly in the 20s...before 29, before the New Cities turned into suspicion states. That's when my body started to react to the radiation. By the time 2030 rolled around, there was so much of it tracking you everywhere. Even the people were tracking each other. I had to get out. So, I bought a new Ford and moved where EMR is not allowed. It's true what they say about West Virginians: We always return home."

At the top of the Great Big Thing, Shaun had argued the cons of the Suspicious Society with Phoenix. Bethany now provided him with a bit of proof. He chewed on brown rice as he turned to Phoenix and smiled. Bethany leaned forward, grabbed one of the silver bags, and pulled it open at the seam. She tipped the bag onto Shaun's plate and a red, ripe tomato rolled out.

Phoenix grabbed a bag and studied it. "I don't think everyone has such negative views of what our country has become." She opened the bag and placed the tomato on her plate. "After the aquifer attacks..."

Bethany raised one hand with a buttered piece of

bread between the fingers. "Nope! That's how they've framed it. That's the excuse they've driven into society. Data-mining and analysis work very well if you know how to use them." She ate the bread and continued, her words muffled by her chewing. "That's what I did. That's what I was good at. That's why everyone told me to leave West Virginia. Marketing and advertising could use the skills I had. New York was the obvious choice. For ten years, I helped powerful people use collected population data to sell not just products and services, but more so ideas, ways of thinking and ways of living."

Both Shaun and Phoenix sliced into their tomatoes at the same time. Shaun took a bite and chewed slowly to savor the flavor. "So, for a time," Shaun said, "you were working for the other side. You worked for all of the liars." Phoenix stopped eating and looked at Shaun as if what he'd said was inappropriate.

"We can all speak freely around here," Bethany said to Phoenix. "The house is pretty well protected except, of course, for the bugs. Your boyfriend is right. But with age comes wisdom." She took a bite of tomato then leaned back and rocked while she chewed and gazed at the ceiling. The trees on the hills outside filtered sunlight through the windows. Intermittent blades of gray shadow walked across her face as she swallowed and continued.

"It wasn't like we didn't see it coming—everyone

giving up one more piece of their privacy—for convenience, for relationships. Unless you are in rural places like Marlinton or Green Bank, it's hard to even find a human being at the checkout line. To have an actual human being to talk to about nothing, to see those groceries pass over the scanner, to have your bags filled for you. As hokey as it may sound, there's so few chances anymore to talk to someone you don't know about nothing that is of any importance. In the big cities, you fill up a cart and walk out the door. All of the tagged groceries are automatically deducted from your invisible bank account. They said Net-tracking gave more power to the people—like we haven't heard that before. It was less convenient, apparently, to wait in a line or whip out a credit card or, for God's sake, use real money. Of course, the real truth is that the Net gives more power to the powerful.

"I created messages that were developed not for the sake of personal convenience. I framed them based on economics and surveillance which, by the way, go hand-in-hand. Think about it. To surveil is to collect data. The more data gathered, the more accurate, the more trustworthy. Economies of scale are purely data-driven. If businesses and governments can analyze the tendencies of its population down to what each person had for breakfast, how many steps each took in a day, where they went, what they did, and how they did it, they can precisely manipulate the economy for maximum corporate profit or greatest opportunity for power of the politicians who take advantage of the agendas set up by the media and other controlling billionaires. Tell enough people who will listen that hate and fear solves problems and you will find entire industries transformed. Tell enough people the same message a thousand times and you can begin to make it the norm so that society will no longer consider opposing thoughts.

"If you know what people think via their actions and the number of actions recorded as data are large enough, you can pretty much predict and therefore manipulate their direction of thought. Predict wrong and all you have to do is add the inaccuracy to the data mass for a better chance the next time. Mind reading and control in the twenty-first century."

Shaun had never heard anyone verify in such detail exactly what he feared in today's world, a fear that he'd been chastised for believing throughout much of his life. At that moment, Shaun wished he could have recorded everything Bethany had just said so he could play it back the next time his mother suggested life was better in the city, or the next time Chris touted Cleveland as a much better choice for his future than Marlinton.

Bethany concluded, "Ironically, if it hadn't been for the massive buildup of electromagnetic radiation from so many data collecting devices, I might still be there, creating the messages that the powerful want you to believe. I would still be in the den of liars." She looked hard at Shaun then smiled and started to rock. "You're pretty sharp for a teenager. Fortunately, I've had a two degree change in latitude and a hundred and eighty degree change of attitude."

A hundred and eighty degree change of attitude, Shaun thought. How eloquent. Bethany was, surprisingly, much more intelligent than he'd given her credit. Based on Phoenix's profile that insinuated she might have a screw or two loose, and by her choice of living arrangements which were about as simple as one could get, he'd not expected her to have such educated thoughts, particularly those that he totally agreed with.

Phoenix leaned forward and finished her tomato before she said to Bethany, "You never told me you were a mathematician."

Bethany stopped rocking and smiled. "There's a lot, a lot of people don't know about me and I like it just fine that way."

Again, Shaun felt the connection. "The less a lot of people know, the less chance for the knowledge to be abused."

Bethany pointed at her plate. "Would you two like the rest of my tomato? They're good, aren't they?" She didn't wait for an answer and leaned forward to cut the remainder of her tomato in half. She forked a piece onto each of their plates then said to Shaun, "The way you think, young man. Don't ever change. Money, power, fame—they ain't worth it."

The room suddenly turned a full shade darker as the sun could be seen atop the hillside through the window above the sewing table. A thimble on the table snatched one fading sunbeam and reflected it onto the coat that hung on Bethany's bedroom door.

They finished dinner and Bethany collected the empty plates. As she walked to the kitchen, Shaun said, "I hope you don't mind, but I noticed your bookshelf over there when I came in earlier."

Bethany set the plates in the sink and leaned against the counter. "You like my choice of reading material? I'll tell ya, if you ever find yourself in my kind of predicament, get those books. Inspirational."

"And I'd need a couple of the frequency meters like the ones you have."

"Damn straight. No matter how complete my cage is, there's always a chance for infiltration. That's how I first detected the bugs."

"Cage?" Shaun asked.

Phoenix intervened. "I think she's talking about a Faraday cage—a purposefully constructed room or building that blocks EMR. We have one at the lab so that all of our control electronics don't escape and interfere with the telescopes."

"Right," Bethany said and pointed around the shadowy room. "Coated window treatments, specialty paint, wire mesh in the walls, reflective storage bags to protect food…even my clothes are made of EMR-blocking fabrics. That's why I make my own."

"And if that's not enough," Shaun added, "you have EMR bombs that'll do the trick."

Bethany nodded. "You were curious, weren't you? You can't be a high-sensitive without owning a few of them gems."

All remaining slivers of sunbeams disappeared which cancelled the thumbnail reflection. Shaun stared at the coat on the bedroom door. "My mom always tells me that's one of my problem areas that needs looking after. She always says that curiosity kills the cat."

"Smart mom," Bethany said.

"So…I'm curious about one more thing. Like you said, if I ever turn sensitive, I'm going to need to know as much as I can."

"You don't have any cats, do you?"

It took him a second to understand. "No. I don't. But not because I'm curious." He smiled and pointed at the coat. "There's a mark on your door—a symbol. It looks like it was burned into the wood."

Bethany walked over, grabbed the coat and laid it on the sewing table. "Yes, I burned it there." She pointed at the symbol. "You probably don't know this. The movement is only beginning to grow. It is incredibly secretive. The Net really doesn't know much about it…yet."

"FM," Shaun said. "That's what I see."

"Faraday Movement. For all those who are rejecting the Suspicious Society, rejecting data collection, rejecting being treated like a commodity for profit. We just don't want our lives controlled."

"We?" Phoenix said. "You are a part of this… movement?""

"Shhh!" Bethany put her fingers to her lips. "It's getting dark. They'll be listening soon, so we have to speak more confidentially."

Shaun would have loved to continue the conversation but he needed to pee. Besides, he thought, if Bethany's bugs were real and they were coming with nightfall, he'd have to take care of business before their arrival. "You mind if I use the bathroom?" he asked Bethany.

"It's okay to call it an outhouse. That's what it is. Did you see it out past the shed?"

Shaun nodded and left. When he stepped outside and into the growing dark, he couldn't help but to look down for any strange insects that might pose a threat.

◉ ◉ ◉ ◉ ◉

Phoenix thought that it was incredible how very little someone could know about another person, especially in today's society. Bethany had carried on a relationship with her uncle for over five years? Bethany was a mathematician who'd worked in New York City, creating messages with data that manipulated people? She'd turned wiser when she'd become EMR-sensitive and now she was a part of some cult called the Faraday Movement that Phoenix had never heard of?

"Why didn't you ever tell me?" Phoenix asked her.

"Honestly, my dear," Bethany said as she walked over and sat on the couch beside her. "You really never gave me any reason. You never believed in hypersensitives. Quite frankly, I always thought you regarded me as a nutcase and that was fine with me until Dr. One pulled you into all of this. Being a renowned nutcase has its advantages. Ignorance causes people to react in unreasonable, involuntary ways, wouldn't you agree?" Bethany patted Phoenix's knee, softly, quickly. "Dr. One was never like that. He knew. He cared. He helped. And he never said a word about it to anyone. Of course, I wasn't about to tar the good name of such an important man by revealing a relationship that no one would understand. Like you. Right now." Bethany leaned over and grabbed one of the wooden matches that rested next to the propane lantern. She struck it against one of the table legs, angled the flame into the lantern's glass globe, turned a knob, and a rush of gas ignited into a bright white glow. She used the knob to reduce the light's intensity. "You ever wonder why none of the horrible side effects of EMR ever made it into the public conversation? Because of media agents like me. We convinced people that wifi and satfi and all the other fies out there wouldn't hurt them—all for the interests of the digital oligarchy. We could never tell the truth: that the invisible sauce they serve through the billions of devices that have defined the twenty-first century really does cause everything from indigestion to nose bleeds, and from irregular heartbeats to cancer." Bethany stood and walked to the kitchen.

Sunlight faded fast and Phoenix looked for Shaun beyond all of the room's darkening windows. "There's proof?" she asked.

"Oh yeah, but good luck ever finding it. We did a pretty good job of hiding the truth, even back when I was involved. Can you imagine the power of deception in today's ultra-connected world? They know just about everything about everyone anymore. And with those damned bugs…well, honey, we can't even be safe from the prying eyes of those who wish to be gods in our own homes." She waved Phoenix over and directed her to look into the narrow cabinet door opening. Sitting on the shelf inside was the glass jar she'd shown them earlier. Most of the cicada was still visible in the dimly lit room but as Phoenix continued to stare, the bug started to change. Tiny, multi-colored specks of light within the insect's body grew brighter.

And as she leaned forward for a better look, her cheek pressing hard against the edge of the cabinet door, the cicada jumped at her and Phoenix yelped.

⊙ ⊙ ⊙ ⊙ ⊙

Shaun stood in the outhouse with his legs spread in an unnatural position; his left foot was forward so that his toe touched the wooden bench seat and his right foot was behind him so that his heel propped the door open to allow what little dusk remained inside. The toilet hole had a hinged seat and lid and, by habit, Shaun shuffled forward to lower both after he had finished. When he did so, his right foot released the open door and it gently swung closed on rusty, springe hinges. He stood in complete darkness, listening to the acoustics inside the outhouse that made the cicada buzz outside sound as if a UFO was hovering over him. It gave him a moment to escape reality and ponder how wonderful a trip in a flying saucer might be—one that would get him the hell out of here and off this bat-crazy planet.

Bethany had sealed the boards inside quite well. Whatever remained of dusk filtered around the closed door and frame, and through a tiny, uncaulked opening in the roof right above him that was less than half an inch wide. He reached up, leaned forward a bit, and with his arm not quite fully extended, swiped the hole with the pad of his finger for no other reason than to see if he could do so. Then he looked down and what he saw made him drop his arm and gasp.

Creepy darkness, just like Dr. One's house had been the night before. Cicadas, buzzing in such numbers as to drown out all else. And a tiny speck of multi-colored lights, just like the one that had floated over Dr. One—it suddenly appeared from what Shaun correctly guessed was the closed, lidded toilet hole. It crawled for a moment across the dark bench, moving only an inch in the ten seconds that had frozen Shaun's attention, before it took flight.

It was a tiny little thing, full of tinier red and green and blue pinpoint specks that could not be seen without such darkness. Bethany's bugs had arrived and Shaun wondered just how far one could fly in less that twenty-four hours.

The speck darted quickly upward and hovered near the small opening in the ceiling which brought it within a foot of Shaun's face. A dozen micro-tiny lights twinkled like a small spectral universe within a grain of sand.

Of course, curious Shaun was unable to keep his hands at his sides. He reached up and the speck shot three, micro-thin green beams away from his face and up onto the low ceiling. The three beams began gyrating, faster and faster, until they formed a triangle against the darkness above.

"Agghhh!"

Shaun shuttered and quickly jerked around. It was Phoenix. He immediately opened the outhouse door but looked up first to see that the green triangle and the speck were both gone.

Carefully, he ran around the house, dodging shadows of tree roots and fallen branches. He pushed open Bethany's front door with a bit too much force and it startled the women inside. Phoenix almost dropped the jar she was holding.

"You want to be the death of me?" Phoenix said. The lantern by the fireplace cast dull light against her face.

"Sorry." Shaun's breaths, fueled by the run around the house and his nerves, came quickly. "I heard you scream." He stepped into the kitchen.

"It was more like a yelp," Phoenix said. "We were just about to check out one if Bethany's bugs."

"Yeah? I've already seen one hovering around in the outhouse."

Bethany led them to the couch and motioned for Phoenix to put the jar on the table near the lamp. "Hovering?" she said. "No. Cicadas can't hover; they're too fat."

"It wasn't a cicada. It was way much smaller. And it shot out tiny green beams." Shaun started to tell them about the similar incident he'd had at Dr. One's but Bethany's comment stopped him short.

"I'm gonna have to check the well water filter," she said. "Might be some hallucinogens making their way into it. My bugs don't hover and they don't shoot nothin'. They just sit in the corners of the room where I can't see them, recording what I say, capturing video frames of everything I do."

"But…" Shaun was silenced by Bethany's index finger.

"Have a seat and gaze into my crystal jar." Her inflection was one that mimicked a fortuneteller. Shaun and Phoenix sat on the couch as Bethany turned the lantern light down. "Watch closely."

As the light faded, so, too, did the cicada in the jar. Its red eyes disappeared until the lantern light blinked out in a tiny flash of orange flame, and then they started to glow—just two tiny red specks, identical in size to those that had hovered in the outhouse. Shaun stared until his pupils had adjusted to the darkness and an additional dozen or so red, green and blue specks appeared inside the jar.

"I'd say it is recording us right now," Bethany said as she kneeled beside the table. Twilight remained enough so that her body could be seen only in shadow. "You can almost see all of its micro-gizmos at work by the tiny flashes." She lifted a shadowy finger. "See… flash…flash…flash. There goes your face onto the Net, and there goes my voice telling you your face is going onto the Net."

Shaun leaned back. "A picture of my dark face? Good. Not much use in that."

"Like I said before." Bethany's shadowed head lifted. "Sharp kid. That's why darkness is preferable. I don't care what kind of new tech they're using but I'm pretty sure none can understand features from a dark, featureless face." Bethany twisted away from them and pointed toward the front door. "Look."

Shaun watched the bottom of the door. His eyes had adjusted enough so that all of the room's general outlines were visible.

"Usually just after dark." Bethany lowered her voice to just above a whisper. "Within a few minutes."

The cicada in the jar jumped against the glass and all three of them yelped and turned. Space inside the jar became a multi-colored menagerie of light streaks as the bug beat feverishly for escape. This lasted a full minute and just when Shaun thought that the cicada would surely break out, it settled to the jar's glass bottom. The colored streaks remained until Shaun blinked a couple of times.

"What's that?" Phoenix said, pointing.

Shaun rolled his eyes toward the floor near the front door. Three separate groups of multi-colored specks sat equally spaced a foot apart. They flashed and twinkled but otherwise remained motionless, and Shaun wondered how fast they could move. He'd turned his attention away from the door for only a moment.

"And over there," Phoenix said and pointed toward the opposite side of the room at the floor near the bedroom door. "Three more."

"Yep," Bethany said. "That should just about do it. So you believe me now? Bugs. Just like I said. And smart little fellers, too. Did you see how the one in the jar created a diversion?"

"Damn," Phoenix whispered. "My uncle said something like this might happen."

"Shhh!" Bethany urged, loudly.

"So, what do we do now?" Phoenix asked. "Just sit here and look at them all night in fear of doing or saying anything?"

"EMR bomb," Shaun interjected.

"Go ahead," Bethany said. "Get the one shaped like a giant cookie."

One of the bug specks sat right in front of the bookcase and Shaun tensed as he approached it. Whatever these things really were, they acted just like cicadas. Any one of them could launch at his face in an instant. They couldn't hover but they could fly pretty fast in a short distance.

Shaun stepped to within a foot of all three bug specks and all three shuffled back a few inches. He didn't like it. They felt…threatening.

"Behind you!" Phoenix urged.

Shaun looked over his shoulder to see that the other three cicadas had moved from the front door and now occupied his left flank.

"They won't hurt you," Bethany said to Shaun. "But they know you're afraid. Go ahead. Get that cookie."

Suddenly, above him, three, tiny multi-colored specks flew into the room through some hidden crack just above the sewing table window. They were miniscule in size compared to the cicada specks. Apparently, Shaun thought, his outhouse visitor had found two friends.

Both Bethany and Phoenix stood from the couch and all three flying specks took positions above all three of their heads. All at once, nine micro-thin green beams, three from each of the flyers, shot straight down then rotated and joined to form a glowing, circular, ten-foot-wide perimeter that surrounded them, a halo of green that reminded Shaun of his own insatiable curiosity and how it had gotten him into all of this in the first place.

Within seconds, two things happened in quick succession. All six cicada bugs scrambled from the room (three fled under the front door and the other three scuttled under the bedroom door). The moment they were gone, the entire home filled with bright light. A car had been silently waiting outside. Its headlights blazed mercilessly through all of the large windows and blinded them. All three lifted arms and hands to shield their eyes as three men stepped from the car and stood as shadows within a blaze of bright white.

"Bethany Higgenbotham!" Red Tie yelled. "May we speak with you?"

Bethany casually leaned over and took a few slow seconds to light the lantern on the table. She told Shaun that there was a box of matches in the top kitchen drawer and asked him to light the two remaining lanterns. "I'm surprised it took them this long," she said.

"What do they want?" Phoenix asked.

"Who knows, this time."

"This time?"

"This ain't the first I been harassed by the Feds. They're always trying to discredit me." She grabbed the lantern's metal handle. "You take one, Shaun, and give her the other. Let's see what they want."

Bethany stepped out first. "You mind turning off those blessed damn lights!" she yelled. As Shaun and Phoenix joined her on the porch, the dark figure closest to the car leaned over and the headlights faded out, leaving only the car's soft electric hum to compliment the surrounding chorus of cicadas.

Red Tie stood in front of the car. He held in his right hand something that looked like a giant marble. He wore a pair of ClearGlasses. "I believe you mentioned something about the Faraday Movement," he said to Bethany.

Shaun saw sudden distress enter Bethany's otherwise cool demeanor. "Fara-what?" she said.

"Let's not do this," Red Tie urged and raised his right arm. "Your impenetrable Faraday cage isn't so impenetrable. You're involved, aren't you? What are you doing? Recruiting new members?"

"I don't know what you're talking about."

The big marble in Red Tie's hand started to glow with a shade that matched his tie. Immediately, Bethany grabbed her stomach and almost dropped her lantern. "It's all psychological," Red Tie said. "You aren't really sick. It's all in your head."

Bethany curled forward and Shaun grabbed her lantern. "EM radiation," she moaned.

"Stop this!" Phoenix demanded. "She said you're full of shit, now leave her alone and get the hell out of here."

White Tie and Black Tie walked quickly forward to stand at the bottom of the porch steps. "We only want to talk to her," Red Tie said. "At least for now." The men climbed the four steps two at a time, grabbed Bethany under each arm, and guided her down the steps. Red Tie removed the CGs and placed them inside his suit coat. In his other hand, the big marble's glow died and he dropped it into one pants pocket. "We'll give her a good place to sleep and good food to eat. God knows she deserves it after living in this dump."

Shaun's nerves flooded his body with fight-or-flight. His lantern shook in his hand. Phoenix was much calmer. She said, "What gives you the right to come to someone's house…"

"I give people the right!" Red Tie interrupted, his voice rising with authority. "You should be careful with whom you associate. Such a decision can change a person's Story in ways that could mark them as suspicious."

Bethany regained enough strength to stand and offer limited resistance. She turned her head to look at Shaun as the men guided her to the car. "Your fate is within the burn!" she yelled just before she was forced into the back seat.

"That concludes our meeting for this evening," Red Tie said. "Perhaps we can do dinner sometime… at Sandy's?" He didn't wait for an answer and turned away. Black Tie and White Tie got into the front seat and Red Tie sat in the back next to Bethany. The headlights snapped on, the car backed up and gently tapped the Ford truck's bumper, then slowly drove away.

Shaun and Phoenix stood there until the red taillights disappeared and nothing was left except astonished, cicada-laced silence.

◉ ◉ ◉ ◉ ◉

They'd decided that the best and safest course of action was to lock up Bethany's home and stay the night at Phoenix's apartment located in a campus-type of community on the observatory grounds. They were too mentally tired to face any more surprises. They would get up early the next day and revisit Dr. One's house to retrieve the hidden data files.

It was little after ten o'clock when Phoenix turned into the apartment complex parking lot. The ten-unit, single story building was shaped like an "L" and three solar lampposts located at each of the building's three corners illuminated the facing sidewalk. Phoenix parked in one of two open spaces and they both got out. She clutched the sleeves of her t-shirt. "Got chilly all of sudden," she said. "Or maybe my nerves are just shot."

She was right on both counts, Shaun thought, but he didn't say anything as he slipped his backpack over one shoulder and followed her along the sidewalk toward the interior corner of the building where a tall, glass Superman-style phone booth sat under the lamppost. Next to the phone booth was a bottled water vending machine that promoted "Greenbrier Tea" as the best tasting natural water anywhere. The vending machine looked like one right out of the 20s, complete with push panels and enticing bright lights. Behind the vending machine and through a large window that was dimly lit from inside, Shaun saw a couple of washers and dryers. Phoenix's apartment was right next to this corner laundry room.

In any other circumstance, Shaun would have been consumed by the anticipation of staying the night alone with a beautiful woman but those thoughts were fleeting. Even the Levis patch on the back of her jeans' pocket did not have the same effect as it had when she'd stood in front of him on the platform of the GBT.

Phoenix pressed a series of numbers on a digital keypad beside her apartment door then turned the knob and pushed it open. Just before entering, she stopped and looked to her right. Shaun followed her gaze to see the receptionist from the lab standing under the lamppost at the far corner. She remained there, looking right at them for only a second, before disappearing around the side of the building.

"Odd, as usual," Phoenix said while stepping inside and switching on a light. "She lives in a complex up the road a bit. I guess she's spreading out the distance that she walks at night." She tossed her car's data key on a small kitchen table next to the door and headed straight for a recliner chair on the far side of the small living space. She fell into it and stared at the ceiling for a full minute before realizing Shaun had not moved from the open door. She tilted her head forward. "You're not going to stand there all night, are you?"

Shaun stepped in and closed the door. A small kitchen with all the necessary amenities was to his immediate right, and to the right of Phoenix and the recliner was a short hallway that led to a closed door. Phoenix pointed at a brown fabric couch that sat along the left wall next to a three-shelf bookcase, and Shaun walked over to sit in the middle of its softness. He placed his backpack to his left on the couch.

"You going to be okay with wearing the same clothes tomorrow?" she asked him. She pointed at his shorts. "We could do a quick load. I don't think I have anything your size."

The question took Shaun by surprise because the encounter at Bethany's consumed his thoughts. What had she yelled at him before being taken away?

Your fate is within the burn.

"What'dya think?"

"I…uh." Shaun blinked. "No. I've gone longer. I can grab something at home, tomorrow."

"You want a shower? You're welcome to it." She thumbed in the direction of the hall.

Shaun's thoughts completely shifted away from Bethany and centered on Phoenix's question. Memory took over with a montage that included the first time he'd ever seen her standing outside Dr. One's house with a potted plant in her arms, how he'd felt as a sixteen-year-old boy with a crush on an older woman he'd never met, how he'd fantasized about her living so close to him before finding out the truth about his new neighbor.

A shower? With her…in her apartment?

Phoenix reacted to his expression. "Thinking about tonight?" she asked.

"Umm…yeah." He blushed a little and habitually

reached up to scratch the thin whiskers of one flushed cheek. "Tonight."

Phoenix looked back up at the ceiling. "What did she mean? I get the fate part. She's saying something about our future—or about your future; she was staring right at you."

"And, 'within the burn'?" Shaun said. "I don't get that at all."

Phoenix gently rolled her head. "The sun burns but why would our future be within the sun? She was talking in code, for sure, with those goons around her. Maybe the burn is something caused by the sun."

Shaun shook his head and noticed that the room had no electronics whatsoever: no flat screen, no stereo, no computer. A single, circular clock with the background of a leaping dolphin occupied the center of the opposite wall. "What happened to her tonight and what was that glowing marble thing they were using on her?"

"EMR radiation as torture." Phoenix leaned over and rested her elbow on the arm of the chair closest to Shaun. She cupped her chin with her hand. "Never heard of such a thing. You know, I never did believe her—not about her illness and certainly not about those bugs."

"Why didn't they take us, too?" Shaun asked. "It wasn't like we had much of a fight even without a glowing radiation ball."

"Good question. That red-tied son-of-a-bitch acted like he could do anything he wanted. I know one thing. If they don't release her, I'm getting the sheriff involved. We were witnesses."

Shaun thought about becoming so involved, about the information that would surely be collected and loaded to the Net. He only hoped he wouldn't have to make that choice. He reached over and grabbed his backpack. "Thirsty?" he asked. "Got some great artisan brew here straight outta Cheat Lake." He unzipped the pack, pulled out two bottles and gave one to Phoenix. They opened them and tapped them together. "If it doesn't kill you, it only makes you stronger."

Phoenix smiled. "I'll drink to that." They both swallowed a third of the contents. "Something your mom always said?" Phoenix licked her lips and added, "Good stuff."

"Almost as good as Greenbrier." Shaun wiped a stray, clear drop from his whisker-stubbly chin. "My mom always said that my dad always said that. She said it's a complete example of irony."

"How so?"

"My father disappeared and was pronounced dead when I was six. The Great Flood got him, they said, but they never did find a body."

Phoenix had moved her bottle to her lips but now stopped and lowered it. She leaned even closer to him.

"I'm so sorry. I didn't mean to bring up…"

"No. It's been almost a dozen years. I really didn't know him too well. I remember he wanted me to play baseball and eat my vegetables but, you know, I'm beyond that. Both mom and me—we got stronger." Shaun moved the backpack from his left to the right and scooted closer to Phoenix. "So, tell me about your uncle."

"Well, Dr. One is my uncle but he's really a distant one," she offered. "He's my mom's much older brother so he's more like a great uncle, one consumed by his own fame. Don't get me wrong. I love the guy for getting me the Green Bank job but that's about as far as I can take that word in relationship to him." She sipped some more water. "He *has* taught me quite a few things: how to work twelve hours every day without a break and feel that it would be incompetent not to do so; how to avoid the media and religious fanatics whenever confronted with questions about his God Light discovery; how to work with a man whose ego was as big as the miraculous claims he'd make; and, apparently, how a man can keep a pretty tight relationship with a local recluse without a damn soul knowing about it."

"Sounds like an asshole," Shaun said.

"We agree on a lot tonight. Might have to break out another couple of bottles."

Shaun's gaze caught the hazel veins within Phoenix's irises. "How do you work with such a person?"

Phoenix blinked. "It's all about what you get out of it." She shifted in the chair and crossed her blue-jeaned legs. "I got to use my programming mojo to discover something new. I got to use state of the art hardware. And, of course, the paycheck ain't too bad either. But I should have known that any project funded by the Feds had jeopardy written all over it. Just when we were getting to the good stuff, and all of this happened."

A long silence between them caused Shaun to ask, "What do you do for entertainment, I mean, when you're not working twelve hours or eating or sleeping?"

"Not really into the media stuff. This apartment complex doesn't allow for such connections on the observatory grounds. There are a few units in another complex that are Faraday-caged for those who just can't live without the programmed world. I read and do research. That's just about the whole of my boring life."

When Shaun had tossed his backpack to move closer to Phoenix, the top of a bottle of water and the corner of his decader had slid out of the opening. Phoenix pointed at it.

"That's an antique," she said. "Back when they were called smartphones. It all started with those things. Can I see it?" Shaun leaned over, grabbed the decader and handed it to her. "I figure these will be outlawed some day. They gave you an option for turning tracking off." She flipped the phone around her fingers. "Not today. Not with CELL technology. That's why I usually keep mine out in the car at night. I guess Bethany's paranoia does have a way of rubbing off on a person."

Shaun asked, "They don't work this close to the telescope anyway, do they?"

"They shouldn't." Phoenix handed Shaun his decader. "You know, other than the tracking, the new CELLs are pretty amazing, if, of course, you are willing to give up your privacy to own one. And I'm not talking about my old V.38 CELL. I'm talking about the new V.41, just out at the end of last year. I went to New Pittsburgh in January with a friend who had gotten one for Christmas. We were at a conference at Carnegie for the day but at night we went downtown. The V.41 can connect straight up with everything in the City. The older HaloLens, CGs, and the new iTacts that are supposed to be released this summer all provide an incredible experience when matched with a V.41. And the processing power…when you've got several thousand V.41s walking around and talking to each other, it's all incredibly real."

Shaun sat staring at her, silent.

"It's a neat place to visit but I wouldn't want to live there. You've never been, I suppose?"

Shaun shook his head. "I've heard about what you are talking about. Not so sure I'd be into such things."

"Because you don't like the cost of the entry fee."

"Registry card."

"You have to get one sooner or later." Phoenix suddenly smiled and tilted her bottle forward. She looked up at the dolphin clock. "Another toast," she said. "In a little more than an hour, you'll be eighteen."

Shaun didn't have any water left but he tapped her bottle before Phoenix swallowed what remained inside. "Actually," he said. "Not until ten past nine in the evening at the Pocahontas County Hospital."

"Well," Phoenix smiled. "Might as well get ready for your big day. You sure you don't want a shower?" She stood and crunched the bottle in her hand, then took Shaun's empty.

Shaun shook his head.

"Mind if I get one? If you're interested in astronomy or computer software design, my bookcase is full of interesting titles. If you're hungry, just feel at home." She walked to the kitchen to trash the bottles then walked back past him and smiled. "Be out shortly."

Her t-shirt with the Great Big Thing on it. Her Levis patch painted on the pocket of her left butt cheek. They disappeared into the hallway and a few minutes later a light came on, a door closed, and the shower water started to fall.

Shaun needed to stand and he needed some air,

especially since a citrus body wash aroma now moved from the bathroom to his nose. He touched his flushed cheek, stepped outside, and left the door open a crack.

Late May was chilly, almost enough to need a light jacket. He looked over at the phone booth to his right. The eaves along the angled rooflines were tall and wide enough that the booth and the water vending machine were under shadow from the yellow haze of the solar lamp above. The booth had a small convenience light on inside but most of it was cast in an emerald green glow from the vending machine's lighted graphics.

His attention shifted out toward the horizon beyond the end of the building's L-wing. Why he'd not noticed it as Phoenix had pulled into the parking lot was a testament to how out-of-it he really was. The Great Big Thing towered between the dark hills in the short distance. White and red lights marked its nightlife outline. Lights from the other smaller telescopes snaked as dots from the GBT, the closest one being just beyond the interior lights of the laboratory across the street.

"Up there," he said aloud while staring at the large, blinking red light all the way up at the top of the Big Thing. "I was up there, where few have gone before. I wonder what it's like at night."

"Unbelievable."

The voice came from his left. He quickly spun on his heels.

"Really unbelievable, don't you think?"

"Dr. One?" Shaun could hardly say the words; he could not believe his eyes. Down at the opposite end of the building where the receptionist had been standing when they'd arrived, stood Dr. One. He wore that same black t-shirt with the big yellow smiley face on the chest. "What are you…?"

"Doing here? Just making sure you are on your way."

Shaun started walking in Dr. One's direction. When the doctor didn't move, he walked faster, thinking that the image would disappear as it did in the tunnel. He got within ten feet before the doctor said, "You taking care of my niece?"

It *was* Dr. One except the smiley face shirt seemed to stretch that truth. Still, those were his eyeballs all set back nice and proper above his nose. "What's going on?" Shaun asked.

"Take care of Phoenix and everything will work out just fine for the two of you."

"And Bethany?"

"She chooses to make the sacrifices she does."

Shaun took a step forward and Dr. One stepped backward. "Are you…dead?"

Dr. One's smile matched the yellow face on his shirt. "What do you think? What does Phoenix think?" He pointed. "Don't forget that I left something for you."

"Shaun!" Phoenix shouted from her apartment

door. Shaun looked over his shoulder and waved and when he turned back around, Dr. One was gone. Shaun quickly ran around the end of the building and beyond the illumination of the yellow solar lamp into a large, grassy backyard but saw no one. He stood in the cloud-covered half moon shadows beside a landscaped group of young white pines and took one last look around. Phoenix appeared in the yellow lamp glow beyond the end of the apartment building. "Shaun?" she said, not loudly.

He jogged back to her. "It was Dr. One."

Phoenix wore a button-up plaid shirt and gray sweats and she blew into her hands for warmth. "What!?"

"You didn't see him, did you?"

"My uncle? My uncle is here? Where?"

"He was…I mean…how fast can that guy run?"

"Come on. I think you must have hit your head on a tree limb or something." She grabbed his arm and led him back inside the apartment. "Here. Sit in my chair. You look like you've seen a ghost."

"It was him. Again."

"Let me get you some water."

"No. That's okay."

"Well, what did he say? If he's coming out of hiding to tell us something, it must be important."

"You don't believe me."

"Did he come to the door?"

"No."

"So?…"

"I was getting some air and I saw him over there."

Phoenix stood and listened politely.

"He said…" He looked up into her eyes. "He said to take care of you."

☉ ☉ ☉ ☉ ☉

Phoenix lay in bed, thinking about Shaun and all of the incredible drama that had been cast upon him… so innocent—knowing of his tragic past and how he'd lost his father in a flood at an early age…so sad. All of it had taken its toll on him. He was seeing things. And in the pit of his imaginary conversation with her uncle, a truth had emerged.

He needed to take care of her.

As Phoenix knew well, stress often pushed people to a point of releasing deep feelings, mostly anger. But, she fell asleep believing that Shaun's stress had released adoration. The young man who had only been a lawn boy to her in the past and was about to turn eighteen tomorrow, had a crush on her.

☉ ☉ ☉ ☉ ☉

Shaun's head was planted in the back corner of the couch when he heard the refrigerator door open. He gasped and shifted a few inches so he could breathe. A pan was removed from a cabinet and it clanged lightly against a stovetop. Shaun rolled over and Phoenix looked at him. She was dressed in blue jeans and a lavender-colored t-shirt.

"Calories for the day. Eggs sound good?"

He pushed himself to a sitting position and scratched his head.

"If you get in the shower now, everything should be about ready in ten minutes."

He'd had a surprisingly good rest and a shower and food would cap his energy revival. "Yeah," he mumbled and cleared his throat. "Sounds good."

"Clean towel is behind the door. There's liquid soap in the shower." She opened the refrigerator. "You don't mind soymeat do you?"

Shaun stood and the blanket that Phoenix must have placed over him while he'd slept fell to the wood floor. "No. That's fine. The place where I work does soymeat really well." He folded the blanket and dropped it onto the couch. "I'll be quick," he said. "What do they call it today? The water conscious five?"

"Yeah, right," Phoenix said as she opened a package of soymeat sausage. "I can't even wash my hair in five minutes."

Shaun closed the bathroom door behind him. He'd never been in a single woman's home, had never slept on a single woman's couch, and he'd never gotten naked in a single woman's bathroom, so he couldn't help the sudden feeling of intimacy as he stepped into Phoenix's shower. It smelled like her. It even felt like her. She liked the color of lavender. Her towels, washcloths, soap dispenser, tissue box cover and even the bar of soap sitting in the bubbly shower dish were all color matched. She also liked dolphins. They were imprinted all over the lavender linens, they were pressed onto the floor of the shower to reduce slipping, and a picture of three dolphins leaping across some vast, flat ocean hung on the wall above the toilet. The smell of breakfast infiltrated the citrus body wash aroma that slathered his skin and Shaun quickly finished, toweled off, dressed, then grabbed Phoenix's tube of toothpaste and swished a small amount with water before spitting it out.

Phoenix had set her small kitchen table with two barstools, two plates that held two whole strawberries on each, and two glasses of water. "Ready in a minute," she said. Shaun sat on the stool closest to the front door. She finished scrambling eggs then brought the hot skillet over to the table. "Happy birthday breakfast. Plate, please."

Shaun lifted his plate and she scooped half of the eggs onto it and the other half onto her plate. She returned the skillet to the stove, grabbed a small dish of round, soymeat sausage patties and sat down. Shaun took two.

They ate in silence until they'd consumed more than half of the meal and Phoenix said, "You know we can't go to Marlinton just yet."

Shaun stopped eating and took a drink of water. He knew what she was going to say.

"We have to know if she's alright."

"And we have to find out what she left for me," Shaun added.

He took a bite out of one strawberry and heard a phone ringing outside the door. Phoenix looked up. "Community phone," she said. "Probably someone expecting a call."

The gentle jingles stopped after a dozen rings, remained silent for a few seconds, then started up again. Phoenix got up and went outside and Shaun followed her to the old phone booth. A young woman about Phoenix's age poked her head out of the last unit on the left. She looked sleepy and angry, and when Phoenix grabbed the receiver, she went back inside.

"Hello," she said. Shaun's concern grew quickly as Phoenix's expression turned from curious to concern to despair. "They're what?" Her mouth, in the shape of a circle, remained open for two seconds longer before she moved the receiver from her ear and looked at it as if she'd never seen such a thing. She replaced it on its hook.

"It was Bethany," she said and let out one long breath. "She's home."

"What's wrong?"

"She said they're gonna take her house."

"Who's gonna what?"

"Those Fed goons. She said they're there right now. We have to call the sheriff." Shaun nodded and Phoenix made the call. When she had finished and hung up, she said, "Someone's already called them about Bethany."

Shaun turned away and walked back to the apartment. "Come on. Let's get going."

◎ ◎ ◎ ◎ ◎

When they arrived at Bethany's, a sheriff's black car was parked in the space where the old Ford truck had been and Sheriff Jamison and a deputy stepped out of the house to greet them.

"What are you doing here, Phoenix?" Jamison asked.

"Bethany called me and said someone was taking her house."

"We got a similar call. The caller identified herself as Bethany but the caller said that someone was trashing her house not taking it. And I've got to tell you, they did a good job of it." Jamison looked at Shaun then back at Phoenix. "Why did she call you two?"

Phoenix told the sheriff and his young deputy that they'd come over for dinner the night before and that the Feds had taken Bethany away. When Phoenix described the three kidnappers, Jamison offered his deputy a concerned glare.

"You think they're the ones that trashed the place?" Jamison asked Phoenix.

"That would be my guess. Either them or they had someone do it. Doesn't seem like they have much concern for the law."

Jamison frowned. "Unfortunately, they do push their jurisdiction as much as possible. Not much we can do."

"Not much you can do about kidnapping?"

Jamison paused before responding. "We'll see what we can find out."

Phoenix put a hand on Shaun's shoulder and said to Jamison, "I left my handbag here last night. You didn't happen to see a shiny gold handbag in there, did you?"

Jamison looked at his deputy who shook his head.

"It's got my ID for the observatory in it. It's a real pain in the ass to replace. You mind if I take a look? It's not like we're going to leave any more DNA than we did last night."

Jamison considered the request for only a moment then walked toward the house. "Only for you, Phoenix Messenger, and for…" He looked at Shaun.

"Shaun Winston," Shaun said. This made Jamison pause once again before he led them inside.

Trashed was the word for it. All of Bethany's handcrafted possessions lay broken, torn, or mangled in scattered heaps. Knowing what Phoenix was probably up to, Shaun immediately started looking for anything that might connect with the last thing Bethany had told him.

Your fate is within the burn.

Burn, he thought. As in the sun?

Phoenix walked over broken furniture toward the fireplace and Shaun stepped through the menagerie on the kitchen floor. Tomatoes lay squashed near silver metallic bags. Kitchen cabinet doors and drawers that had been ripped from their hinges and rails lay broken and scattered across the countertop. Splinters had collected in the sink and covered the dirty plates from last night. The jar with the cicada was gone.

At the end of the counter and poking out from under a ball of fabric that had been tossed along with the rest of Bethany's sewing table, was the box of matches he'd used to light the lanterns.

Burn, he thought. As in lanterns? As in matches? Bethany left something inside the box of matches?

Shaun swiped his hand through broken pieces along the counter, pretending that he was looking for something other than the matches, until his fingers fell on the box. "You find it?" he said to Phoenix. This drew Jamison's and the deputy's attention away long enough for Shaun to pull out the match box inner tray and dump the contents over the cabinet splinters. Matchsticks rolled in every direction. Some hit the floor and this drew Jamison's attention back to him.

Shaun tilted the match tray over and tossed the box. "Nothing over here." He looked at Jamison. "You guys could help, you know. It's not very big is it, Phoenix?"

"Nope," Phoenix responded with a knowing grin. "But it's gold and should be easy to spot."

Jamison and his deputy began shuffling around the room and Shaun moved to the corner where Bethany's empty bookcase still stood in one piece. All of her books were scattered among the rest of the debris, but her fancy meters and EMR bombs were gone.

Shaun turned toward Bethany's open bedroom door, thinking that the answer to the *burn* might be inside. He grabbed the door to steady himself and it swung a bit forward through broken pieces of wood.

That's when he remembered: the symbol on the back of the door. Bethany had said that she'd burned it into the wood.

Casually, so as not to create attention, he wiped his hand over the blackened engraving. The ends of his fingers wrapped around the engraved edges of the F and the M and when he pushed against them, he felt something give and the wood between his fingers loosened. He kept his hand in place and said, "Did you check the bedroom? It's got to be in there." Again, he gave Phoenix the look and she led Jamison past Shaun and into the bedroom. The deputy studied Shaun for a moment then started searching around the fireplace.

Shaun peeked behind the door as he wiggled the loose wood between his fingers until it suddenly turned counterclockwise and popped out. He tilted the F and M circle of wood to find a small, silver metallic bag underneath. As stealthily as he could manage, he brought both the wood circle and the bag toward his shorts pocket, angled the wood so the bag slid inside, then replaced the wood and twisted to secure it.

"You have something there?" the deputy asked.

Shaun pushed the door as far forward as the floor debris would allow and removed his empty hand from behind it. "Nothing," he said to the deputy. "Phoenix," he added and looked into the bedroom. "Maybe you left it somewhere else. I just have this burning feeling all of a sudden."

Phoenix nodded. "I guess you're right. I think I'd lose my head if it wasn't attached." She and Jamison exited the bedroom. "If you do find it, you'll call me?" she said to Jamison.

"You can expect a call, that's for sure," Jamison said. "You'll be around if we need you?"

Phoenix nodded. "Where else would I be? You know me and the GBT. Inseparable."

Jamison and his deputy led Shaun and Phoenix

back to her car. "You'll check on Bethany," Phoenix said before getting in.

Jamison nodded. "We'll let you know."

◉ ◉ ◉ ◉ ◉

Phoenix waited until she was off of Bethany's access road and back onto the asphalt; she waited until she had driven past Observatory Road and through the short stretch of Green Bank's town center; she waited until she felt comfortable that they were not being followed before she said, "You found it." Shaun reached into his shorts' pocket and pulled out the silver bag. "That's not a tomato," she added.

"It was behind the symbol," Shaun said. "It was hidden inside the door behind the burned symbol."

"Well?"

Shaun pulled the bag at one seam and tilted it. A flat strip of flexible metal about a half-an-inch wide and six inches long fell out.

"Shhh!" Phoenix urged. "Wait a minute. Let me see that bag." Shaun offered it to her and she reached below the seat to her left and brought forward her CELL. "Open it." Shaun did so and she dropped the CELL inside. "Fold it closed." Shaun closed the bag and shoved it under one thigh. "You know what that is?" She whispered and nodded at his lap as she slowed the car for a series of hard curves. "If anyone knew we had it, we'd be with Bethany, wherever she is, for sure."

Shaun flipped the strip of metal in one hand and also lowered his voice. "This is a visaBand. Saw them in the news not long ago. It's for people who aren't registered. It allows them to go places registered citizens can go."

"What do you think, birthday boy? Custom made just for you?"

"Should I put it on?"

Phoenix reached over and grabbed his wrist. "No. There's only one way a visaBand could be floating around without its owner and that's if it's hot—if it's a forgery."

"Why would Dr. One want us—want me to have a forged visaBand?"

"Maybe your fate is somewhere only registered citizens can go."

"*Our* fate," Shaun corrected. "*Our* fate."

Phoenix smiled. "Why don't you put it in the bag with my CELL for now."

Shaun did so then he placed the silver bag in the small, zippered front pocket of his backpack.

He didn't take his eyes off the side view mirror for most of the twenty-minute drive to Marlinton. Until now, he thought, they really had nothing more on him than guilt by association. The counterfeit visaBand changed all of that. If anyone found that he had it—

anyone, even Chris or Adam or his mom—they'd think he was a terrorist. Who else would have such a thing? The thought made Shaun suck in a deep breath. Is that what Dr. One was into? Terrorism?

"What is it?" Phoenix asked. She slowed to a stop behind a long line of traffic about a mile outside of town.

"Nothing. Just a little paranoid." He looked over at the side mirror.

"No one I can tell followed but with all the traffic…Memorial Day weekend is pretty popular around here."

"You don't even know. It's like a small beach town in the middle of the mountains. It'll get worse." Traffic moved in chunks as the four stoplights in town paced vehicles through busy pedestrians.

"Look at all of them," Phoenix said. "But Marlinton is such a quiet town."

"It is during the months that you've been here."

Phoenix turned to him. "Keeping tabs on me?"

Shaun didn't look away from her this time and he didn't blush. "Small town. People notice. Especially when anything is going on at the misguided mansion.

"Misguided?"

"The previous owner who built Dr. One's house. He was misguided to think mansions by the Greenbrier were a good investment. When he left, everyone just called it that."

Phoenix stopped at the final light before the Great Flood Memorial Bridge crossed the river. In the pedestrian walkway were lots of visitors, made apparent by the lawn chairs they carried and the words emblazoned on the shirts and hats they wore: Richmond, D.C., Baltimore, Pittsburgh.

"How cute," Phoenix said and pointed. "Your school colors must be maroon and gold."

Shaun scrunched down in the seat. Two girls he knew very well played with the graduation cords that hung around their necks. Each wore a maroon and gold robe and they skipped and beat each other with the cords until they passed in front of Phoenix's car. They stopped and looked at him for a moment but didn't offer any sign of recognition.

The light turned and the girls scampered out of the intersection. Phoenix didn't look at him. She didn't say a thing.

◎ ◎ ◎ ◎ ◎

It was all too convenient. The Ties and their co-conspirators—maybe even the Marlinton white suits—were setting them up. Phoenix already suspected that the house was bugged but she also knew where her uncle had stashed a few EMR bombs. She could prevent outside surveillance from recording them but did that really matter? Once she had the drive, they'd show up as uninvited guests to rob her of the evidence she knew it contained. But Phoenix had a secret: though everything she'd worked on for the last two years, and all of the evidence that would provide blackmail material if the need arose would be permanently lost, she could erase the entire drive with one touch of the kill switch. She parked at the end of her uncle's gravel driveway closest to the side entry door.

"You haven't said so, but you're probably as nervous as I am." She got out of the car and Shaun followed with his backpack in one hand.

"Hell yes, I am," Shaun said and slipped the pack over one shoulder. "That's why this is coming with me. I can't imagine what those goons would think if they found a counterfeit…"

"Shh!" Phoenix urged. "They might be listening." She turned toward the house and the backyard and the trees that surrounded it, and raised her voice. "And if you are, you should know that I can erase the entire drive if you try and take it from me."

"Clever," Shaun whispered. "But you really wouldn't…"

"You bet I would," Phoenix shouted at the house and they both walked to the side door.

"You think the entry code is the same? All of the alarms will be on."

"We have three tries before the alarms trip," Phoenix said and pointed at the digital touch pad to the left of the door. "Try yours first."

Shaun tapped his five-digit entry code on the pad and the entire display flashed red. "Nope," he said.

Phoenix reached out and entered her code and received the same red-flash response.

"We won't have to worry about anyone listening if the alarms go off," Shaun said.

Phoenix studied the black, square display filled with green digital numbers and… "This is different," she said. "The red line down here designates that bio-scanning has been enabled." She leaned forward and stared at the display, then placed all five fingers of her right hand against it. The entire display flashed green and the door unlocked. "Someone reprogrammed it since the last time I was here."

"Since the last time I was here, too," Shaun added. "And now, the house knows we're here."

Phoenix opened the door and stepped inside. "Interesting way to put it. So, the question becomes: will the house tell anyone?" She was almost certain that it had. Whoever had changed the touch pad knew they were there. That's why she'd made the threat. There really was a kill switch that, when pressed and held for three seconds, would effectively melt the chips inside. Basically, she told anyone who might be listening that the drive was her hostage. She doubted, though, that she'd really destroy all of her work and hoped, when the time came, her bluff would not be called.

The interior of the house was immaculate, a polar opposite of how they'd found Bethany's place. Shaun stood just inside the door and dropped his backpack on the floor.

"Wait here," Phoenix said. "I'll be right back."

Last month, when she and her uncle had stashed the drive, Dr. One had told her to think about the observation platform at the top of the Great Big Thing, how being up there cradled a person in total freedom from all of the vibrations of interconnectivity. He told her that his house in Marlinton was the antithesis of that rare, experienced feeling. He told her that the house might be one of the most watched residences in America because a man who'd claimed he'd found God in the distant universe owned it. So, her uncle had stashed a handful of EMR bombs in his bedroom.

Phoenix removed a framed, twelve-inch-square picture of a starry night sky from the wall next to her uncle's bed. The picture was an original that had been printed the night of his God Light discovery. Behind it was a boxed hideout that had been built into the wall. Inside, were three, foot-long stick bombs. Phoenix tossed the picture onto the bed and grabbed them.

When she returned to the living room, she found Shaun sitting on the couch. He saw the bombs in her hand, pointed, and said, "One of those is the reason I'm here in the first place."

Phoenix tossed two of the EMR bombs to Shaun

and strangled the one she held. It cracked and vibrated and transformed from dark emerald to fluorescent green. A halo quickly enveloped the entire living room. "We have about fifteen minutes," she said and tossed the glowing stick to the floor at her feet. "I'll go get it."

Phoenix walked through the large kitchen, around the kitchen's center island, and continued through the double-screened sliding porch doors. She shuffled around the porch deck, sat on the porch bench swing for a few minutes to look around the yard's perimeter, then stood, grabbed the potted red petunia closest to the swing and took it inside. She placed it next to the couch and sat.

Phoenix slid her hand down the stem, pressed her fingers into the soil, and gently moved the plant, its roots and most of its black soil to the floor. She brushed her hands together with a clap then dropped her left hand into the pot to release its false bottom. She pulled out a black panel, set it aside and looked down. At first, she thought it was gone and this sent a spike of adrenaline through her chest. But the small device was as black as the pot's bottom, and when Phoenix stuck her hand back in, a tiny blue light in the center of the backup drive came on. She grabbed it and withdrew a block of black that was identical in size to a pack of Wrigley's Classic gum that fit in the palm of her hand.

"You know how much these little puppies can hold now-a-days?" She flipped the drive in her hand.

"It's not even half full."

The small dot of blue light in the center of the drive started flashing erratically. It grew brighter and pulsed harder with an intensity that made Phoenix cover the light with her thumb. At that same moment, the EMR bomb stick died and the tiny drive throbbed like a heartbeat. She pressed it. Expecting some reaction that never happened, Phoenix tilted her head up and looked around the dull, sunlit room.

"What?" Shaun asked.

"Not sure. I don't know. You better crack another EMR bomb." Shaun did so and Phoenix waited until it came to life before continuing. "Like the entry pad outside, the backup drive is different than I remember."

"You pressed it. Was that the kill switch?"

Phoenix gasped. She'd honestly not thought of that possibility. The blue light had throbbed and she'd responded. The kill switch was on the top left corner but had someone reprogrammed it, too? Had she just unintentionally erased everything that she'd struggled to accomplish under the dogmatic eyes of Dr. One?

Both of them stared straight down into the empty petunia pot. The couch provided a chunk of dark shadow that added to the pitch of darkness within the false bottom. Inside the small, rectangular recess, Phoenix saw something that looked a lot like Bethany's bugs: a tiny grouping of even tinier, multicolored specks.

"It's just like what we saw at Bethany's," Shaun

said. "Not the cicada bugs but the smaller flying bugs, the ones that were good."

"Good ones?" The speck of specks was so small, Phoenix had to squint and lean forward to make sure it was real.

"Yeah. Watch. Let it do its thing. This could be the same one that was here the other night when I found your uncle."

"A Bethany bug was here in Marlinton?"

"I didn't know what it was at the time. I guess I really didn't believe what I saw. It was really dark in here that night and I could see it really good. It shot those same green beams that we saw those three at Bethany's do last night. It used them to scan your uncle's…you uncle's body." Shaun frowned.

"No," Phoenix said. "That's okay because he's not really dead, is he?"

"I've seen him twice since then. He talked to me both times. I just don't get it."

The tiny speck started to move across the pot's black bottom and they both leaned closer just as the speck disappeared.

"Where'd it go?" Phoenix said, peering intensely at the floor.

"It took flight. Look."

Shaun raised his hand, palm down, and Phoenix refocused on the back of his wrist. Something incredibly small landed right below the knuckle of his middle finger. She leaned to within a few inches of it as did Shaun.

"A mosquito," Shaun said.

"But where did the little speck go?"

"This is the speck. You just can't see its internal works without complete darkness."

His suggestion, if true, would be phenomenal. Because of her clearance while working for Dr. One at the observatory, Phoenix knew that very small drill drones had been developed by the energy industries to help manage deep and dangerous exploration but those things looked like drones and they were three times larger than even Bethany's cicada bugs. "Looks like a mosquito to me," she said. "I guess there's only one way to find out."

"We need as near to complete darkness as we can find," Shaun suggested. "I don't think this thing is going to wait on my hand until the sun goes down."

"My uncle's bedroom closet. It's large enough for us to stand in and it's a complete Faraday cage."

"Okay…so I just tiptoe in there and hope our Skeeter doesn't fly away?"

"Perhaps we can catch it like Bethany did her cicada. I'll see if there are any jars around here. I just hope it stays put."

"I don't know," Shaun said, staring at the mosquito. "I think it wants to cooperate."

Phoenix was about to ask him why he thought

such a thing, but time was essential right now. She dropped the black drive into one of her jeans pockets, walked into the kitchen and searched through cabinets that didn't have much to offer. There were no Mason-like jars, but there was one empty, glass baby food jar with a partially eroded label that read *Bartlett Pears*. She returned to the living room with it. "Still there?" she whispered.

Shaun nodded.

"This is small but it should work." She showed him the baby food jar as she gently sat on the couch beside him. "So what's the procedure, doctor?" Her voice dropped even lower.

"I guess we just go for it. I don't know. Can you distract a mosquito?"

Phoenix removed the metal lid from the jar and turned the jar upside down. She slowly moved it next to Shaun's hand and said, "You sure this is a good one? I mean, perhaps it's not meant to take things away like surveillance data. Maybe it's programmed to leave something instead. It's a mosquito after all."

Shaun's eyebrows rose with an expression of sudden helplessness. The mosquito's proboscis hovered over one skin pore. Its tiny body and its tiny, long and crooked legs tapped the skin. "Really?" he said. "I'd like to not think about that." His eyebrows remained in heightened alert. "So, can you get it off me?"

"A good one, eh?"

Shaun frowned and Phoenix slowly lifted the jar's upside down mouth over Shaun's hand, moved it above the mosquito and dropped it down hard enough to make a knuckle-to-glass thud.

"Ouch!" Shaun said and pulled his hand away. Phoenix quickly capped the jar. "You get it?"

She looked in the jar and smiled. "Sorry about the knuckles. Didn't want it to inject you with anything." She slapped the back of his hand. "Come on. Let's check it out."

◎ ◎ ◎ ◎ ◎

Phoenix led Shaun through her uncle's bedroom and into his ten-foot deep walk-in closet. Why the man needed such a big closet, Shaun could not understand. There was nothing in it other than a bathrobe, slippers, one pinstripe suit, and a pair of shiny black dress shoes.

Once inside, Shaun closed the door and Phoenix asked him to switch off the light. The transformation was immediate. Phoenix held the jar out in the palm of her hand and rubbed off some of the remaining paper label with one thumb. A little bit of light entered from under the closet door, creating near pitch-blackness that sharpened the dozen or so tiny pinpoints of red, green and blue lights within the jar. There it was, Shaun thought. Just like it had been the night he found Dr. One, except much clearer.

"Incredible," Phoenix said. "Turn the light back on for a moment."

Shaun hit the switch. Inside the jar was a regular-looking mosquito. "Our Skeeter is a chameleon," Phoenix said. "Just incredible. It must be bio-digital or bio-mechanical or a combination of something like that."

Shaun turned the light off. "You mean, it's not real?"

"Part real. Part assembled. But my god, such microscopic assembly…it's like a biological microdrone."

"Also known as Bethany's bugs," Shaun added.

"Uh-huh." Phoenix leaned in closer until the tip of her nose touched the glass. "I wonder what it knows? All those tiny, blinking lights…just like neurons."

The wonderment that filled Phoenix's wide-open eyes was magnified by the glass jar. Her gaze reminded Shaun of the *E.T.* remake he'd seen as a first-grader. He remembered that his dad had taken him to see it the summer before the flood. He remembered its magic, particularly the part when the little E.T. creature lifted its finger and said "Ouch." The kid in the story whose name was Elliott had just cut his finger and he'd leaned forward to watch E.T.'s finger glow. Cast in the halo of the extraterrestrial's finger, Elliot expressed wonderment that came with witnessing something impossible. That's exactly how Phoenix's face looked right now.

Suddenly, she blinked and looked down. "Something's vibrating," she said. "Here, hold Skeeter."

Shaun took the jar as Phoenix shuffled around in the dark. "You need the light on?"

"No, no. It's the drive. It vibrated in my pocket. Here."

Phoenix moved the drive and its blue light toward Shaun's hand and the closer it came to the jar, the brighter the blue light grew. "It did that before and you pressed it," Shaun said.

"Okay. I'll bite." The bright blue light dimmed as Phoenix covered it with her thumb and pressed.

At first, nothing seemed to happen other than the drive's blue light that completely died. This brought Shaun's and Phoenix's full attention on Skeeter. All of the specks of red, green and blue stopped blinking and froze. Phoenix's nose touched the glass on one side and Shaun's nose touched the glass on the other. This brought their foreheads so close, his dark hair tangled into her blonde bangs.

It was his imagination of course, but at that moment, Shaun saw Skeeter look up. Two tiny blue specks were the eyes in an incredibly small face. "Did you see that?" Shaun said. "It winked at me."

"Great imagination but I don't think…"

All of Skeeter's tiny light specks blinked off then on again. A second passed and Skeeter did it again. And again. And again.

"I think it's Morse code," Phoenix said. "Yes… dot-dash-dot-dash."

"Can you read it?"

"Let's see here. I'm a bit rusty. Haven't been challenged with this binary language since college. Hmm…not much sense it that…wait. There's the repetition. J-A-C-K."

"Who's Jack?

"Not just Jack. Hold up…"

Shaun waited and watched the flashing light reflect against Phoenix's moist pupils. After more than a dozen seconds, her eyes faded to black as she moved her head away from his hand and the jar.

"You can turn the lights on, now," she said. "I think I got it." Shaun did so. "This little guy has, indeed, been programmed," she continued and reached out to snag the baby food jar from Shaun's hand. "It has awareness."

"Awareness? You mean it can see?"

"See or smell or hear or maybe even touch. It did land on you. It allowed itself to be captured. It waited until it was in a dark place. It waited for me to press the blue button."

"The drive and Skeeter are connected?"

"Connected by my uncle. Planned perfectly. It all

makes sense."

Phoenix held the jar and marveled at the little mosquito inside but didn't say anything until Shaun asked, "What?"

"It flashed: Jackrabbit Johnnie." Phoenix continued staring at it. "I heard my uncle talk once about this guy he knows who is supposed to be an expert in drone tech. It was a while back and I remember it being a part of a conversation that had no value to me other than for small talk, but I do remember the name: Johnnie. I remember it because it wasn't just John, but Johnnie. And, I remember it because of where my uncle said Johnnie worked, which seemed strange for a drone tech wizard. He worked—and probably still does—at Kennywood Amusement Park outside of New Pittsburgh. It would appear that my clever uncle programmed the drive to send instructions to his little drone when I pressed the blue light."

"To tell you about someone at Kennywood?"

"To tell us that our next stop is on a rollercoaster."

Shaun didn't immediately understand.

"Come on. Let's get out of the closet." She stepped around him, opened the door, and walked through and out of the bedroom. Shaun followed. She leaned against the living room couch and said, "You're going to want a change of clothes before we go."

Shaun just stood and stared at her.

"Grab a light jacket, too." She looked down at the

mosquito inside the jar then up at Shaun's bewildered eyes. "Don't you see? He's been leading us all along. He got you involved and somehow made you think that he was both dead and alive. You came to me. Bethany was his go-between. Through her, he left you a counterfeit visaBand which I'm sure he intended you to wear when we head north to the Jack Rabbit rollercoaster at Kennywood Park. He wants us to deliver the Skeeter drone and the drive to Johnnie."

"I guess you know him better than I do but why the hell involve me? You were going to have to recover the drive anyway."

"You said it yourself already. To protect me."

All of this revelation amassed too fast and too furious through Shaun's mind and he started to get angry that he'd been used in such a way, until Phoenix reminded him of his encounter with Dr. One outside her apartment.

Take care of Phoenix, he'd said.

The thought immediately shifted his focus from anger to chivalry. He felt a rush of adrenaline. Inadvertently, he sucked in a big breath and stuck out his chest. His first big test in the eighteen-year-old adult world would be to protect a young lady.

Phoenix smiled. "You know you don't have to go with me. There's still enough free will left in this world for *you* to decide. So far, you've done a pretty good job. The Feds haven't taken us in yet and, I suppose, that's a good thing."

"You have the drive. Surely, they'll…"

"I don't think so. Not now. But I'm sure they're not going to leave us alone anytime soon."

"And I'm supposed to protect you from them," Shaun said.

Phoenix leaned closer to Shaun's face, causing his adrenaline rush to peak. Her tantalizing citrus body wash smell enveloped him. "Kinda looks that way," she said. "You want the job?"

Shaun nodded.

"You think your mom is going to mind you taking off like this?"

"I figure she's already working the early brunch crowds. People like to drink early during the holidays, I guess. Besides, we'll be back as soon as we deliver the drive, right? Might even be back before she gets off work."

Phoenix shrugged and her stare promoted mystery.

"Okay. Well, I can always text her."

"I'll wait while you go and get some clothes. Bring a change, just in case. Then we'll head back to Green Bank, grab a few things from my apartment and move on."

"You know," Shaun said, stepped away from Phoenix and turned to leave. "I think you're enjoying this. You've had this strange little smile in the corner of your mouth ever since Skeeter Morse-coded you."

Phoenix lifted the small jar. "This is amazing stuff. I can't wait to see what's on the drive."

Shaun grabbed his backpack by the door and left Dr. One's house, wondering which drive Phoenix meant: the one in her pocket or the one that awaited them across 200 miles of Appalachian roads.

◎ ◎ ◎ ◎ ◎

As soon as Shaun left, Phoenix started imagining how effective such a tiny microdrone could be, particularly in the wrong hands. What if there were hundreds of them? Thousands? Tens of thousands? What if all of the cicadas she heard buzzing outside the house were all bio-digital? There would be no safe place to hide from the prying eyes of the Suspicious Society.

"Ridiculous," she said to the mosquito in the jar, not really caring anymore if anyone was listening. "Someone would have discovered such a conspiratorial scheme by now. You and your buddies back at Bethany's are the only ones, aren't you? You have to be."

Phoenix took one last look around her uncle's home, grabbed the one remaining EMR bomb stick that Shaun had left on the couch, and went outside to put the jar and the bomb in her car. But, as soon as she opened the passenger side door, she looked up to see a pair of black SUVs heading along the access road. She quickly closed and locked the door, and ran into the surrounding tree line in the direction of Shaun's trailer park.

⊙ ⊙ ⊙ ⊙ ⊙

What Shaun felt as he ran from Dr. One's he couldn't quite understand. So many new emotions had been jacked into his system that even the basic definitions of fear, anxiety, bravery and desire were muddled. He was afraid of his desire and his newfound bravery made him anxious as hell. How could a person handle all of that emotional weight? It sat like a rock right in the middle of his chest.

What Shaun did understand, though, is how he felt as he entered his mom's trailer. She wasn't there, of course. She hadn't left him a note. There wasn't, in fact, any evidence that she'd even been home all night. It didn't surprise him; it didn't make him sad; it just was. He'd gone beyond high expectations at home long ago. Love nor hate nor remorse nor regret had any bearing. You did what you had to do. You survived. You became stronger. And strength meant that you had to control your emotions.

This defense mechanism, which had been wound up so tightly inside his very soul, was now coming apart. It no longer controlled emotions that strengthened his resolve. Phoenix (and her uncle), in less than two days, had made that impossible. It was, in fact, the break from routine, mundane, single-parent lifestyle that, now, made him feel stronger. It was that rock of emotion pounding in his chest, which could only be described as *the unknown*, that fueled his young passion. He wanted nothing more than to get out of Marlinton and explore new adventures with someone who needed him more than just as a son. Remaining safe no longer felt safe. The trailer, his mom, the bike shop—the time had come. And so fittingly on his eighteenth birthday.

It took him less than five minutes to change into blue jeans and a button-up short sleeve shirt, and stuff his backpack with a second change of clothes and a light windbreaker. He shoved the same cash he'd been carrying around since yesterday into one pocket and glanced around the room one more time. The U.S. Citizen registration form still sat on his small study desk. He quickly turned away from it and left the trailer.

⊙ ⊙ ⊙ ⊙ ⊙

Unbeknownst to Phoenix, she knelt in the exact location where Shaun had hidden two nights ago. She witnessed a nearly identical scene when four men dressed in white uniforms entered Dr. One's house.

Phoenix set the baby food jar on the weedy grass beside her knee and considered Skeeter inside. If the microdrone really had awareness and could detect her, the white suits would have followed her into the bushes, unless…

Perhaps Shaun had been right. Maybe Skeeter was a *good one*. Maybe Skeeter was on their side.

"Are you good?" she whispered at the jar.

"I am." Shaun startled her and crouched down.

At that moment, the four white suits exited the house, took a few moments to digitally unlock Phoenix's car and started searching it.

"Looks like we're going to have to find a different ride north," Phoenix said. "They'll bug the hell out of that thing."

"I got a couple of friends at the bike shop…"

"No." Her voice rose enough that one of the white suits looked up and over the hood of the car. She waited until his attention returned to the car before lowering her voice and continuing. "We don't want to involve anyone else."

"What about a shuttle? There's regular service to Green Bank over the holiday. You know how we can get from there to Kennywood?"

"Yes. I believe so."

"Come on, then. We might have just enough time to catch the twelve o'clock run."

◎ ◎ ◎ ◎ ◎

The shuttle stop was at the street corner directly opposite Jennifer Outfitters where he and Phoenix arrived, breathing heavily, just as the driver closed the shuttle bus doors. Shaun led Phoenix by the hand and they rushed across the street through the pedestrian crowd. They ducked and dodged a white suit in their path, bumped through a couple of old women who cursed at them and brought the white suit's attention in their direction, paused in front of the shuttle with their backs to the white suit until the man looked away, then Shaun knuckle-tapped the shuttle's glass doors and the driver let them in.

Half of the twenty seats were occupied with no one Shaun knew and no apparent government agents, though one middle-aged woman dressed in a white pants suit did give them a long, concerned look. Shaun led Phoenix to a pair of open seats two rows back from the pants-suit lady because he wanted to keep an eye on her. He sat next to the window and placed his backpack between his legs, and Phoenix sat next to him.

As the shuttle slowly crept through town, Shaun pressed his head against the window and gazed at the congested streets of home. It was extremely hard to maintain composure. If the shuttle had been able to get out of town quickly, everything would have been okay. With each short block they passed, Shaun's breaths grew heavier and the big rock of congested emotion leaked a whole bunch of memories that careened through his body and made him shiver. A single tear fell from welling eyes and he sucked in a quick gasp when Phoenix grabbed his hand.

"You okay?" she said.

Shaun wiped the tear away before he turned to her.

"I am, umm…" Those crazy rivers of hazel veins in Phoenix's eyes lured Shaun's face closer to hers. "I think they call it waxing nostalgic." Her eyes pulled him even closer and he shifted his gaze to her lips. For the first time since he'd met her, he gave them considerable attention. "I was thinking that…"

Phoenix turned away from him and for a moment, he thought he'd gotten too close, thought he'd stared too long, thought his tear had turned her off. But she'd turned because of the pants-suit lady who was staring at them across the back of her seat.

"Can I help you?" Phoenix said and scowled.

"Get a room," the woman said and abruptly turned back around.

"Well, this is going to be an interesting ride." Phoenix raised her voice purposefully loud then looked at Shaun who, again, had his forehead pressed against the window.

◉ ◉ ◉ ◉ ◉

Shaun said very little the rest of the way to Green Bank and Phoenix supposed it was because of the lady two rows up. But some part of her wondered: had this young birthday boy made a move on her? She already suspected some attraction and, to be totally honest with herself, she shared that feeling for him to some degree—but a kiss?

No. That would ruin everything. There was no time for romance with what was at stake and it would be her responsibility to throttle the young man's urge if they were to succeed. Possibly, she thought—just possibly—after all was said and done, the timing might be appropriate. For now, it had to be all business.

The shuttle let them off in front of the observatory Welcome Center. The pants-suit lady followed the rest of the riders inside, but Phoenix walked with Shaun toward the lab.

"Wait out here. I'll go and see about our ride," she said to Shaun whose attention was everywhere else except on what Phoenix had just said. "Space to Shaun." She grabbed his arm and he finally looked at her. "Did you hear me?"

"Wait. Yeah, sure."

A tour bus rolled up to the Welcome Center behind them. On its marquee were the words: Carnegie Science Center.

◎ ◎ ◎ ◎ ◎

His backpack wasn't really that heavy but the psychological weight of its contents made him drop it from his shoulder to the asphalt as he waited at the curb a hundred feet from the front of the lab.

It was the visaBand that had suddenly consumed his thoughts. He stared at the front flap pocket where it lay hidden inside the metallic silver Faraday bag.

What the hell was he doing? Getting out of Marlinton, of course. Protecting a pretty young woman who was likely to be threatened sometime between here and Kennywood. Trusting a tracking device that was full of information that he knew nothing about. What if, when he put the band on, a terrorist alert went out across the nation? The waves of caution just kept coming. Helplessness was the predominant nag right now. His mind was a mess to the point of feeling numb.

When Phoenix returned with an Asian woman who looked to be her same age, Shaun just stared without expression. "Shaun. This is Dr. Yang from the Carnegie Science Center. She said we are welcome to join her and her students on their trip back to New Pitt."

Shaun stood from the curb and managed a polite smile. "Nice to meet you," he said.

"They're going to hold the bus up for a few minutes while I run over to the apartment to grab some things."

Shaun nodded, still politely smiling.

"You can come with me or, she said, you can wait

with her on the bus."

Shaun nodded. Dr. Yang and Phoenix exchanged a look of curiosity.

"Go or wait?" Phoenix asked.

"I think I'll stay right here. That way I can watch you…you know…just in case."

Phoenix said to Dr. Yang, "Thank you for waiting. We'll be over in less than ten minutes."

Dr. Yang quickly walked in the direction of the bus just as several people exited the Welcome Center and boarded.

"Shall we educate ourselves in what is known, and then casting away all we have acquired, turn to ignorance for aid to guide us among the unknown?"
— Michael Faraday

"Reality leaves a lot to the imagination."
— John Lennon

The need for self-sustaining cities had been realized throughout the first three decades of the century but it had been the Aquifer Attacks on Thanksgiving Day in 2029 that had not only accelerated the momentum for their need but also had fundamentally changed the reasons for pursuing them. A self-sustaining city could survive, for the most part, on the resources it generated and recycled, but a New City had the added benefit of complete control of security. No one could enter a New City without proper credentials, the most recognized being that of a Registered U.S. Citizen, and no one could function in a New City without them. Tracking of everything and everyone was essential and was openly accepted—a cost for the protection and opportunity the New City provided. No purchases could be made without an eCash account, which was only available to those with credentials. Even if a person illegally entered the city perimeter and somehow avoided the eyes and digital reporting of the suspicious city population, just the fundamentals for survival would be unattainable.

The New Cities had naturally grown up around major fresh water resources. Those nested against the Great Lakes had been some of the fastest to develop through the 30s. With them had surfaced old territorial boundary disputes as Canada made claims to the lake water. Great tension had been the result. Water walls had been suggested but had not yet been built since doing so would have placed a physical division to the North American partnership and would have escalated tensions further.

New Pittsburgh was a shining star among all of the New Cities, mostly because of its location away from the Great Lakes tension at the convergence of three major rivers. The fresh river water not only sustained the city and most of its suburbs, it provided thousands of jobs at its numerous water filtering mills from which fresh water was distributed to much of the drought-stricken West in a trade agreement from 2035. Tanker drone colonies transported the precious liquid from Pittsburgh in exchange for agricultural commodities that would be converted to food and fuel sources for the city. Added imports from the West weren't a necessity for New Pitt's survival; it could live on its own resources for as long as a year. But so many of the states west of the Mississippi were in big trouble. Some scientists had even predicted that in the decades to come, the U.S. would resemble the Australian outback with tremendous deserts in the center and most of the population dispersed on the coasts. So, the trade deal had been less about the resources the West provided New Pitt and more about locking in the ten-year supply deal. State governments and a couple of major corporations had worked together to create several safe water trade routes. For Pittsburgh, it was the city's second industrial revolution but instead of supplying the country with steel to construct its modernity, it distributed the lifeblood that kept people alive.

New Pitt's incredible security was also a major allure. With rivers providing a barrier around much of the city, and a wall that had been built between the Monongahela and the Allegheny Rivers through the suburbs to the east, tracking of the inhabitants within this perimeter was the best in the country. For five years straight, New Pittsburgh had been named as the President's "Safest City," an American honor.

Being the safest had attracted all kinds of business interests. The Zon had relocated its central headquarters from the west coast to New Pitt. The brains behind the V.38 and V.41 CELL technology and much of the development of virtual reality before that now lived in and continued to develop in New Pitt. It was not only the center of the mighty water distribution networks, it was the center of well-being for those who did not want their valuable interests destroyed by riots; it was the center for a lifestyle grown out of the minds of the virtual world.

◎ ◎ ◎ ◎ ◎

Shaun looked down at his backpack for the umpteenth time, a gesture that had increased in repetition as they'd gotten on the northbound interstate. They were only thirty minutes away from the city's outer interchange from where he and Phoenix had planned to leave the bus for a FasTrain to Kennywood. That's when he'd have to put on the visaBand.

The academic air of questions and answers from the Carnegie students to Phoenix had occupied most of the trip. She sat with Shaun in the aisle seat three rows back and this had given many curious minds the opportunity to turn in their seats to surround Phoenix as she energetically talked about the observatory and her experience with software engineering.

Shaun had pretty much zoned out, his attention away from the conversations that were well above his education, and had tried to grab snippets of rest between thoughts of high school friends and living dead scientists and tiny drone insects and federal agents who loved to wear ties. He tried to make sense of it all one more time before finally concluding that the counterfeit visaBand was the only thing worth his immediate concern.

The questions from the students finally stopped and Phoenix settled back into her seat. She smiled until she saw Shaun looking down between his legs.

"I got carried away," she said to him. "Sorry. It's just that when I get going…"

Shaun sat up and turned his attention to her. "That's okay. It was really interesting talk—kind of like being in a classroom. Besides, it made the time go by."

She stared at him for a moment before placing a hand on his forearm. "You're getting uneasy. I can tell. I guess the first time in a New City can do that."

Both of the students sitting in the row ahead of them looked over the back of their seats.

"You've never been to New Pittsburgh?" the male student asked. "I can't even imagine." He had pudgy cheeks full of freckles and his eyes bulged incredulously. The Latino female student beside him could not seem to close her astonished mouth.

"Nope," Shaun said. "Never been. Never really had to."

The female student looked at her red-haired friend

and both said simultaneously, "But wouldn't you want to?"

Phoenix squeezed his arm. "You guys are jealous, aren't you?" she said to the students. "It's one experience that can never be duplicated with any software or hardware. You took a ride to the top of the telescope, didn't you?"

Both nodded.

"And?..." She looked at one and then the other. "Tell me you can duplicate that experience anywhere in New Pitt."

"Well, kind of," the male student said. "But, I guess, not exactly. The smells are different. It's like your skin can breathe up there."

"The thought right now is even exhilarating, isn't it?"

The students looked at each other and then at Shaun. "I wish we were visiting for the first time," the male student said. "I was born here so I would never be able to know how excited you must be."

When Shaun didn't respond, the two students turned back around.

"No worries, Shaun," Phoenix whispered. Her hand squeezed his forearm. "I know you have to be thinking about what's on the visaBand. After all, once we get to Kennywood, you're gonna have to deal with it. But I don't think my uncle would have hauled us all the way up here just to put you in jeopardy with tainted credentials. I'd say its Story would be one that could only help us."

"I shouldn't worry, should I?" he said to the back of the seat in front of him. "A part of my upbringing, I suppose."

"It's new. It's a mystery. You're eighteen. I'm guessing you'll never get another chance to experience it all with someone else's Storyline."

Shaun *had* been focusing on most of the negatives since leaving Marlinton. He'd accepted that the reason was a heavy dose of homesickness. A big part of him didn't want to be here and that was the part that had fueled his fears up to now. But Phoenix had a really intriguing point. Whatever was going to happen and whomever he was going to be would become shared Net pieces of a life that he'd be able to throw away once he left the city. He'd be the persona that the visaBand had been programmed to represent. He'd be able to walk around as Shaun Winston but not really be Shaun Winston. Perhaps his name wouldn't even be the same. Phoenix was right. When would he—or anyone—ever get such a chance? To do anything you wanted in a city full of opportunities. What had Phoenix asked the two students in front of them? Even the thought was exhilarating.

Phoenix seemed to sense this change in him as she squeezed and pulled his arm and smiled and eased back into her seat as the suburban lights of the approaching

New City grew colorfully numerous outside the bus's tinted window.

⊚ ⊚ ⊚ ⊚ ⊚

The Fort Washington T-interchange was one of the two largest hubs for those going in and out of the city, the other being the Eastern T-interchange along the city's suburban boundary wall. The T-interchanges controlled what traffic and which people were allowed within the New Pittsburgh perimeter. In addition to having traceable personal identification such as a CELL or temporary visaBand, you could only physically enter the city via the preferred T-metro array of available buses, taxis, subways and FasTrains, or in a commercial or personal vehicle that matched exact quality standards such as zero carbon emissions, self-driving automation and a hundred percent uptime tracking via V.38 tech or better. Trying to enter the city without such prior approval would lead to immediate arrest. And with the eyes of the city constantly on you, arrests were aggressively fast.

The tour bus parked between buses of equal size and Shaun and Phoenix stood. Phoenix turned a full three-sixty and said, "Thank you all for having us and taking the time to stop here. Dr. Yang…I hope to have you all back very soon. There'll be some fantastic events in the skies this summer." Dr. Yang, who was sitting in the back, waved, smiled and nodded.

Phoenix grabbed the duffle bag she'd packed with extra clothes and Shaun followed her into the aisle with his backpack over one shoulder. Students sat and smiled up at him and Shaun returned their friendliness until he came to the front row. Two female students sat and smiled at him from the two seats to the right but the one girl sitting behind the driver was not looking up. She was hunched over and talking to her lap.

The bus doors swooshed open and the metro interchange's complex aroma of city smells rushed in. Phoenix started down the two exit steps as the girl behind the driver rose in her seat. "Very beautiful," she said, still looking down. Her finger stroked it.

Shaun's gasp was loud enough for the entire busload to hear. The sound made the monarch butterfly that had been sitting on the girl's lap take flight. All eyes behind him watched the butterfly wag and flutter right in front of Shaun's face. They all heard him say, "Tony? Is that you?" And they all watched with dismay as the tiger-striped butterfly quickly flapped over Phoenix's head and out of the bus.

"No!" the butterfly's young keeper said. "She's been sitting there all this time. It was amazing. It was like nothing that could ever be duplicated."

⊙ ⊙ ⊙ ⊙ ⊙

How could it be true? Shaun thought. Beyond the wild notion that the monarch he'd seen fly from the bus into the suburban madness was the same one he'd first met on the river trail, and even if those seconds when the butterfly had momentarily hovered in front of his face had not really been some attempt at communication, how could it be true that just a simple, non-stalking, real-to-life butterfly would travel four hours as a docile occupant on some girl's lap?

The fact was: it couldn't be true. There were more than mosquitos and cicadas that had been converted into—what was it Phoenix had called them—bio-digital microdrones, he thought. Perhaps Tony was a butterfly microdrone. The complexity of such a thing boggled his mind, which was an appropriate precursor to the experience of the T-interchange.

"You can put it on now or wait until we get to Kennywood," Phoenix said to Shaun, "but I'm gonna need my CELL so we can pay for the ride."

Shaun dropped the backpack and unzipped the front flap. "And so the tracking begins," he said as he grabbed the silver metallic bag, unfolded it, and gave the CELL to Phoenix.

"That began when we stepped out of the bus. You've been captured a dozen times already, I'd say. The Net knows there's a new face in town. It just doesn't have much of a Story to go with it, yet."

The CELL screen started up and displayed in

white across a black background the words: **Phoenix Messenger**. Next to her name was a green icon of a circle with an arrow pointing right in the two o'clock position. A green smiley face glowed in the middle of the circle. Shaun pointed at it.

"The smiley face means I'm not going to destroy the city," Phoenix said and grinned.

Shaun considered the visaBand at the bottom of the bag. "I think I'll be me for as long as possible," he said then folded the metallic bag and zipped it back up in his backpack.

He'd seen commercials and had watched a few documentaries about it while in school but the experience was much different. What surprised him the most was the efficiency of the transportation hub. Few people stood in lines. Entry and exit gates seemed non-existent. A row of three kiosks shaped as eight-foot-tall black monoliths stood against a wall near the FasTrain tracks with small screens full of information such as weather, financials, sports and entertainment. When Phoenix tapped the middle kiosk with her CELL, the cost of passage on the train for both of them was deducted from her account. There were no tickets. System tracking knew everyone's location. It made walking through the terminal seamless and easy.

The FasTrain car they got on was filled with youngsters who, by the topic of their combined chatter, were headed to the Memorial Weekend Kennywood

Spectacular. None of them looked older than ten and they were all sitting politely on their seats. Many of them wore CGs and those that did tapped the air in front of them as they manipulated some augmented reality that only they could see. The sea of tapping and swiping fingers in the vacant space around them made Shaun think about blind people who reach out to test the path in front of them. More than once, the hand taps even crossed the personal air space as some of the kids shared their own experiences.

Shaun sat in one of two empty seats next to the window and Phoenix sat next to him. Other than the entertainment he got from watching the passengers play with their technology, Shaun felt comfortably overwhelmed by the FasTrain car's interior. Much of its brightness came from the many digital screens that were built into the curved walls. Directly in front of him, the entire wall between the car's two sets of double doors displayed a map of all of the FasTrains, depicting them as colorful lines that moved along dotted routes within and around the New City perimeter that was boldly displayed in red. The train they were on was a blue line on the map screen and it traveled in parallel with the Monongahela River just below the red perimeter line that ran down the middle of the river's even bluer digital representation.

On the wall screens in other locations glowed a collection of ads that promoted New Pitt celebrations for Memorial Day weekend and information that revealed international financial data, world news and local weather, which noted that the weekend would be overcast with a chance of showers.

For most of the ride to Kennywood, Shaun had his face planted against the window. It was heavily tinted but he could still make out the security boundary stations located on both sides of the river that passed to the left of the train every five hundred yards. There were few boats on the Mon: a couple of them looked like sightseeing vessels; several others were personal watercraft that zipped along a surprisingly clear water surface. Beyond the river and looking back toward the city, Shaun saw four giant water tanker drones flying slowly over the distant city spires. They looked a lot like blimps but moved with more purpose than a blimp could navigate. Far behind the tanker drones, out near the horizon, the white dots of airplane landing lights dropped from and rose into the gray sky with timed efficiency.

About five minutes into the ride, the scenery outside turned stark dark as the train moved through large non-residential areas then suddenly brightened as the train passed one of the massive water-filtering mills. The illumination from the riverside facility revealed a tanker drone as it sat idle on the ground next to a white building from which wide, flexible pipes filled it with fresh water from the Mon. New Pittsburgh's eastside perimeter wall started at the bank of the river directly opposite the water mill and snaked away through the lighted suburbs in the direction of the Allegheny River a dozen miles away.

A few minutes later, activity on the FasTrain grew busier as it began stopping at numerous stations outside and through Homestead. Only a couple of passengers either entered or exited their car and it remained mostly full of anticipatory children. Phoenix's CELL lit up and the display told her that the next stop was Kennywood Park. All of the youngsters who were wearing them, removed their CGs and joined the others who were pecking away at their CELL screens until the train came to a stop. When the doors opened, they all rushed out, shouting their preferred destinations within the park as two, tired adults followed.

Shaun and Phoenix exited onto a platform that resembled an Old West steam train station. *Welcome to Kennywood* was etched into a large wooden sign under which were three monolith kiosks much like those in the T-interchange. A dozen or so park employees who were all dressed in identical navy blue uniforms roamed near the kiosk entry. None stopped anyone who entered but it seemed they were stationed there just in case, a kind of amusement park version of the hired white suits that roamed Marlinton. Two of them looked in their direction as soon as the FasTrain departed. Public restrooms were to the left of the park entrance and

Shaun immediately headed in that direction.

"I'll be right back," he said to Phoenix then walked ten yards around the men who still stood and stared. No one was in the bathroom so he locked it after he entered. Quickly, he dropped his backpack on the floor, unzipped it, yanked the silver metallic bag out and took the visaBand from inside.

Someone pushed on the bathroom door. A man's voice said, "Hello?"

Shaun thought about it for one more second before he wrapped the flexible, metal band around his right wrist and pressed the two ends together which sealed in a way that only cutting the band would remove it.

"Hello, sir. The door is locked. Please unlock it." Knuckles rapped against the door.

Shaun repositioned his backpack before unlocking and opening the door. "Sorry," he said to the first blue-uniformed Kennywood employee he saw. "Didn't realize it locked."

The man looked at Shaun's visaBand then at his own wrist, which had strapped to it what looked like a compact version of a CELL device. "Winston," the man said. "Welcome to Kennywood. I see it's your first time here. Forgive the intrusion."

Shaun saw the word **Winston** displayed in white on the man's CELL and looked down at the visaBand to read the same word displayed in white along the length of the vertical strip. "Yeah. Thanks. Sure thing."

Shaun stepped from the bathroom and the park man nodded toward his male companion. "Do you need any help with your bags? We have secure lockers for them at the station entry gate. No charge."

Both men walked with Shaun to stand beside Phoenix. "We need to check our bags," Shaun told her.

"Of course we do," Phoenix replied.

"Phoenix Messenger," the park man said to Phoenix after looking at his wrist. "Glad you could return to the park and thank you for bringing a new guest. Enjoy yourselves." The park man bowed a bit and waved his hand toward the entry, and Shaun and Phoenix moved in that direction."

Shaun whispered, "Looks like I'm not a terrorist, at least."

Phoenix giggled. "Of course you're not."

They walked between the monolith kiosks with a group of youngsters and were met by two different park men. They smiled and welcomed the children as they skipped and scuttled by, then one of them told Shaun that he would help him with his pack. Shaun removed his windbreaker from the backpack then gave the backpack to the park man. The second park man took Phoenix's bag after she removed a lavender-colored jacket from it.

The park men thanked them and Phoenix grabbed Shaun's elbow and spun him around. "Come on," she whispered and shook the jacket. "What we brought is in here."

◎ ◎ ◎ ◎ ◎

One thing was certain, Phoenix thought. Time was short. Whether they'd lost the Ties and their contacts in Marlinton was no longer important. Turning on her CELL had certainly flagged her current location and some unwanted stalkers were bound to show up.

She did wonder, though, if Shaun's location was known on the Net. Any other visaBand would certainly have tracking, but his was a Dr. One special. Making Shaun invisible from controlling, digital eyes made sense.

Kiddieland was the first section of the park they entered and it gobbled up most of the youngsters around them. The skies had grown twice as gray since they'd departed the T-interchange and the temperature had fallen ten degrees. A sudden rush of chilly air whipped around her as the classic kiddie rides created a tunnel of airflow.

Phoenix slipped on her jacket, one of her favorites and one of the only gifts her uncle had given her that she actually cherished. The lavender cotton fabric had three pockets, two that zippered at the hips and one at the left breast. It was thin and flexible and perfect for a cool, city evening. Her favorite thing about the jacket, though, was her uncle's proof that *he did* know his niece at least a little bit. Centered across the back of the jacket was an embroidered yellow and orange dolphin surrounded by a stitched halo of yellow light. It was spectacular in its definition. She'd never worn it much around the observatory so as to avoid too many niceties with her uncle. The backup drive was in the breast pocket; the baby food jar was in the left hip pocket and her CELL was in the right. Phoenix adjusted the jacket but didn't button it.

Shaun also put on his windbreaker. It was forest green in color and had the logo of Jennifer Outfitters sewn into the breast. It looked much thinner than what Phoenix wore but it seemed to be enough for him.

"Very cool jacket," Shaun said. "Looks like others think so, too."

Phoenix watched the faces of those who sat on the numerous wooden benches around them as they walked through a food court plaza. Some, who were wearing CGs, pointed at her and smiled. "Wow!" one man said. "Very pretty," his female companion added. "Can you get me one, honey?"

Maybe the jacket wasn't such a good idea, Phoenix thought. It stuck out like a beacon—like that really mattered in a place that watched her with more than the suspicious eyes of its guests. She was on the Net. Did it really matter what she was wearing?

They escaped the scrambling menagerie of people in Kiddieland and came across one of the park's newest attractions: *The Walk On Water Experience*. A large pond of water sparkled as lights from its depths beamed up through the gentle surface waves and surrounded a long, rectangular building that cantilevered fifty yards over the water. A digital billboard promoted possible "experiences."

Play with Dolphins
Hook a Mighty Marlin
Escape the Jaws of Jaws
Walk on Water
All Now V.41 Enabled

A long line of people waited for their own experience. Most of them had CGs either on their face or were holding them. As Phoenix and Shaun squeezed through, screams erupted from within the rainbow-sparkling walls of the building. Everyone in line yelped and clapped with approval.

Across the pond, Phoenix saw the top of the Jack Rabbit and she led Shaun in that direction, passing by the Grand Carousel on the right. It had been magnificently maintained to preserve its century-old history. The horses' expressions were time-stamped and engaging. A fine, polished sheen created reflective glints of happiness, surprise and determination in the many circling horse eyes.

"Want to take a ride?" the carousel operator asked them. He wore a black, Lincoln-era stovetop hat over short black hair that formed into heavy sideburns and a short beard and mustache. A blue jean jacket that had the sleeves torn off revealed the short cuff of a white t-shirt above a complex tattoo that depicted a carousel horsehead stretched across his bicep. He turned and looked right at Shaun. "You've not ridden one before have you, Winston? Come on. It's like taking a trip back through time."

Phoenix was going to have to get used to it. She was sure Shaun was having a tough time. Since everyone was connected with everyone else in the park, some knowledge of each individuals' Stories would be available. Shaun, who was apparently known as Winston to everyone else, had not been to Kennywood and he'd not ridden a carousel. Anyone who might be interested would know such easily accessible information.

"Maybe later," Shaun said. "It is really beautiful."

"I polish them myself," the operator said.

"No." Shaun pointed. "I mean the tattoo."

"Take a look with CGs for the total effect."

Phoenix and Shaun both shrugged.

"That's okay, Winston." The operator smiled but only his incisors were visible. "Perhaps, next time.

Enjoy your day and God Bless the United States of America."

"He knows me," Shaun said while walking away.

"Uh-huh," Phoenix responded. "All of the park employees are going to know about their guests."

"Gives them a particular advantage for persuasion, don't you think?"

"Goes with the territory. It's one thing you have to be aware of, constantly: them knowing what you might need before you know it. Welcome to the Suspicious Society suburbs of the New City."

"Predictable," Shaun said and continued around the bright, shiny pond toward the Jack Rabbit rollercoaster.

◎ ◎ ◎ ◎ ◎

Yeah. He was spooked. Phoenix was wrong in suggesting he'd get used to it. Having complete strangers know you before ever meeting them was unnerving in the least and downright scary. Some part of his freedom seemed to have been taken from him. And he was beginning to realize that those with more recent technology could access information faster and with greater depth. The visaBand provided him with no information about those he met. He pressed it with one thumb. His name **Winston** disappeared from the screen and a Kennywood marquee replaced it. A tiny, yellow exclamation point glowed with a gentle pulse. Beside it were the tiny, yellow glowing words **Locker Key**. He pressed again and the screen reverted to the black home screen with the white text **Winston**.

"You know how to work one of these?" he asked Phoenix. They'd arrived at the back of the line for the Jack Rabbit.

"Press and swipe," she said.

"Yeah. Pinch, too, but not much happened."

"Limited readout. It's not the purpose of a visaBand. It's more one way. Others know of you but you can't interact in the other direction. I have my CELL if we need it. I doubt it's going to help us locate Johnnie, though. I figure he's the type that can control his own Story."

Several couples entered the line behind them as they stepped a dozen feet forward. Coaster cars clicked by in the opposite direction beyond a wooden fence to their right. Like the carousel and the Kiddieland rides and just about every other attraction in the park, the Jack Rabbit had been diligently preserved. The wooden coaster latticework, towering forty feet to his right, shook as a coaster car train hit a turn that led to a big drop from above. When Shaun looked up, he wondered how the train even stayed on the track; he wondered why he was about to get on it. A dozen seconds later, another train zipped by beyond the wooden fence and the passengers' screams reminded Shaun of the

Water Experience outburst, except no one clapped and cheered in the Jack Rabbit line.

A change in the glow from the visaBand made Shaun look down again. A tiny, pumping red heart icon read: **90 bpm.**

"Never been on a rollercoaster either, I see," Phoenix said, looking at Shaun's wrist. "You don't need any more info than that."

Shaun grabbed the elastic at the end of his windbreaker sleeve and pulled it over the visaBand. "I don't need to see it, I know it."

Most of the chatter in line centered on everyone's anticipation for two things: the legendary airtime for which the coaster had been famous and the new VR Tunnel that offered additional experiences for those who were V.41-enabled.

Shaun stepped up onto the wooden coaster platform first and Phoenix followed. Ahead of him, a single line of people snaked through three back-and-forth railings. From them, he'd heard enough about "coming out of your seat" and his heart now raced a little faster. Even if his nerves did completely fail him, he thought, there were too many people for him to escape.

And as the suffocating feeling of claustrophobia closed in, he turned to look at the line behind him. Back near the end of it, in about the same location where he and Phoenix had entered the line, were three men wearing what looked like ClearGlasses that were darkly shaded. All three wore matching casual jackets that were the same blue color as the park men's uniforms but heir faces were turned away.

"What do you think?" Shaun nodded in the direction of the three men and Phoenix looked. "Tailing us?"

The line moved ahead and Shaun followed Phoenix forward, but the three men remained where they were standing.

"Waiting," Phoenix said. "They're not gonna bother us, yet. I sure hope Jackrabbit Johnnie has a plan."

◎ ◎ ◎ ◎ ◎

Riders filled the next train which left Shaun at the front of the line with a new dilemma. He'd never ridden a rollercoaster and he had his choice of seat.

"The front's the best," Phoenix said.

"Damn straight," a teenage boy of about sixteen said behind her. He'd dyed his rather hairy sideburns aqua blue. "It's even better with the VR." He twirled a pair of CGs in one hand. A girl of about the same age stood beside him and twirled her pair with a smile. She looked a lot like Phoenix, only more petite.

"We've never done a front ride VR with no heads in our way," the teen girl said. "Yuns gonna VR?"

Phoenix shook her head.

"Mind if we get fronts?" the teen girl asked. "The back is also great for first-time Jack Rabbit riders." Her smile widened as she looked right at Shaun.

"Yeah," the teen boy said. "The negative G you experience back there is more intense. Just hold onto the bar if you don't trust the seatbelt. I didn't the first time and I thought I's gonna fly off into the trees."

Phoenix shrugged and Shaun said, "Sure. We could always ride it again."

"Thanks, Winston," the teen girl said and reached out to touch his hand. "Your bio says that you are thoughtful person."

The girl's boy friend didn't seem to care about her little flirt. He smiled in gratitude and placed his CGs atop the bridge of his nose as the coaster train clattered to a stop. The teen girl put on her CGs and tapped the small CELL strapped around her wrist. When she walked passed Shaun, she purposefully brushed against his chest. "I wish you were my bodyguard," she whispered to him, then followed her friend to the front of the nine rows of double seats. Phoenix grabbed Shaun's hand and led him to the back and the teen boy shouted, "It was really great to meet you, Winston." He waved and jumped onto the train beside the girl.

Shaun sat to the inside and Phoenix dropped beside him and adjusted her jacket before pulling a two-inch-wide seatbelt across their laps. She pressed the buckle against Shaun's knee to lock it then placed her hands on the black knee bar that was anchored to the seat in front of them just a few inches above their thighs. "He's right," she said. "The Rabbit is known for great airtime. It's really evident if you don't hold the bar, but the part about flying off into the trees—I think that's stretching it a bit…bodyguard."

Shaun was testing the flexibility and strength of the seatbelt when he looked up. "What did she mean by that?"

"I guess you look like a bodyguard."

"I'm just not going to get used to people knowing me who don't know me. She said my bio says I'm thoughtful."

"She's right. I'd say it's one of your better keywords."

"Great. My life reduced to a digital collection of keywords."

The coaster operator stepped to them and looked down. He smiled a set of white teeth that glistened with the reflections of the surrounding multi-colored coaster lights. A thin line of black whiskers encircled his lips but his jawline sported no other growth. Her wore baggy jeans and a Kennywood blue jacket over a black t-shirt.

"All strapped and ready?" he said and leaned forward to test the seatbelt with one finger as he gazed at Phoenix. He had that same gleam of knowing in his eyes that Shaun had seen from the teens and he grinned as he rose. "Have a good one," he said and walked to the front of the train. A second later, they were off. The operator pointed his finger at Shaun as they passed, then curled the finger so that it pointed at the first left turn in the tracks. He nodded and winked.

The ground-level coaster rails skirted the perimeter wooden fence where the line to ride formed on the other side. It was tall enough so that you couldn't see who was standing there but a space at the bottom of the fence allowed a view of the shoes. At the point in the turn where the three men had been standing, Shaun saw six loafers, all of the same style. He wondered if the men could see him. He wondered if the coaster operator had been pointing at them.

Around the turn, the coaster dropped thirty feet into a valley then rolled up an incline that led straight for the tunnel. It wasn't arched at the top like Sharp's, but the approaching rectangle of black reminded him of the railroad passage.

Several of the riders ahead of him who wore CGs held one hand against the side of their heads to keep the devices in place. Above the tunnel was a digital 3D sign that promoted the kinds of experiences the VR tunnel enabled. Life on another planet or under the sea, or perhaps a brief encounter with something personally beautiful or fear-filled—it was the VR rider's choice.

The ride through the tunnel was seconds-brief.

Though there was plenty of overcast light outside, the tunnel's interior was pitch black. Screams of fascination and fright mixed in with the hallow acoustics that magnified the clacking of train wheels against metal. Shaun, of course, could not engage in the digital experiences but in those brief moments, while feeling quite alone in all of the intense blackness, he did see something. A memory, perhaps. Dr. One stood at the mouth of the tunnel, surrounded by a halo of white and several micro-thin beams of glowing green light. When the coaster exited the tunnel, Dr. One disappeared and Shaun's seat fell from under him as the train dropped from the boxed tunnel down a steep decline. He pulled the seatbelt tighter as the train grabbed the lift chain and hauled them to the top of the coaster. Phoenix reached down and loosened it a bit.

"Not too much," she said. "You want to experience what this baby is known for."

The train gently rounded the turn at the apex of the coaster and this gave Shaun a magnificent view of the bright pond, Kiddieland and the FasTrain station on the far side of the park, and the Grand Carousel that rotated under a canopy of trees. He saw a stovepipe hat wander among a crowded set of heads and he expected the operator to look up at him, but he didn't.

Down the steep drop they went, leveled off, then dropped again. Shaun had significant airtime and he did think that he might spring right out of his seat, though the tops of trees were not where he thought he might land. Against the coaster's wooden tower boards was a more likely destination.

They rolled around one more hundred-and-eighty-degree turn, dropped one more dramatic time, then clickety-clacked into the coaster station and stopped.

"Not so bad," Phoenix said and popped the seatbelt clasp. "Now your Story includes a ride on the Rabbit."

When she stepped up and out of the car, the operator was there to help her. He offered Shaun a hand and Shaun took it. The operator walked with them toward the exit where the riders massed to leave in a single file. The teen boy and girl stood there and the operator took off his Kennywood jacket and gave it to the boy. "Chuck should be in at six," the operator said. "He'll take over then." The teen boy quickly walked across the train platform and began ushering riders to their seats. The operator then urged the three of them closer to him with twiddling fingers. He didn't quite whisper. His voice was only loud enough to hear over the audible tremor of stressed wood and human exuberance.

"Phoenix Messenger," he said. "I'm J.J." When Phoenix didn't immediately respond, he added, "Your uncle's Johnnie." He scrunched forward as if not wanting to be seen, and all three of them followed his lead. "Your jacket," he said. "I need your jacket… Quickly."

Phoenix removed her jacket much too slowly for the operator and he helped her pull her arms through. He gave the jacket to the teen girl who put it on and ran out through the exit.

"But she has…" Phoenix started to say, her voice rising to the point that J.J. had to shush her.

J.J. turned and walked away from them to look back along the waiting line. He held one finger up for several seconds then walked back over. "Two of them took the bait," he said. "The other must be waiting for you, Winston." He tapped a CELL that he held in his hand, said to them, "Hold right here for a couple," again walked over to look back along the waiting line for at least a full minute, then returned. "Let's go," he said and led Shaun and Phoenix through the exit.

They jog-walked quickly from the Jack Rabbit to a neighboring restroom building. Shaun looked back over his shoulder to see the one remaining stalker standing between two park men who looked to be aggressively questioning him. J.J. ushered them into the men's room where they found a couple of men who didn't seem particularly surprised to see a woman in their bathroom. Both gave J.J. the thumbs-up and then both stood at the bathroom's exit. J.J. went to the last stall and stepped inside while Shaun and Phoenix waited. The stall doors rattled and the sound of escaping air preceded J.J.'s face that appeared from behind the stall door. "Come on," he said.

The opening in the back wall of the handicap stall was only hip high and Shaun had to crawl into it, behind J.J. and Phoenix. Once inside the hidden room's dark chamber, the opening closed behind Shaun's feet.

⊙ ⊙ ⊙ ⊙ ⊙

A bunch of popcorn cooked somewhere nearby. The buttery, toasted smell permeated the darkness and made Phoenix's stomach growl a quieter rumble than her thumping heart that beat between her ears. Everything had happened so fast. J.J. Johnnie had certainly made a plan. Unfortunately, it had included the departure of the valuables she'd stashed in her jacket.

"Hold for another moment," J.J.'s voice whispered in the dark.

Phoenix was about to ask about the jacket when a sound beyond the closed access panel that they'd just crawled through stole her attention. A toilet seat dropped and someone shuffled around in preparation of doing some business. A strip light suddenly flickered on overhead to reveal a large, vacant crawl space. It was tall enough for them to crawl toward a set of lighted steps that descended from the back of the crawl space floor. J.J. scuttled forward, turned his body feet-first, and walked backwards down the steps. Phoenix followed him and Shaun followed behind her. The contrasting sounds of defecation and smell of popcorn began to turn Phoenix's stomach. J.J. laughed. "Welcome to Kennywood," he said.

At the bottom of the concrete staircase that Phoenix thought might double as a missile bunker was a standard-height, gray metal door. J.J. pressed his hand against the center of it and the door clicked open and swung inward. All three of them stepped through and into a brightly lit five-foot corridor that opened into a much larger and much longer room; it ran perpendicular to the corridor and looked like a trailer-sized white laboratory. The room was deeper to the right than it was to the left. Shaun pushed the door closed behind him.

Phoenix immediately asked about her jacket, even though the lab was filled with technological gadgetry that only a scientist could love. "You know my jacket had in it the reason why we're here," she said as Shaun walked passed her and stood behind J.J. to marvel at a huge, digital screen anchored to the back wall of the lab.

"Yes. I figured as much," J.J. said and scratched his chin. "Can't be too careful in a place like this." When Phoenix didn't respond, J.J. added, "The jacket's right over there." He turned and offered an open hand to the left. Draped across the high back of a cushioned rolling chair was her lavender jacket. Phoenix stepped quickly to it and searched the pockets. She nodded at J.J. then turned her attention to J.J.'s hidden lab, twenty feet below the food court picnic tables.

Right beside her, in front of the chair and sitting on a long table against the wall, was a big white cube about three-feet wide. A clear glass panel on the face of the cube revealed enough technology for her to know that it was a 3D printer. Two sealed, ceramic-looking containers, each about the size of a cookie jar, sat next to the printer. One was labeled *Resin 111* and the other was labeled *Resin 390*. To the right of the printer and containers sat a thirty-six inch digital touchscreen monitor that was completely dark.

Beyond J.J. and Shaun, near the back of the right side of the lab, another table supported a very exotic and expensive-looking microscope and an assortment of small hand tools. To the right of this table was what looked like a filing cabinet and a few smaller tables that supported equipment that Phoenix had never seen before. She walked over to stand with Shaun and J.J.

Directly in front of her was the huge screen that continued to consume Shaun's attention. It occupied nearly all of the wall's height. A 3D-layered map of Pittsburgh seemed to jump from its glass face. A title at the top of the screen read in green text: **EMR Details: New Pitt: 50%.**

The current magnification showed the entirety of

New Pitt, its security boundary markers and much of the eastern suburbs, including Kennywood, without any topographic detail. A transparent green layer covered everything except a dozen or so irregular spots, one of which was over Kennywood.

"I'm guessing the open areas in the EMR overlay are where radiation is not used or its detection is blocked in some way," Phoenix said to J.J.

"That's right," J.J. said.

"It looks familiar," Phoenix continued. "I mean the detail of detection. Even the dark spots seem pretty precise…like this one." She touched the word **Kennywood**. "This is about where we are." The map zoomed in and she touched it again. "Everything around the Jack Rabbit is dead. You have some kind of cage going on?"

J.J. didn't answer the question. Instead, he said, "You know, his pictures don't do you justice."

J.J. was a couple of inches taller than Shaun so Phoenix had to look up a bit. "What do you mean?"

"He showed me a picture just in case someone tried to ghost you. I'm sorry that he's dead."

"What makes you say that?" Shaun asked.

"That Dr. One is dead? Through the grapevine and you being here confirms it. He said that if he ever died, he'd send his niece with valuable data he'd collected."

"*We* collected," Phoenix corrected him.

"Of course. Hell, it's your software that's got us

this far. I bow to the greater codemaker." J.J. bowed a bit.

No wonder the fine details in the map data looked so familiar, Phoenix thought. It was her program running the whole thing. Anger for her uncle began to surface and J.J. saw this.

"He never told you. Not surprising. That man was always full of surprises."

"We don't think he's dead," Shaun offered. "Do we, Phoenix?"

"Not based on what you told me," she said.

J.J. stared at Shaun. "Winston, is it?"

Shaun looked down to see that the elastic armband of his windbreaker had scooted above the visaBand. "According to that…yes."

"You have great Story markers," J.J. continued. "Your overall U.S. Citizenry rates a perfect green smile." The two stood face-to-face and Phoenix thought they looked a lot alike. Shaun had a more mature beard, though scruffy, and J.J.'s face was filled with at least ten more years of age than Shaun's, but the similarities in body shape were very close.

"I still can't get used to people knowing me so well even if what they know isn't entirely accurate," Shaun said. "I'm not even registered yet."

"Not according to Winston's Story. Your basic bios are the same but your history has been augmented a wee bit." J.J. reached out and dropped his hand on

Shaun's shoulder. "You're a registered citizen who is turning twenty-one today. Congratulations."

"Twenty-one?" Phoenix said.

"Uh-huh." J.J. shook Shaun lightly. "A twenty-one-year-old bodyguard, visiting New Pitt for the first time." J.J. removed his hand.

"Someone else called me that. The two riders at the front. Your people, I suppose."

"My people. Yes. That's what they are. And there's a whole lot more like them."

"My uncle told Shaun that his purpose was to protect me," Phoenix said. "To basically, be my bodyguard."

"So, he is alive?" J.J. asked.

Shaun interjected by telling J.J. that the day after he'd found the doctor dead, he saw him on the river trail, and then a day later, saw him outside Phoenix's Green Bank apartment. "So, I've guarded her up to this point…now what?"

J.J. grinned. "I don't think you understand what a bodyguard is, at least not so far as the city understands. A bodyguard is one who is hired to control a person's Story. You're an expensive commodity to have but a lot of the, how do you say, upper-tier individuals can afford to make sure their Story is recorded in a measured way."

"What else is there about me that I should know?"

"I'm going to have to show you a few hacks that you can perform in case someone questions your coding chops, but all of that we'll get to later, Winston."

"You know you can call me by my first name," Shaun offered.

"Your Story says you're Winston."

"Who in the world came up with that name?"

"I did," J.J. said. "I programmed your counterfeit visaBand."

◎ ◎ ◎ ◎ ◎

He'd been flung three years into the future and, as Winston, would be celebrating his twenty-first birthday…today. That, plus the knowledge that he was some special code hack known as a bodyguard only heightened his sense of fantasy. He wondered, only briefly, if J.J. could change all of that with just a few taps of a Net device. Could J.J. make him whomever he wanted to be?

At the same time that Phoenix offered J.J. the backup drive, Shaun's attention was drawn to the right side of the room. He walked passed a long countertop full of small tools like a jeweler might use, scattered digital parts he did not recognize and a very exotic-looking microscope, and headed straight for the far white wall. Nothing stood in front of it. Creases formed the shape of a door that was built into the wall. He placed his palm in the middle of it but nothing happened.

He turned ninety degrees to examine the second thing that had drawn his attention: a six-foot-tall, black-as-coal box that could have been a filing cabinet except that it had no apparent drawers. Shaun stood in front of it to find three equidistant glass openings, each about the width of a pair of eyes, along its vertical face. He bent forward to look in the top-most window then stooped to look in the second and the third. Through each, he saw nothing but complete darkness.

"This is what we were able to pull of the servers about a month ago," Phoenix said to J.J. and gave him the drive. Shaun shifted his attention to J.J. who dropped the small backup drive into a recess in the countertop below the smaller touchscreen. He didn't plug it in to anything; he just set it there. The blue light in its center immediately came on and the wall screen changed to one filled with black. In the very center of it was a blinking white question mark.

J.J. pressed the small control screen with one finger and a band of light appeared above the counter in front of it. It expanded and redefined itself as an augmented reality keyboard.

"It's all yours," he said.

◉ ◉ ◉ ◉ ◉

Phoenix had never tried to remember complex, precise passwords. Instead, she remembered an easy phrase and applied a quick algorithm that she could do in her head. The formula amounted to replacing each of the characters in the phrase with another that was some mathematical difference in the programmed character set: a form of Turing cipher she'd learned in college. The easy, base password phrase was *vibrations of interconnectivity*. She applied the algorithm in her head and tapped the augmented reality keyboard. White asterisks rolled across the width of the big black screen. There were so many of them that two asterisks dropped to the second line. Phoenix tapped the keyboard's translucent Enter key.

J.J.'s EMR map was almost identical to the one that now replaced it, and Phoenix could tell that he'd been using an older version of her software. The newest software provided finer detail in not only the location of EMR bursts but, also, what was actually causing them by data-mining the frequencies that the Green Bank telescopes had helped detect and log. The map was also different in that its magnification was zoomed all the way out to show the entire border of the United States as a yellow, glowing, jagged outline. Each state and any borders with Mexico and Canada were also represented as yellow lines. A blue color identified the water on the map in two shades: very dark blue colored the oceans and any other saltwater sources, and light blue denoted freshwater sources. Phoenix's attention was drawn straight to the light blue, finger-like glow of the Great Lakes. Surrounding the shorelines on all sides of the lakes were brightly glowing masses of green light. The green grew darkest the closer it came to the light blue lakes, but even the lightest shades of green, which represented lower density EMR emissions, extended a good two inches beyond the shorelines. **New Duluth, New Milwaukee, New Chicago**—each named black dot was suffocated by the green EMR overlay. The Canadian border cities were not named **New**, but their black dots were just as dark green. The representation was similar in the area on the map around **New Pittsburgh.**

In great contrast, on the west side of the map, there were only sporadic pockets of EMR green, mostly located in the northern states. The California coastline remained as a prominent EMR source but much of the inland areas had very little. The southwest and Midwest looked to be the starkest on the map. A dozen years ago, the Plains and Desert cities might have glowed a bit greener but today, the absence of water meant the absence of populations.

"This down here is a lot different than the old data I have," J.J. said, pointing at the southeastern states.

"My uncle began giving a lot of time to watching that area of the country several months ago," Phoenix said. "The wide disbursement of EMR sources in the south made it a little easier to programmatically detect individual frequencies. From what I see here, he must have updated the backup from a month ago when we hid it in his house. The buildup in just that time is amazing."

From Florida to the Mississippi River in Louisiana and all the way up into the southern part of the Appalachians, scattered swaths of very light green, ragged patches were painted on the screen like islands of electromagnetic noise in a sea of tech-free silence.

"Lots of changes here," J.J. said and took two fingers to pull a zoom in on the area south of West Virginia. A large section of it appeared and a new window of information popped up on the right side of the screen that contained a list of the EMR-emitting devices detected in that area, from AM radio to microwaves and CELL usage. "Don't know how they're getting this stuff so fast. The communication towers have increased faster than they could reasonably build them and there's an incredibly wide distribution of V.38 and V.41 CELLs. That takes money and from the looks of it, a whole lot."

"So, they're beginning to invest in new tech," Phoenix said. "So what?"

"Let's take a closer look." J.J. double-fingered another zoom and the light blue lines of many rural rivers appeared. Most of the magnified light green EMR pockets ran along these rivers. "That's what we expected."

"The government is starting to set up a protective grid around freshwater," Phoenix said, "Makes sense."

"It's not just the government," J.J. said. He backed away from the screen and Shaun walked over from the black cabinet. "Why do you think the last dozen years have moved us into this all-connected, all-suspicious society?"

"Water shortage," Shaun said. "And the thought that terrorists could do more damage."

"Yes," J.J. said. "Good reasons, don't you think?"

Shaun and Phoenix both nodded.

"Just a matter of convenience, though, for what the government and big business really have as goals."

Shaun and Phoenix remained silent.

"Let me put it to you this way. If you knew that a group of people born right here in the U.S. were so dead set on destroying the prosperity of their own country that they'd poison its major sources of underground water, and if you knew more groups of individuals who shared similar domestic terrorism beliefs had grown dangerously large and were massing in parts of the southeast to guard their own freshwater sources, what would you, as the U.S. government think?"

Phoenix took both hands and swiped them against the big screen to zoom out. All of the green masses along the light blue river lines now looked like a military map that depicted the front of an opposing strategic force.

Shaun pointed at several green dots that snaked up from Virginia and continued along the Greenbrier River through the mountains. "Those are government," he said. "I've seen them myself."

J.J. nodded. "That's what Dr. One thinks, too. They are creating a boundary…a perimeter."

"For what?" Phoenix asked. "No…wait. The government thinks there's gonna be an invasion—a war?"

J.J. remained calm and collected. "The government. Your uncle. Me. This isn't the kind of information those that try to control the information wants the country to see. The New Cities provide hope in an otherwise very bleak future."

"But Civil War!?" Phoenix exclaimed. "Isn't that a bit much? People have families everywhere. No one wants to blow up their kid sister with a missile."

"Who said anything about blowing people up? You really thought about what Civil War might look like today? We took all of this time to start making things right for everyone, building up the infrastructure by building up data on its citizens. We wouldn't want to destroy all of that. There's gonna be things blowing up, don't get me wrong. But in the end it will be about control. Today's Civil War will be won by controlling the masses."

"Then, what we have is proof," Phoenix said. "The Feds took it off our servers to conceal the truth. But why would they give us money to detect something they wouldn't want made public?"

J.J. just stared at the map and its depiction of a future growing more separate. He was offering her a chance to, first, think about an answer. The brain of a scientist, Phoenix thought. A computer mind. Always looking for ways to exercise the neurons… "Computer programming," she said. "The value isn't so much the data collected; it's the software that collected it—my software."

"And once they break any security measures you took to protect it, they'll not only be able to see this kind of detail, they'll hack it to make it better. The movement will no longer be invisible."

"My uncle gave them my software?" Phoenix mumbled.

"Wait," Shaun said. "You said, the movement. You wouldn't be talking about the Faraday Movement would you?"

J.J. put both hands in his baggy jeans pockets. "Winston. I didn't write anything into your Story that included such knowledge."

"That's because Shaun knows stuff that Winston doesn't," Shaun said.

"As he should. Bethany told you, didn't she?"

Phoenix interjected. "She didn't say that an operator of a rollercoaster outside of New Pitt had anything to do with it."

"Sworn not to," J.J. said. "But you do understand our purpose? We're tired of laws that demand our ever-present data just to be a 'citizen' and enjoy all of this country's freedoms while using that same data against us—to control us—to manage any possible dissension—any possible uprising. We've created so many cracks in their plans already, that they've become ever more determined to seal them…to seal me and this lab."

"What are you going to do with it?...the EMR data on the drive?"

"Share it with contacts in the city and hopefully use Dr. One's second layer of data to continue perfecting the microdrones."

Phoenix stared right at Shaun and Shaun shrugged. "So, two things," Phoenix said. "What do you have to do with microdrones and what do you mean by second layer of data?"

"I make microdrones and your uncle encrypted a second layer of data that includes some much needed tech specs on them that he'd developed. He said that you would have the password to decrypt it."

"First I've heard," Phoenix said.

"Down here. Look." J.J. pointed at a tiny icon at the bottom left edge of the big screen. Its shade of gray was such that the two letters were almost invisible:

FM

J.J. pressed it and the screen went black. It reset, again, to show a blinking white question mark.

"That doesn't help me. I don't know of any second layer password."

"Odd," J.J. said. "He said you would have it."

Shaun walked over to Phoenix's jacket and reached into one hip pocket. "We might not have a password but I think we have something else you might find interesting." Shaun's closed palm hid the small jar as he walked back to J.J. and lifted his hand to eye-level. He uncurled his fingers and J.J.'s reaction of marvel and shock was immediate. He leaned in closer.

"May I?" he said. Shaun nodded and J.J. took the baby food jar and brought it to the bridge of his nose. "That's a mosquito."

"We call him, Skeeter," Shaun said.

One of J.J.'s eyebrows rose in curiosity. "Appropriate. Where'd you get it?"

"Dr. One's place in Marlinton," Shaun said. "It was there the night he died. At least, I think it's the same one."

"Same one?" J.J.'s other eyebrow rose. "You mean there's more?"

"We saw three at Bethany's."

J.J. shook his head. "You know how hard this must have been to create?"

"All three of them shot tiny green beams just like this one did two nights ago. They protected us from the Feds' cicadas."

"Whoa!" J.J. lowered the jar and held it at his side. "I think you gotta fill me in on a few more details."

Shaun told him about their evening at Bethany's and how the Feds had taken her away. He told him about the night he'd found Dr. One.

When he finished, J.J. walked toward the large, black cabinet on the right side of the room. "Come here. I want to show you something." Once they were all standing in front of the cabinet, J.J. continued. "When you looked in, what did you see?"

"Darkness," Shaun said.

J.J. reached around the back of the cabinet and a light turned on inside the top chamber. "Look now."

Shaun bent forward to look through the small, glass window. "Ah, yes. Cicadas. Two of them." J.J. turned the light off. "Uh-huh. That's them. Cicada microdrones."

"And now the middle chamber," J.J. offered.

Shaun looked. "Lots of them in there." J.J. turned on the light. "Eww. Cockroaches."

J.J. snickered. "Not one of my better successes," he said. "Bio-digitally very sound but testing revealed a high casualty rate. People like stomping on roaches. Besides, we found that insects that fly are much more effective. It's the flight mechanisms that the doctor was working to perfect along with greater EMR shielding. The sudden appearance of the cicadas from hibernation gave us a chance to experiment with limited flight, just like the government is doing. But it's the intricacies of something as small as a mosquito that could really give us an advantage." J.J. lifted the jar and looked at Skeeter. "You are a little miracle," he said to it. "Let's see what you're made of."

J.J., again, knelt behind the cabinet, pressed a panel near the bottom, unscrewed the jar but left the lid loose of top, and set it in the dark, bottom chamber before taking the jar lid and closing the panel. He shuffled on his knees to the front of the cabinet to look inside. "Tiny, tiny, tiny," he said. "Come on little guy… fly. Yes. There you go." J.J. rose from his knees. "You want to see if it will talk to us? Maybe it knows the password."

Phoenix hadn't thought of that but it made perfect sense from a Dr. One point of view. Even if the Feds had intercepted them on the way to Kennywood, she wouldn't have been able to decrypt anything.

All three of them walked back to the huge wall screen. J.J. typed commands on the AR keyboard projection that replaced the blinking question mark on the big screen with a 3D-360 spin of the contents of the microdrone cabinet's lower chamber. A mass of tiny red, green and blue specks (made larger by the screen) bobbed and rotated and landed and walked and flew playfully.

A long moment of silence tuned Phoenix's senses to the rumbling of the floor and the very faint screams of riders on the Jack Rabbit. The Skeeter's small dot of multicolored specks landed and remained still for a second before slowly flashing in unison, on then off, so that Phoenix could read the coded message. "Hello… Johnnie…" Phoenix said. "It…would…appear…" The lights started flashing faster than Phoenix could track.

"Morse code?" J.J. asked her. "I'd forgotten all about that ancient language."

The Skeeter specks flashed so fast that all of them became one small, glowing spot of white. Above it, in the right corner of the wall screen, a smaller window popped up and the pixelated face of Dr. One stitched into a coherent headshot portrait. The lips started moving below a frosty white mustache. Heavy eyebrows, also frosty white, hovered over stern, wet, gray eyes that were set within a sea of wrinkles.

"Hello, Johnnie," Dr. One said. "It would appear that I am in your lab; at least, that's what my mosquito senses are telling me."

"How did you do it?" J.J. asked the video but Dr. One continued.

"I know you must have a billion questions. Unfortunately, my programming is a one-way conversation. Never got a chance to try out my impromptu response mechanisms.

"First, let me offer an apology to my niece. You must be quite upset with me, Phoenix…even more so than historically usual. I had to *borrow* your incredible program so that the government jerks would stay off my ass." Dr. One's face leaned forward for a moment. "They never got the really good stuff, so, at least the magic of your program is still ours…" The face leaned back. "…is still yours. It shows some pretty worrisome stuff, proof of what we've believed to be true for some time."

Dr. One's lips closed and he stared as if waiting for a response.

"Yes," he continued. "Civil War."

J.J. looked at Shaun and then Phoenix and nodded.

"The ones that control the digital Net are profoundly advantaged. And so I give you the mosquito microdrone. What do you think, Johnnie?"

"He never calls me J.J," J.J. said and shrugged. "For whatever reason."

"Small, quick, flight-enabled, hard to catch, hard to see, most people want to avoid them. Perfect for the carrier of mobile MIXR technology. Yes, Johnnie. Mobile MIXRs in flight. It's what we've been talking about for some time."

Dr. One's finger appeared from beyond the bottom of the popup window and he pointed at Phoenix, though Phoenix thought it was pure coincidence that the recorded video had done so. "Go ahead, Johnnie," Dr. One said. "Take a minute and explain. I'll wait." Dr. One swiveled in the high-backed chair he was sitting in to show them the back of the chair and the top of his white hair.

J.J. said, "Your uncle and I have known each other for some time…five years at least. He was always fascinated with sophisticated surveillance equipment and how he could render their collected sophistication useless. When he found out about the government's microdrones, well, that really put him over the edge. He was going to create a way to block them and he asked for my help."

Dr. One turned back around inside the popup window. He had a big smile on his face as if he knew what J.J. had just said. "You want to know why?" he offered but did not wait for an answer. "As much as the power brokers hate to admit it, we're still an open society, one that's gotten so open, there are many cracks that have developed. That seepage is what we call 911, the Eastern European Scare, and the Aquifer Attacks. The cracks have developed in such numbers that those hungry for control will seal them. It's all a part of their engineered Suspicious Society, where you get the people to do the work for you. Make them fearful of each other. Give them easy ways to capture and store data about each other on the Net. But even that isn't enough. It's those last little bits of data they don't have, that aren't shared, that can't be easily collected outside of controlled areas like the New Cities. Tiny, unsuspecting microdrones—thousands of them, maybe more—crawling through your house to make sure your Story is as complete as possible, particularly those parts of it that could flag you as a possible threat."

Dr. One paused to scratch his mustache and J.J. said, "That's the reason for this lab."

Dr. One continued, "Not a very pleasing thought, is it? Every insect, a cause for suspicion. You'd be looking in corners, wondering. You'd feel caged."

Phoenix thought of Bethany and how her fear of the "bugs" had caused her so much paranoia. She thought it would be a horrible thing for entire populations to live that way.

"Lucky for us, Johnnie got a good bit of experience back when he worked for the energy brokers and managed their exploration microdrones. Coupled with my breadth of knowledge of frequency emissions and Phoenix's detection software, Johnnie created our own experimental factory right here, right under their noses. They want to collect data and we want to prevent it, so we are creating microdrones that can not only escape the limits of flight, but can also generate an EMR-deflecting field around anything close to it. I believe you saw evidence of this at Bethany's house. The drone you are now interacting with was one of the first three I created."

"I didn't know you were doing your own thing," J.J. said to the big screen.

"Sorry, Johnnie, for keeping it a secret but these are secretive times, as you know. I am proud to say that the first test at Bethany's was a success. The triangulated EMR-deflection from the three mosquito drones effectively created a mobile Faraday cage, one that could follow a person pretty much anywhere. No more need for stick bombs or any other less mobile deflection devices. But that's not the icing on the cake. I suppose I should make a second apology…this one to you, Shaun, or is it just Winston?"

Dr. One leaned back in his chair and rocked a couple of times while staring at the ceiling.

"Not only have I been perfecting mobile faraday cages and working on the smallest of drones that can fly, I've been playing around with the new V.41 MIXR technology in other ways and I think the integration into my microdrones was a success, don't you think, Winston?"

Dr. One suddenly rolled backward in his chair to reveal a body shot from his sitting waist, up. He wore a black t-shirt with a big, yellow smiley face right in the middle of it. Shaun's shocked expression drained a little blood from his face.

"Yes, Winston. It was me on the trail and in Green Bank, but it really wasn't me. You saw my mobile MIXR."

On the big screen, the white glowing Skeeter dot moved a few inches to the right and sat directly under the video popup window. Suddenly, it blinked and three tiny green beams shot out from its center and landed in the dark part of the screen to the left. A fuzzy, holographic-looking image started to appear. It morphed from translucent to a solid, three-dimensional projection of Dr. One as he lay dead in his house on the night that Shaun found him. Phoenix gasped.

"You were concerned, weren't you, Shaun? You really thought I was dead, as did the white suits and my favorite three Ties who came directly from our government's central agencies.

"Forgive the graphic nature of my imagined murder but it seemed to illustrate what I'd hoped would transfer into your minds as a mystery…one needing solved. Shaun didn't follow the exact path I thought he would in becoming Winston, but you all made it here where I need you.

"You'll understand why I never did give any of you the password key. Everything that will help our cause is on that drive. Go to the Theatre District. Find the Pompadour. Then, Phoenix, you can use the dolphin algorithm to gain access. Be sure to take my mosquito with you."

The video popup window disappeared and the solid white Skeeter dot divided into a dozen tiny red, green and blue specks. Both Shaun and Phoenix turned to J.J. as he tapped the keyboard projection and the big screen again displayed the U.S. map zoomed into the Mid-Atlantic EMR hotspots. "Faraday Movement," he said.

⊙ ⊙ ⊙ ⊙ ⊙

What doesn't kill you makes you stronger. His father's quote was one of Shaun's most cherished memories of a time before the Great Flood. Shaun had lived by that wisdom and now thought, after listening to all of the revelations that had consumed the past hour, he was about as strong as a person could get. But it was his father's other quote, the one he'd not needed to apply much in his life so far, that had Shaun reminiscing about his youth.

Don't let others get you knee deep in their shit. That's where Shaun was now. Knee deep in it, at least. In reality, he was up to his neck in some covert, super-secretive society known as the Faraday Movement and he felt that it was either impossible to pull himself out now, or the opportunity to do so was quickly fading.

J.J. opened a drawer under the countertop where the 3D printer sat. From it, he produced two CELLs and set them on the counter. He then pulled out two

ClearGlasses and placed them beside the CELLs. "As a bodyguard, you are going to need a CELL. Besides, you wouldn't want to experience your twenty-first birthday in the New City with limited or outdated technology."

He grabbed a pair of scissors from the drawer, quickly snipped off Shaun's visaBand and tossed the band in the drawer before closing it. He then began thumbing through the screen of one of the CELLs as he walked over to Dr. One's backup drive, moved it from the countertop cradle, and put the CELL in its place. He tapped on the projected keyboard. "Winston, the bodyguard," he said to the keyboard. "Now you have the highest U.S. Citizenry rating and, let's just say and overly sufficient eCash account."

At that moment, the exit door to the right shook from the beating of knuckles against metal. J.J. removed the CELL from the cradle, gave it Shaun, and tapped the keyboard. A split screen of footage from six surveillance cameras appeared on the big screen. One showed riders boarding a Jack Rabbit coaster car train. One showed riders racing down the Jack Rabbit's anti-G drop. One showed the front of the restrooms where they'd ran to find entrance to J.J.'s lab. One showed the storage area of some back room that Shaun did not recognize. One showed a dimly lit, narrow hallway that split in two directions at the point where the camera was located. The one J.J. was most interested in was the split screen in the lower right corner. The teen boy with aqua blue sideburns and his girl friend stood on the other side of the exit door. They smiled into the camera. "Time to go," the teen boy mouthed. J.J. stepped to the door, placed his hand in the middle of it, and it clicked and swung outward. In the door's frame stood the teen boy. "You've got to get moving," he said. "Our diversions ain't working no more."

"Time to get on a new ride," J.J. said to everyone.

J.J. tapped a few more commands on the keyboard and it disappeared, and Phoenix snatched the backup drive from the countertop and put in her jacket. J.J. shuffled by Phoenix to the microdrone cabinet, knelt behind it, and used the baby food jar to remove Skeeter from inside. He gave the jar to Phoenix. From a hook on one wall, J.J. grabbed a tan bomber jacket that was covered with patches depicting an assortment of old, prop-engine aircraft and put the two CGs and one remaining CELL in its pockets.

"I think we're ready," J.J. said and walked with the teen boy out the exit door. Phoenix followed and Shaun took up the rear.

Outside the lab, while standing in a cool, narrow concrete hallway that was only dimly lit, Shaun conceded that the shit he was now walking in could not be escaped.

◎ ◎ ◎ ◎ ◎

They walked through the narrow corridor for only thirty yards before coming upon a second door. The teen boy, who was in front, opened the door by placing his hand in the middle of it. Once they were all through it, Shaun pushed the door closed behind him.

"You got a lot of hand-reading doors around here," Shaun said.

"Wait till I integrate proximity detection," J.J. said. "You'll be walking through just like in *Star Trek*. Shoosh!"

The five of them stood at an intersection in another concrete hallway that was identically lit from the ceiling as the one they'd just exited but was just a few feet wider. Shaun immediately looked up to see the surveillance camera that had streamed one of the split screen shots back in the lab. In both directions, the hall continued for several dozen yards before meeting turns that hid both destinations. The teen boy led them to the right. Shaun looked back as he followed and thought that it would be nearly impossible to know that a door to a hidden hallway existed in the wall.

The hallway snaked an underground path and the further they traveled it, the louder the rumble of the Jack Rabbit became overhead. The smell of oil also thickened. They quickly scooted for at least a hundred yards before the rumble above softened and the oil was replaced by tastier amusement park aromas.

A set of wooden porch steps greeted them at

the end of the hall. The staircase rose twenty feet to a closed wooden door with a regular, old-fashioned, round metal knob. The teen boy grabbed it and pushed against some weight on the other side. He pushed a little more so that he could peek beyond the foot-wide opening then forced the door open enough for him to pass through it.

Shaun followed Phoenix into what was certainly a storage room, one that he immediately thought he'd seen in one of the split screens. Stuffed toys were everywhere. Four big plastic bags full of them sat in disarray at his feet. When J.J. closed the door, he stacked them against it. More stuffed animals occupied a wall of shelves to the left. Boxes of numerous sizes were stacked against the wall in front. The right side of the room had a myriad assortment of prize-winning toys and knickknacks ranging from the cheapest 3D stylist pens and a stack of rolled up posters, to glassware that looked expensive but probably wasn't. The room was so full of stuff that it was hard for them to comfortably stand without rubbing elbows.

From beyond a three-foot-wide passage in the wall in the far right corner, the loud, joyful sounds of arcade games and many people at play was briefly interrupted when a portly man wearing desert camo pants, a red plaid shirt, and a black ball cap that read *Tamarack* walked through it. He tripped on a four-foot tall stuffed white rabbit with the toe of one of his hiking boots.

"Damn mess," the man said. "But great camouflage. You kids alright?" The teen boy and girl nodded. "And you guys? Got you away from those three stalkers right good, didn't we?"

"This is Bob," J.J. said. "He runs the Penny Arcade."

Bob was at least eight inches shorter than J.J. and the pudgy hand he offered Shaun sported some rather hairy knuckles. "How's the Greenbrier these days?" Bob asked. "I grew up outside of Charleston."

"Very popular," Shaun said, shook the hand and released it; it felt rubbery.

"Well, enough with the pleasantries," J.J. said. "We good to the street?"

"As of now," Bob said and turned to lead them through the opening from which he'd appeared.

In its holiday weekend primetime, the Penny Arcade was packed. Dusk wouldn't fall for a couple of hours but the big open doorways and windows beyond the tops of the arcaders' heads revealed a cloudy gray start to the evening.

Shaun tried to stay wary of the path everyone took in front of him and the more curious-looking people they passed, but his attention was consumed by the flashing lights, clinks of balls, and all of the rings, jingles and tinkling sounds coming from the many arcade setups. It was a retro game junkies utopia. Decades-old games that, in Shaun's mind, were too valuable as artifacts, were being punched, slapped, screamed at and shaken. They even had ancient PacMan and Asteroids freestanding game consoles. Each had plenty of original wear-and-tear scars but the coin slots had been augmented with a touchscreen for payment.

"You next, sir?" a boy no older that ten asked him. A couple of red licorice sticks poked out from above the boy's mostly zippered jacket.

"I haven't played one of them in forever," Shaun told the boy.

"Pretty simple: right, left, thrust, fire. Score the daily high and get entered to win the daily Big Snag. Tonight, it's a great one." The boy pointed to the right and Shaun craned his head up to see a shelf built into the far wall with a digital sign above it that read: Big Snag. A brand new, boxed pair of ClearGlasses sat on the shelf, bathed in yellow light. "I got a bunch of digiTickets at the basketball shootout and Skeeball but not enough yet to enter." The boy reached into his jacket pocket, pulled out an older V.38 CELL and thumbed through it. "I don't know if I should spend my allowance on more chances at Asteroids' top score or for more chances at tickets. What do you think…let's see here…it's Winston, right?"

"Hey!" Phoenix's head and arm appeared above the crowd near the front of the arcade. She waved.

"Save your money," Shaun told the boy. "Then, you can buy your own."

The boy disappeared in the crowd as Shaun pushed through toward the entry. Phoenix stood with J.J. just outside the arcade but the teen boy and girl were gone.

To the right snaked a very long line for the Jack Rabbit and just a bit to the left of it, the Water Experience building and pond glistened in the distance under the overcast sky. People were everywhere.

Phoenix grabbed the sleeve of his windbreaker. "Come on," she said.

J.J. led them to the left through a thick crowd that was headed into the park from the street side entrance just ahead.

"What about our bags?" Shaun said to the back of J.J.'s head.

J.J. continued his quick pace and looked over his shoulder. "Took care of it. We can pick them up at this gate."

"What about the visaBand I checked in with?"

"Don't need it with the CELL I gave you. Remember, you are Winston, now."

Two park men met them at the black iron exit gate. One of them immediately walked up to Shaun and Phoenix. "We're sorry," he said, "but your bags have been misplaced. We can set you up with a complimentary dinner if you'd like to wait, or we can notify you when they are found and deliver them to you."

"You must be new," J.J. said. "I run the Jack Rabbit. When you find my friends' bags, just let me know. I'll make sure they're returned."

"Yes, sir," the park man said. "Again, we're sorry for the inconvenience. We pride ourselves…"

J.J. turned away and Shaun and Phoenix followed him through the iron gate. "That's bullshit," he whispered to them. "Hope nothing valuable was in them."

Phoenix tapped her jacket pocket with one hand and said, "We have what we need."

Outside, four buses were lined up at the curb and dozens of people exited them. Behind the last bus was a line of yellow taxicabs. J.J. led them to the first cab that had a small digital panel on its roof; it read, in yellow: **#22**. He opened the back door for Shaun and Phoenix to get in, then jumped into the passenger seat and closed the door.

Two park men stood outside the iron gate, watching. Behind them, the three Ties stepped forward. They'd traded in their blue suits for more casual attire that was also blue and included bow ties of the same black, white and red colors.

Red Tie watched the cab doors close then lifted his right arm and tapped his CELL. "They're on their way," he said to it.

◎ ◎ ◎ ◎ ◎

Would you like a driver? the cab's interior male voice said. The accent was more northern Massachusetts than western Pennsylvania.

J.J. looked back from the passenger seat. "You more comfortable with a human or do we just throw caution to the wind?" J.J.'s smiling goatee provided reassurance. "The real trip is sitting up *here* with no one next to you in the driver's seat. And you thought the Jack Rabbit was a thrill. You wanna give it a try, Winston?"

Shaun felt enough uncertainty already from the thought of loosing his backpack and from the absence of a head over the seat in front of him. "Maybe on the way back," he said. "I'll just enjoy the scenery for now."

"Cab 22," J.J. said to the driver's seat. "No driver."

Destination?

"The Point," J.J. responded.

Would you like information on tonight's activities at the Point?

"Sure," J.J. said. He turned in his seat toward Shaun. "Might as well start there to celebrate Winston's twenty-first birthday."

Tonight, the cab said, *you've got a virtual concert at the Waterspout featuring the 1965 Beatles. Can I purchase you a seat?*

"Yes," J.J. said. "Three, please. Use Winston's account."

Would you like three admissions deducted from your account, Winston?

Shaun was about to ask how much it would cost when J.J. interjected. "Yes," he said.

Confirm, Winston?

"Yes," Shaun said.

One hundred and fifty dollars has been deducted from your account. Coupons for free beverages can be obtained at the concert venue.

Shaun gasped. He'd never stashed that much cash anywhere, especially not on the Net.

"Happy birthday, Winston," J.J. said. "You have a generous gift account courtesy of Dr. One and yours truly."

Happy birthday, Winston, the cab said. *New Pitt has a bunch of opportunities for those celebrating their twenty-first birthday. Would you like me to add that information to your account?*

"Yes," Shaun said.

Transfer complete. With current traffic, time to destination is approximately twenty minutes. Engage in music or other in-cab entertainment?

Shaun looked at Phoenix and shrugged.

May I suggest the invisible roof? the cab said. *It's popular with first-time Yellow Cab riders.*

Shaun immediately looked up at the roof of the cab that was less than a foot away from his face. He touched its slick, plastic-fabric surface. "Absolutely," he said.

Shaun had to blink because he couldn't believe what he saw. The entire roof of the cab turned into a giant digital screen that transformed into a mirror image of the cloudy gray skies above. The windshields and vertical pillars holding up the roof and all of the passenger-side windows were still there and this made the experience even more surreal.

Shaun lowered his hand and leaned back with Phoenix, as if they were in a convertible, to stare as the clouds passed overhead. "Cab driver," Shaun said. "Play the sounds of New Pittsburgh, please."

After a few seconds, the cab responded. *Please define your request or tag your preferences in your account.*

"What music is popular in the city tonight?" Shaun asked.

The cab thought for a few more seconds. *CrissCross and City Rock are the styles most listened to since the beginning of 2041.*

"Define CrissCross," Shaun said. Above him, the clouds opened up enough for the fingernail moon to peek through.

CrissCross is the production of live, original content performed in a virtual space.

J.J., looking over his shoulder, clarified. "You can perform with an archived, live Beatles concert, virtually, from anywhere across the country. The audio recordings are pretty amazing but the video productions are much more popular. Cab driver, please show us the most popular CrissCross in New Pitt."

Centered in the roof at the front of the cab, a foot-wide window popped up against the gray, crawling clouds and featured performers he did not recognize. *We built this city*, the lead singer sang, his lips kissing a microphone. *We built this city on rock and roll.*

"Only the lead singer and guitarist are performing live," J.J. said. "The other three are a virtual integration from a recorded concert by a group called Jefferson Starship. Can you imagine how much talent the live singer and guitarist must have to create such an original sound from music played by a group that is no longer alive?"

"Convenient, too," Phoenix said. "You only need one or two people to have a band."

"You'll have a chance to give it a try in the city," J.J. said. "Maybe the two of you will become the next CrissCross stars."

"Doubtful," Phoenix said. "My parents gave up on finding any musical genes in me long ago."

"And I can't sing," Shaun added.

"You don't have to CrissCross with a band," J.J. explained. "You have lots of choices. You'll see."

This sparked Shaun's curiosity enough that he reached into his windbreaker pocket and pulled out the V.41 CELL that J.J. had given him. With it, he'd intended to explore what J.J. was talking about but, instead, became more curious about the word he pressed under the name **Winston**. It read: **Storyline**.

The screen changed to a list of choices pertaining to Winston's Story. To the left of each line of blue text, serving as a bullet, was a small green circle with an arrow in the two o'clock position. Two green eye dots and one green nose dot in the center of each circle bullet made them look like smiley faces. Above the listing was the title screen text: **Winston Storyline**. The listing read:

- ☺ **Financial**
- ☺ **Personal**
- ☺ **Health & Well-being**
- ☺ **Social**
- ☺ **U.S. Citizenship**

He pressed the first listing to find that Winston had **$19, 850** in his eCash account. Below the larger green numerical text, smaller white text noted his recent transaction of **$150 to Pitt Point Entertainment**. He swiped the screen back to the **Storyline** listing and pressed **Personal**.

A new, blue text list gave him choices to explore Winston's **Demographics**, **Education**, **Newsworthiness**, **and Employment**. He quickly scanned through each to find small discrepancies between the recorded life of Winston and Shaun.

His birthdate and age were different under Demographics. His high school graduation date was wrong in the **Education** section.

The **Newsworthiness** selection brought him to a screen with a single icon that looked a lot like the circle-arrow-smiley face bullets except this one was red, the arrow sat in the nine o'clock position, and there were no green-dotted eyes or nose.

As for **Employment**: Winston had never worked at Jennifer Outfitters. Instead, Winston's current employment was listed as **Personal Bodyguard**. A small red padlock icon glowed to the right of the two white words and when Shaun pressed it, a blinking white question mark replaced the text in the middle of the CELL screen—a password to find out more about his position as a personal bodyguard, Shaun thought. He tried a few he'd used in the past but none worked so he swiped back.

At that moment, the popup video performance on the front edge of the cab roof ended and the video window disappeared. In its place was the skyline of the city that was visible partially through the invisible roof and partially through the windshield. To the left of the cab, vehicles sped along an expressway that Shaun had not realized they'd entered. Each was equally distanced in their travel but those in the left lane moved a little faster. To the right, a FasTrain sped in the opposite direction along rails that bordered the river.

Time to destination, the cab said, *is approximately five minutes due to heavy traffic in the Fort Pitt Tunnel.*

The cab slowed as the city skyline was interrupted by a hillside with a steep rocky face of dynamited earth. All cars traveled within a car's length of each other but both lanes now moved at a residential pace. The expressway started down a shallow valley toward the tunnel entrance, and the face of the hill created a backdrop behind a FasTrain that had caught up to them and was now slowing for the tunnel turn.

The Fort Pitt Tunnel allowed no traffic other than public transportation and vehicles that had already cleared the city's security and environmental checks. Cabs slowed to a crawl in both lanes as the expressway and FasTrain curved to the right. Shaun pivoted from staring at the mostly yellow cab line of cars on his left to the FasTrain on his right. It moved slow enough that Shaun could see beyond Phoenix's head to the occupants in each train car. Seats were filled and many people stood, holding onto something overhead that Shaun couldn't see.

In the last train car, two faces were pressed up against the window glass that made both look pig-like. It was the teen boy with the aqua blue sideburns and his reliable female companion. Both waved.

◎ ◎ ◎ ◎ ◎

Phoenix knew very little about the Faraday Movement other than the scant information she'd learned from Bethany the night before, and that all six of them were now involved in it, including her uncle and the two teens she saw on the FasTrain beside them. She suspected that Bob, the jolly arcade assistant, and perhaps even the stovetop-hatted carousel operator were also members of a group she was sure would continue to present themselves as the evening progressed.

She'd sat, quietly thinking, up until the time Shaun had pulled out his V.41. She'd seen the invisible roof trick before so her impression of it wasn't as mesmerizing as Shaun's. Instead, she'd thought about Dr. One's request that she use what he called the dolphin password. She knew of no such thing. The only animal nickname she'd given to any of her algorithms or passwords was **Bu!!dogSa]]ie**, in reference to a stray bulldog she'd wanted to keep as a child. She'd named it for the one night that Sallie had stayed, but the next morning her parents had told her that pets weren't allowed in their leased house. She'd never shared her depressing experience on the Net, so it was safe from social knowledge and, therefore, safer from password hackbots. But dolphin?

When Shaun had started to thumb through the CELL J.J. had given him, Phoenix was a bit amused with his reaction, one filled with emotions that she'd experienced many times: curiosity, surprise, uncertainty.

Handling new technology always thrilled her but she was one who acclimated quickly and could, because of her love of tech, figure out new gizmos no matter how complicated. Phoenix was one who always helped the heavy Luddites who didn't know, and who could really care less, about navigating the digital world they so desperately wished had never taken control. Most of the time, she was happy to help those willing to take the time and listen.

Shaun was no Luddite but Phoenix did notice that he navigated the CELL like a newbie and she thought that he might ask her for clarification about what he was seeing, especially when it came to the Winston Storyline listing. But he never said a word and Phoenix continued to shy away from watching him, even though the glow of the CELL's digital screen in the dark cab begged for her attention.

Once the FasTrain managed the turn into the tunnel, it sped up, but the line of vehicles next to it continued to crawl. The invisible roof showed the boring tunnel in full one-hundred-and-eighty degrees; numerous brake lights gave it a fuzzy red hue that brightened and faded as the traffic crept.

"How should I act as your bodyguard in the city?" Shaun asked her.

Phoenix blinked away her attention to the tunnel. "I guess you'll make sure no one gets me into trouble," she said.

J.J. turned around and leaned between the middle of the seats. "Your value as a bodyguard isn't so much as what you will do but who you are. Remember that everyone knows everyone in the city. A bodyguard label gives you credibility that needs no action. You'll have a bit of a pop star aura around you, one that is respected and envied. A bodyguard can hack the Net and that makes people less willing to treat you with ill will."

"They'll be scared of me?" Shaun asked.

J.J. smiled. "I would be." He turned back around in his seat.

The end of the tunnel, a gray, unimpressive rectangle of brake light mystery, was fifty yards away and slowly closing. Phoenix turned toward Shaun, wondering how he would handle his unexpected thrust into adulthood. Shaun never looked at her as he shoved his CELL into his windbreaker pocket and stared straight ahead.

◎ ◎ ◎ ◎ ◎

The Fort Pitt Tunnel quickly reminded Shaun of his two recent encounters in similar places, but it was the gray-shrouded exit ahead, which was so dissimilar to the bright white exits of Sharp's and the Jack Rabbit's tunnel, that had him reminiscing another moment in his youth.

He remembered the day that Marlinton had honored a monument to the Seneca Tribe. The ceremony had been an endnote to the five-year reconstruction after the Great Flood. The town had decided that Fresh Water would be the central brand that drove tourism to them in the 30s, but making the town square a historical landmark was sure to add to Marlinton's appeal.

The dedication was fitting to the post-2029 country as it memorialized the Seneca Trail, also known as the eighteenth-century Great Indian Warpath. Way back then, the Trail had been the division between the British Crown's singular interest in colonizing the eastern territories and the much-unexplored West. Settlements beyond the mountains were forcefully discouraged because they represented expanse beyond the ruling class's control.

That had been five years ago and the entire populations of the local elementary and high schools had been there. Shaun remembered that he'd respected the ceremony much more than most of his own classmates who'd had their attention planted at downward angles toward the decader smartphones they'd held. He remembered that the rectangular monument had been covered by a gray sheet that two high-schoolers held in place as the mayor delivered his speech. He remembered thinking that what would be revealed once the mayor was finished would look like all of the other monuments he'd seen. But when the gray shroud was removed, even his attention-deficit classmates looked up.

The monument wasn't stone. It was one of those, back then, new-fangled, environment-proof, 3D digital billboards. What everyone had thought would be boring turned out to be gasp-inspiring. The brilliant colors and crisp depth that had pulled the viewer into the displayed video of Seneca Tribe history was something few had apparently experienced. It had been a sign of what was coming. It was a monument to a world both within and outside Marlinton.

The gray shroud over the Fort Pitt Tunnel exit wasn't lifted in one swift motion as it had been over the Seneca monument—the cab was creeping too slowly. Instead, the magnificence of New Pittsburgh faded into view. The cloudy day made all of the lights much more spectacular.

Shaun's head pivoted in all directions. The invisible roof made the exploration of new senses even more dramatic. Thankfully, traffic moved slowly enough so that Shaun could attempt some acclimation. He tried to remain calm but his hand tapped nervously against his thigh. He sucked in a couple of deep breaths and Phoenix's hand covered his leg-tapping fingers.

"My bodyguard," she said to him.

Shaun managed a piece of smile as he looked at their clasped hands. Really, he thought, that's all it took—just a simple gesture and reminder that he was something more now. *Winston* wasn't supposed to be scared of New Cities. These were places where bodyguards thrived.

Traffic moved faster as the cab reached the middle of the Fort Pitt Bridge but it was still much slower than the FasTrains that sped by in both directions to the right. The cab inched into the left lane and this gave Shaun a better view of the three-river convergence beyond the yellow steel bridge girders.

Several large, brightly lit boats moved gently over the Monongahela and there were quite a few smaller ones anchored off the Point that blazed with activity. The concert stage was over there as was the sparkling, majestic spray of the Waterspout. Beyond the Point, across the Allegheny River, a baseball game was in progress. Fireworks exploded overhead to celebrate a homerun.

As soon as the cab escaped the bridge steel overhead, the breadth of the cityscape, through the invisible roof, came into full panoramic view. Lit up stuff was flying around the tall spires of colorful skyscrapers. A giant tanker drone hovered over the tallest building and a thin tether anchored it to the roof. At ground level, rows of streetlamp-lit roads divided the city structures. Shaun felt like an avatar that had been dropped into a first-person fantasy world. He'd seen pictures but the experience…

Time to destination is two minutes, the cab said.

Your concert starts at eight. Refreshments can be enjoyed at many locations. Would you like a map?

"Sure," Shaun said to the driver's seat then looked at Phoenix and added, "Might as well add an interest in bar crawling to Winston's Story."

A social map of gatherings at or near the Point has been added to your account.

It wasn't necessary, but Shaun felt the urge anyway. "Thank you," he said.

J.J. didn't turn around this time. "Trying to get your psychographic courtesy metric in the green, Winston? Not sure manners count with digital devices."

"Maybe," Shaun said. "But it's hard to take the country out of the boy."

⊙ ⊙ ⊙ ⊙ ⊙

Traffic moved in three directions on the New Pitt side of the Monongahela. The right lane of vehicles and FasTrain rails continued onto an overpass that split into a west and east bound loop around the city. The left lane dropped under the overpass and continued straight toward downtown where it became two lanes at the first streetlight intersection. A slow line of cabs and buses gave Shaun the opportunity to measure what he thought the city would look like and what he actually saw.

Looking up through the roof, he thought that most

of the buildings were as expected. Except for a couple, standing tall in the distance, that had plentiful plant life growing on their exteriors, it was hard to tell that any of them had been converted into self-sustaining structures. What did surprise Shaun about the city heights were all of the small drones he saw darting around. They'd land on balconies and float outside windows to deliver the small packages they carried.

At street level, everything sparkled with an enormous magnitude of color. The stoplight at the intersection ahead was a simple square of digital green that changed to red as hundreds of people stood at the four corners waiting to cross. Shaun's cab stopped as the first car in the left lane. More than half of the people that crossed in front of him were wearing ClearGlasses. They pointed at invisible objects in front of them and swiped through visions that Shaun could not see. At one point, a man and his male friend accidentally smacked hands together as they waved them frantically. They stopped in front of the cab as other pedestrians parted around them, smiled, laughed, hugged and kissed before moving on.

When the traffic light square turned green, the cab turned left and followed a line that entered a large parking garage two hundred yards straight ahead. The huge structure, which looked like it could accommodate thousands of vehicles, doubled as the T-interchange at the Point. The expressway and FasTrain rails traveled over the structure and connected to a bridge that crossed the Allegheny and an elevated byway that ran along the nearside east bank of the river. The FasTrain station platform was built into the left side of the parking garage and one train sat idle as passengers shuffled around it. As far as following the efficiency provisions of the city, the parking garage was a perfect example. It served not only as a central downtown parking location, it provided the support structure for the bridge and the busiest T-interchange inside the city perimeter.

The cab drove itself into the garage and followed the traffic line up five stories. One by one, the vehicles ahead parked neatly in rows, leaving no open spots between them. Shaun's cab parked between two other yellow cabs.

Welcome to the Point, the cab said. *Do you have an estimated return time?*

"No," J.J. said.

Please acknowledge your return five minutes before departing. You can also request for pickup at any location within the city.

"The cab is just gonna wait for us?" Shaun asked.

"Public transportation is a bit different around here," J.J. said. "Having a dedicated personal cab makes getting around much more efficient."

"Everyone can't have their own cab," Shaun said.

"No. But there are those who can afford it. In many ways, it helps with inner city congestion. All of the cabs know where all of its riders are at any given moment. Having a personal cab doesn't mean that this one is going to wait here all night, but it does mean that we are its priority and we'll not have to switch to another cab all night."

"Ahh!" Shaun said and opened his door. "That means we'll be able to get to know our driver better."

J.J. flashed a quick smile then he and Phoenix followed Shaun out of the cab.

Cordiality was not one of the virtues that best described the mass of people who walked across the parking garage deck toward a central location of elevators, stairs and escalators. Those who had exited the cab right beside them hadn't even acknowledged how close their doors had come to slamming into each other. They'd not even said "Hello" because the CG experience they were engaged with was much more important.

They joined the mass of humanity that collected in front of the escalator. Everyone stood shoulder-to-shoulder. Those that were wearing CGs talked to no one. Those who didn't, engaged in casual conversation or stared, like Shaun did, at the brilliant festivities accumulating around the Waterspout at the very tip of the Point.

Shaun's windbreaker pocket suddenly vibrated. J.J. and Phoenix were in front of him as he stepped onto the escalator and pulled out his CELL. Below the word **Winston** was a blue, glow-throbbing spherical icon that had a tiny face set in the middle of it. Below the sphere was the word: **Hello**. Shaun touched it.

The tiny sphere spun and expanded to fill the top half of the screen. The woman's face that appeared was three-dimensionally rounded. She looked to be about Winston's age. A tanned complexion of smooth cheekbones and forehead magnified the woman's alluring brown-eyed expression. Below the face was the blue word **Hello**, and below that was a blue horizontal slider that Shaun swiped with his thumb. As he did so, the woman's 3D face rotated so that he could see earlobes with small silver earrings peeking out from below her shoulder-length blonde hair.

Hello flashed and Shaun touched it. The screen was replaced by a conversational text session.

My name is Arlena. Can I buy you a drink to celebrate your birthday?

A round of firecrackers exploded out near the Waterspout and Shaun looked up. The descent of the escalator neared a platform where another mass of people were either moving left toward the T-interchange station or were continuing down another escalator to ground level. Phoenix turned to him, looked curiously at his CELL, and turned back around. Beyond her head and immediately to the left, traveling up the escalator in the opposite direction, was the woman who'd just, basically, asked him for a date. She didn't look at him as she rose from below and ascended past him. At the bottom of the escalator, Shaun looked back and up to see the woman disappear in the crowd.

Shaun couldn't deny the anxiety he felt for being hit on, especially from someone he'd never met…at least not in the rural West Virginia way where courting remained traditionally physical. Responding to a date request without knowing the requester beyond a fleeting glimpse of them was a feat filled with more uncertainty than Shaun was willing to accept at this point. He was struggling enough with being someone he wasn't and entering a world that had seemingly left him, and those like him, behind. He shoved the CELL back into his jacket pocket and followed J.J. and Phoenix down the second escalator and into the Point's Memorial Day celebration.

He'd not walked a dozen steps across grass that looked too perfect to be real before the vibration of his CELL, again, tickled his hip. When he pulled it out and looked at it this time, six blue spheres filled with five different female faces and one male face, filled the screen. The word **Hello** glow-throbbed below each one. Phoenix stopped in front of him and looked back.

"You getting these things?" he asked her.

"Thank God no," she said. "My V.38 doesn't integrate so well." She pointed at Shaun's CELL. "It's hard enough dealing with real people and that's a bit creepy, don't you think?"

All of the faces in the blue spheres smiled. "What do I do about them?"

"Nothing. Responding means interest. Are you interested in any of them?"

The question made Shaun wonder, for only a second, if Phoenix was jealous. "Are you kidding? My only interest, right now, is getting through tonight with a little sanity left. How do I turn them off?"

"Press and hold your name. It'll go dark, then all of those ladies and gentleman will know you have other plans."

"And to stop the annoying vibration?"

"Just squeeze it for a second."

Shaun did so.

"Whatever happened to a simple Hello?" Phoenix said and turned toward J.J. who had left them behind and was waving above the crowded heads a dozen yards away.

Shaun pocketed the CELL and, as he followed Phoenix through the crowd, imagined seeing all of the faces he passed as tiny headshot profiles within blue, glow-throbbing spheres. All of them knew him but how many really cared?

◉ ◉ ◉ ◉ ◉

Phoenix buttoned up her jacket and checked that the zippers on its breast and hip pockets were closed.

The last thing she needed was to become the victim of a pickpocket. Even the phenomenal security Net within the city couldn't prevent all crime but most of the serious felonies were kept to a minimum. The promise of a lifetime in one of the VR rehab centers located underground just outside the city perimeter deterred most of them.

In front of her, Shaun and J.J. and a growing crowd stood near an entrance that had been constructed by temporary fencing and two eight-foot-tall black monoliths that resembled those she'd seen at the T-interchange and Kennywood. The crowd split into two lazy lines and beside each monolith, a male attendant wore CGs and tapped on invisible displays that only they could see floating at waist-height.

"Welcome to our V.41 breakout party," each attendant said as people in line passed them. When Phoenix walked by, the attendant greeted her the same way then added, "You can pick up your complementary drink at any one of a dozen locations. A token has been added to your account." The attendant tapped the air with one index finger. "Locations mapping has been added to your account. Enjoy your evening, Miss Messenger."

Phoenix followed Shaun as she pulled out her CELL to view the map. The V.38 wasn't as fancy as the new model but it was still the most popular. It did what was necessary to manage the New City and even integrated with ClearGlasses, though experiencing a MIXRized world through them was not part of the V.38 software.

Three-dimensional graphics noted her name **Phoenix Messenger** at the top of the CELL screen and two icons, one a green dollar sign and the other a square map thumbnail, glow-throbbed below it. She pressed the dollar sign to reveal her free drink token, swiped back, and pressed the small map. It expanded to show the refreshment locations around the Point as red dots. The closest was just ahead and to the left. She touched that dot.

Party Tent
Your first stop for the
V.41 Memorial Day Point Celebration.
All drink tokens accepted.
And don't forget:
Check out the Brand New! MIXR-enabled V.41
At the demo before the concert.

A shoulder brushed against her own hard enough to make her fumble the CELL and almost drop it. She looked up and back but the crowd was too dense to know who it had been and no one acknowledged her.

"You coming?" Shaun said and turned her around by the elbow. "There's a place for drinks just over there." He thumbed in the direction of the Party Tent but was looking above her head in the opposite direction. "That guy bumped you pretty hard. He didn't even apologize."

"Who?" Phoenix asked and turned around.

"He's gone. Maybe you can look up the tag words *rude behavior* on the CELL to find out possible suspects."

"I'm afraid that list would be too long."

Shaun suddenly wrapped his arm around Phoenix's shoulders and walked with her through the crowd. "Well," he said. "Let's make sure Winston isn't on that list."

The crowd shuffled around a huge space to the right that had been temporarily fenced off. Hundreds of cushy white fold out chairs were set in neat rows in front of a concert stage that had a solid black background towering above and behind it. None of the seats were occupied but several stagehands were setting up. A bit farther beyond the stage was the towering parking garage T-interchange. FasTrains and heavy vehicle traffic moved methodically slow across the top of the parking structure. Assembled like a massive mural on the garage wall facing the Point was an interlocking puzzle of digital billboard displays. They worked in unison to provide an animated advertisement for the concert's headline promoter.

V.41 MIXR TECH!
More Realistic Than Ever!
Efficient and Fast!
Trade In Your V.38s and older!
Decaders accepted!

To the left of the stage and several hundred yards away, the Waterspout at the point of the small peninsula shot a steady, thick jet into the air that looked just like what might escape from a whale's blowhole. Boat lights cruising across the mouth of the Ohio created colorful, dancing sparkles within the city's geyser monument to its plentiful freshwater resources.

A hundred-foot-square canopy covered the temporary setup that was the Party Tent. Underneath, a long bar sat in front of shelved cabinets that held a wide variety of liquor bottles. All of the stools at the bar were occupied and dozens of people stood between seated customers, waving their CELLs over their heads.

Beyond the right side of the bar, in a twenty-foot corner space under the canopy, a small counter displayed the new V.41. Two demonstrators had a handful of people engaged in their product.

J.J. was standing a couple of people back from the bar when Shaun, with his arm still wrapped around Phoenix's shoulders, joined him. At that moment, the tall, male bartender closest to them raised his hand in the air and exclaimed, "Happy birthday, Winston!" He looked right at Shaun. "For your twenty-first birthday, your drinks are on the house."

Several of the people standing nearby and both of the women who were sitting on stools in front of them looked down at the CELLs that were either in their hands or were strapped to their wrists. Almost simultaneously, they turned and looked at Shaun. The two women reached out arms that gently moved the crowd aside to create space for Shaun to join them. J.J. winked at him and Shaun dropped his arm from Phoenix's shoulders and walked to the bar between them.

Knowing that they'd no longer have a chance at ordering a drink from the space that Shaun now filled, most of the thirsty crowd shuffled to the right and began waving their CELLs again.

J.J. poked Shaun's ribs with one finger. When Shaun didn't turn around, he said, "How about a couple of drinks for your friends?" Shaun still didn't turn around, but he did ask the tall bartender to get them drinks.

"We only have Water City on tap," the bartender told Shaun and J.J. "But we have just about any liquor you might want."

"Beer okay?" J.J. asked Phoenix and she nodded.

The bartender returned rather quickly with two biodegradable cups full of beer and when he handed them over, he had to stretch his arm out beside Shaun's head because Shaun was too engaged in conversation to notice.

J.J. poked Shaun in the ribs again, leaned forward, and said, "When you're done, birthday boy, we'll be out at the Waterspout. Join us in a few?" Shaun nodded and J.J. led Phoenix from the Party Tent. "Maybe we outta give him some air," he said to her. "It's not every day that you get to have the house serve you free drinks in Pittsburgh on your eighteenth birthday."

"He'll be okay, won't he?" Phoenix asked and tried hard not to bump anyone with her cup as they walked by the fenced-in concert chairs.

"You mean with those women or just by himself in the city?"

Phoenix elbowed him with the arm without the beer. "You know what I mean."

"I haven't gotten any warnings about bad actors being present," he said, "and I don't think we will until later. I think he can take care of himself. Besides, *he's* supposed to be protecting *you*."

It was an odd feeling, Phoenix thought. She'd not been this far apart from Shaun in more than a day. The growing distance from the Party Tent made her feel unsettlingly vulnerable, particularly since she didn't know J.J. much at all.

She looked back for a moment and sipped some beer but Shaun had disappeared behind the crowd.

◎ ◎ ◎ ◎ ◎

Apparently, everyone at the bar knew he was not only twenty-one, but was also a bodyguard from West Virginia. This intrigued many of them. A bodyguard from outside the city seemed important and it garnered more questions than Shaun wanted to answer, particularly since much of J.J.'s programming of Winston was unknown to him. Some of the most curious questions concerned the information that should have been publicly available but couldn't be found within their access of Winston's Story.

What did you do before you were a bodyguard? How much education do bodyguards need? How much money does a bodyguard make? Are you married or do you have any girlfriends? At least a dozen women, ranging in ages from twenty-one to forty, asked him that last question.

He accepted one mixed drink that the tall bartender called a Steel Kiss but it was too sweet and too strong for his liking, so he sipped from a cup of Water City beer instead and tried to handle all of the attention with abstract answers that sounded correct. Everyone was extremely nice to him and this made him uneasy.

After about ten minutes, he'd had enough socializing with false smiles, told the two women sitting on either side of him that he'd "hook up with them later if he had an opening," and waved goodbye to the bartender whose face was no longer smiling and whose eyes were no longer looking at him. Shaun grabbed his beer cup, turned from the bar and ran face-first into the Three Ties. The crowd under the canopy had formed a semi-oval around the men who had ditched their failed Kennywood undercover attempts of a casual, bowtie look for their Yes-we-are-Feds standard blue suits and I-don't-care-if-you-know-it Windsor-knotted ties. Those standing at the perimeter of the semi-oval opening closest to the three men expressed concern and fear, and they slowly backed away to create even more space. The two flirting women sitting on either side of him got up and quickly left. The tall, male bartender moved to the right side of the bar in an effort to keep some of his customers from leaving.

Red Tie's mustache seemed heavier than it had been the last time Shaun had seen him in front of Bethany's house. "Fancy meeting you here," he said, his white-toothed grin hiding within thick, black whiskers.

Shaun glanced around at all of the curious faces that remained. He should have been afraid, but he wasn't. He knew that if they'd wanted him, they would have had him by now.

"Just a coincidence?" Shaun asked.

Red Tie's grin widened. "Let's have a seat, shall we?"

Shaun stepped back and sat on one of the barstools

that had been vacated by the two women. Red Tie sat on the other one to his right. Black Tie and White Tie stood a couple of feet behind them to maintain the open perimeter. Much of the loitering crowd beyond the tent stopped momentarily to look over at the bar then down at their CELLs before continuing on.

"I know why you're here," Red Tie said and pointed at the tall bartender who grabbed a cup, poured a beer and set it in front of Red Tie with a frowning smile. "Refill?" he asked Shaun.

Shaun told the bartender, "No thank you."

"Should we tell him you are really eighteen, Winston?" The bartender squinted then quickly walked away.

"Like you said at Sandy's in Green Bank…reality is what the Net says it is."

Red Tie turned and stared straight into Shaun's eyes. "You learn quickly which makes me wonder why you still don't know why you're here."

"Celebrating Memorial Day in the New City," Shaun replied.

"With your friend, Phoenix Messenger. Yeah, yeah…I think the whole city knows that."

Shaun took a sip of beer and set the cup down. Red Tie no longer smiled. His lips disappeared under his mustache and could only be seen when he talked.

"You look very mature sitting there, drinking your illegal beer, with all of those older women flirting with you. Shit. They even made you a bodyguard. It's a great Storyline but that's not really you, is it? You're just some country asshole that's being used to screw with the people I work for." He chugged half of his beer in one swallow. Foam remained on his mustache and he didn't wipe it away. "They're using you, dumbass. Surely, your little high school pee brain has figured that much out."

Some of the people who remained at the bar stared with apprehension. "I don't know who you're talking about," Shaun said, holding his nerves as still as he could to avoid a quivering voice. "I think you have the wrong person. You've made a mistake." Simultaneous gasps from the onlookers created an echo under the canopy.

Red Tie ignored them. "Bravery. It's not becoming of you…Shaun."

"The name's Winston. Even the Feds can make a mistake once in a while."

Red Tie downed the rest of the beer and slammed the cup on the bar so hard it crushed and scattered stray drops. New foam doused his mustache and, this time, he casually wiped it away. He licked his finger, smacked his lips, and lowered his voice.

"Your other friend…the new one…the one you picked up at Kennywood. We know he has some hidden operation going on and he's roped you and your girlfriend into it. All he wants is her software. As for you—you're disposable. You should have stayed in Marlinton to celebrate your graduation. It's so much more peaceful and less life-threatening in the West Virginia hills, don't you think?"

Shaun sucked in a deep breath and did not whisper his response directly at Red Tie's face. "You go on with your little fantasy conspiracy and leave me and my friends to enjoy our evening or else I'll hack your Story and put you in jail."

Red Tie didn't flinch. "Who are you trying to impress? Even if you had the skills, your attempts would be futile. I, on the other hand, have no such limitations." Red Tie pulled out a V.41 CELL from his suit coat pocket and started thumbing through it. "Access Winston," he mumbled at it. "Access Story. Uh-huh. Change bodyguard to toilet cleaner." Red Tie's thick eyebrows scrunched downward as he repeatedly tapped the CELL. "Change," he mumbled three more times."

It was apparent to Shaun that Red Tie was having some difficulty. "Trouble?" he asked and stood. "I think you outta leave me and my guarded body alone."

The crowd no longer looked fearfully apprehensive. Several stepped closer and Black Tie had to forcefully nudge one stocky, bearded man who had a Mountaineer mascot stitched onto the breast of his jacket. "Leave him alone," the man said.

Red Tie stood and grinned again. "You've done

well for your first time alone in the City," he said to Shaun. "Too bad they don't know who you really are." He looked at Shaun's beer cup before turning away and added, "There's some pretty serious penalties around here for peeing in public."

The Three Ties walked together through the crowd that was no longer willing to give them much space. Immediately after they left, the Mountaineer man led a dozen people to surround and congratulate bodyguard Winston for standing his ground.

Shaun did what he could to appease his new fandom while he stared over their heads toward the Waterspout, thinking:

Was he here just to protect Phoenix, or did she and J.J. really have some other agenda?

⊙ ⊙ ⊙ ⊙ ⊙

The first thing Phoenix did when she reached the river's edge was pull out her CELL and search for the name "Johnnie." A total of **1,281 possible results** displayed in blue text. She searched for "J.J." People named J.J. in the city were about half of those named Johnnie.

"You won't even find me in those long lists," J.J. said. "How you know me and how the Net knows me are two different things."

"Sounds familiar." Phoenix pocketed her CELL

and looked at J.J. "So let's talk about that."

"Talk about…"

"You." Spray from the Waterspout moistened her cheeks and she squinted. "Who are you? What's your connection to my uncle? And just what the hell is a Pompadour?"

"Rest assured that what I told you is the truth. I was as surprised to see your uncle back at Kennywood as you were. I really thought he was dead."

"He still may be. But you knew he stole my software and gave it to the Feds, didn't you?"

"That's not the least of it. I think we have more in common with your uncle than you think. He's not the most trustworthy as far as what he tells you…or me. But the cause is just. And if he is dead, what you are carrying becomes even more important."

"The micro…"

"Shhh!" J.J. brought a finger to his goateed lips. "You gotta remember there might be ears. The Feds already know what I just told you, but they also know something that I didn't. In fact, very few people know."

"What's that?"

J.J. pulled out his V.41. "This," he said and waved it in front of her. "They really should have called this the Phoenix."

Waterspout spray hit her in the face again but with greater density. She had to wipe it from her eyes. "Not getting you," she said.

"Remember, I'm just the messenger…uh…no pun intended. Dr. One has been offering up your software to those who controlled the money at Green Bank for some time. Your early algorithms were the foundation from which V.41 tech was created. Your software has, in a way, enabled a whole new level of experience and a whole lot more possible data points that the Net can collect to make its citizens' Stories more complete."

Anger welled and Phoenix scowled at J.J. "You mean all of my work on EMR detection was all a big farce?"

"Not at all. That turned out to be significant, too. But Dr. One saw greater potential in your software to become the building blocks of mobile MIXR technology."

"So, he did steal it."

"A long time ago."

She could almost hear her uncle laughing at her from the grave or from wherever the coward might be hiding. For how many favors had he sold her out? How much money had they given him? What value was there in a new CELL system that was about to change the country? "And now your cause *and* Big Brother have it."

"There can't be one without the other. At least, that's how I see it. But don't feel too horribly bad. Like I said, we have a lot in common. I'm certain he stole my early drone designs. You have that proof right there."

J.J. pointed at the round jar bump in her jacket pocket.

Phoenix suddenly felt very uneasy. She looked around for Shaun and when she didn't see him, used her CELL to search for "Winston." Immediately, the name appeared above a small map of the Point. A red dot showed that he was still at the Party Tent.

"I swear to you right now," J.J. said. "As God is my witness. I'm not going to hurt you or your friend. I am just as innocent to our evening's fate. I know what you know. We're to go to the Theatre District where we'll be able to create a few diversions until we can…" J.J. looked around at the crowd. "…until we find the Pompadour which, I'm guessing, is just another code word for something we'll not understand until we need to."

"Or until Dr. One's or Big Brother's plan reaches its goal."

"We can't argue about the Suspicious Society's influence on us, can we?"

Shuffling through the crowd along the riverbank's paved sidewalk upriver was the teen boy with the aqua-colored sideburns from Kennywood. Behind him, the mass of small boats that she'd see from the Fort Pitt Bridge sat anchored and bobbing. People walked across the boats to share in the party atmosphere.

"There's three of them confronting Shaun right now," the teen boy said to J.J. as he walked up to stand beside them. "He's handling his own, though."

"I didn't get any proximity warnings," J.J. said.

"Must be blocking them," the teen boy suggested.

"Everyone knows everyone until someone says they can't. Typical," J.J. said. He looked at Phoenix. "But we have other, old-fashioned methods: real, human eyes."

The teen boy nodded. "We should be all set shortly after the concert. We're stationed pretty good along the river walk."

"Pretty good isn't good enough," J.J. told him. "Double them up, if necessary."

Phoenix thought the teen was a bit too young to be coordinating some covert trek through the New City, but she didn't say anything. Instead, she asked, "Where's you girlfriend?"

The teen boy smiled and laughed, once. "She's no girlfriend…hell no. She's my sister. She's going to join you at the concert and, afterward, escort you safely. I'll catch up along the way."

J.J. nodded and the teen boy walked off in the direction of the parking garage. Just about midway passed the fenced-in concert seating, he ran into Shaun. Phoenix watched them talk for a moment before the teen slapped Shaun on the shoulder and continued on toward his next assignment.

☉ ☉ ☉ ☉ ☉

"That was a treat," Shaun said as soon as he joined them. "I suspect our aqua blue friend told you."

Phoenix thought Shaun stood a bit more confident of his New City experience than when she'd left him at the bar. "What did they say?" she asked.

"Just a bunch of intimidating, but Winston helped a lot. You were right, J.J. A bodyguard in the city garners respect. You should have seen all of them come to my side when the Fed failed to hack my account. Whatever you did to it, worked."

J.J. smiled. "You can't hack a hacker…well, most people can't, anyway."

"And that brings me to a question," Shaun said. "Can a bodyguard hack a Fed, since I just threatened to do so back at the bar?"

"Fantastic!" J.J. said. "I would have liked to see him squirm."

"He didn't, but he did get pretty angry."

"Well, the short answer is, yes. It is possible to hack a V.41 owned by anyone since we have been in possession of the code that runs it for some time."

Phoenix hadn't thought of that. Of course, there could be a bunch of backdoors to her software that the thieves, which now included the behemoth V.CELL manufacturer, had not found.

"If we get a chance," J.J. continued, "I'll show you a few—just a simple hack that can change anyone's current employment so that the next time you threaten him, or anyone, it'll be more than just a threat."

"So, I could change that son-of-a-bitch federal scum bag to toilet cleaner?" Shaun asked and giggled.

"Creative," J.J. said. "Very creative."

As dusk started to settle over New Pitt, a large, river cruise ship drifted into the mouth of the Ohio and blared a foghorn that caused just about everyone on the Point to look in its direction. Its size was double that of any other boat on the water and its three decks were so brightly lit that the glistening waves reflected a moat of rippling light a hundred yards around it. It anchored smack dab in the middle of the three-river convergence several hundred yards beyond a platform that also stood still atop the water. A small boat floated next to the platform and several people busied themselves with setting up a fireworks display.

On their way to the entrance into the concert venue, they ran into a flock of people who surrounded two young men in a semi-circle whose wardrobe contrasted the multi-colored spectacle around them. Both were dressed in identical, gray Edwardian collarless suits and a pair of shiny black Beatle boots. Phoenix guessed that they were a part of tonight's performance.

One of the fence partitions had been removed from the temporary perimeter around the concert venue and two black monoliths stood on either side of the opening. Attendants stood beside them, pecking at the air, just as the two at the entry to the Point had done.

The aqua teen boy's sister waited for their approach near one of them.

"This is gonna be somethin'," the girl said, her perky voice rising above the crowded chatter. "A live CrissCross with the 1965 Beatles." They entered the venue and took four adjacent chairs, five rows back and on a center aisle that separated the seating into two sections. The teen girl sat nearest the aisle, immediately put on her CGs and said, "It ain't real CrissCross without your special peepers."

"And V.41 Phoenix tech," J.J. added. He reached into the pocket of his jacket that had a big, four-prop B-17 Flying Fortress bomber patch sewn onto it and pulled out the two pairs of ClearGlasses he'd stashed there back at the lab. He gave one each to Phoenix, who sat beside him, and to Shaun, who sat between Phoenix and the girl. He then pulled out his CELL from the opposite hip pocket and thumbed through it. "I switched the account on my V.41 so that you can enjoy the fruits of your efforts," he said and gave it to Phoenix.

A tiny, rotating 3D image of a pair of ClearGlasses glow-throbbed on the screen and she pressed.

Multiple pairings available. Physical pairing is necessary.

"Touch the CELL to your glasses," J.J. said to her.

When Phoenix did so, the glasses didn't make any visual response to being paired but the clear, thin, almost weightless strip vibrated for a fraction of a second. The CELL displayed in green text, **Success**!, then reverted to the home screen with her name at the top.

"You can do a bunch of things to make the experience more personal but we can explore that a bit later," J.J. offered.

Shaun had followed along with J.J.'s instructions and was now paired with the CGs he'd already placed across his nose. "Wow!" he said. "You can make this more personal?"

"Sure," J.J. said and leaned forward to look at him. "With the virtual stage, you can compliment a number of special effects with one's you choose."

"We can all watch different concerts?" Shaun asked.

"In a way. You can't change the virtual Beatles and you can't change the live performers, but stage lighting and the mixed reality background can be. You want to see a mighty eagle flying across the treetops in a mountain scenery behind a song such as *Ticket to Ride*, there's a way. But for now, since it's your first time, I think you'll be overwhelmed with the performers' choices of entertainment as it is. You'll be doubly challenged just to get around the MIXR integration you'll see all around you, excluding the stage."

Shaun looked around. "Yeah. Double wow!" He started pressing invisible objects that only he could see in front of him. "This is so much easier. Chris never told me it could do all of this."

"Chris?" J.J. asked.

"My friend back home. I guess you can't get this kind of immersion in a town that's not well connected."

"No," J.J. said. "You wouldn't. The interconnected power of all the CELLs in the City makes it possible."

Phoenix slowly lifted the CGs to her face with anxious anticipation. The experience would be as new to her as it was Shaun.

The rectangular V.41 in her hand, now floated three sizes larger as a mixed realty object within arms' reach in front of her. Her name titled a solid black, 3D-realistic screen. Down in the lower right corner was the tiny ClearGlasses icon. When she reached out and touched it, the pad of her finger felt the gentle pressure of something that really was there. The MIXR display immediately disappeared and she looked down at the CELL in her other hand to see the ClearGlasses icon, but the word **OFF** had been added above it. She pressed and the MIXR, again, appeared in front of her.

"They all have blue bubbles over their heads," Shaun said.

Phoenix followed Shaun's gaze across the crowded seats. Above each person's head was a blue sphere, and in the center of each one was a tiny face. The spheres littered an entire layer of space over them. There were too many.

"You can control all of the things you see…here," J.J. said and reached over to press Phoenix's name on the CELL. Above her **Storyline** and the green smiley face next to it were the words: **MIXR Control**. "You can go in there and change what you want." J.J. showed her and Shaun how to make all of the MIXR-enabled blue spheres disappear.

"This can be immensely clutter-filled," Phoenix said.

"Yes. Just like life, don't you think? Thank God we still have choices."

J.J. and Phoenix both looked up from the CELL and their eyes locked with shared human understanding. The stare, only fractional to the speed of the MIXR world around them, told Phoenix that J.J. was much more a rebel confidant than she'd previously thought.

Shaun also looked up and turned toward the two of them. The expression on his face was one that Phoenix, in all of the few hours that she'd been with him, had not seen before. She didn't need V.41 tech to show her that there was a giant question mark glow-throbbing above his head. And she wondered, if only for the same fractional, expressive moment that had codified J.J.'s true feelings: was Shaun jealous?

◉ ◉ ◉ ◉ ◉

Help! I need somebody.
Help! Not just anybody.
Help. You know I need someone. Help.

The choice for the opening set was as strangely unsettling to Phoenix as the appearance of Ringo and George, 1965-young, standing behind two men who were not Paul or John. She'd anticipated something that looked more holographic, kind of like the projected keyboard that J.J. had used back at his underground lab. The programming needed to project images of display screens and floating, blue headshot spheres that looked amazingly realistic was elementary to the trillions of data point subroutines it must have taken to create what she was seeing. She had to lift her CGs above her eyes to make sure the drummer and guitarist were not really alive and for a moment, she relished the thought that all of this was possible because of her stolen software.

Ringo's and George's gray suits matched the two CrissCrossers in color, hue and density. Even the stage lighting cast shadows across all four performers at visually appropriate angles when they moved which, of course, was constant. When John (who was not John) sang, his virtual band members hit the appropriate guitar riffs and drum beats in perfect sync. Even the sound was seamless. Phoenix closed her eyes and concentrated on nothing but the music. Except for the CrissCross vocal impressions that could never perfectly duplicate the long dead voices of McCartney and Lennon (and it was this variety in recorded CrissCross that made it so popular), it all sounded crisp and unbroken. The instrumentals from 1965 meshed perfectly with the voices and guitar play of 2041.

When the song ended, a roar of applause erupted from the seats. Phoenix stood with J.J. and Shaun and just about everyone else.

CrissCross John clapped in appreciation before he whispered into his microphone. "How's everyone feeling tonight?" Applause roared again. "Let me ask you. Do you feel fine?" And off they went with their next song.

Baby's good to me, you know.
She's happy as can be, you know
She said so.
I'm in love with her and I feel fine.

◎ ◎ ◎ ◎ ◎

Forty-five minutes passed in a flash. The MIXR experience assaulted the senses with illogical precision that struck some carnal desire for more. At moments, during *Ticket to Ride*, Phoenix really did see an eagle fly above the stage against a moving 3D backdrop of water and mountains and sunshine that reminded her of the country she'd left just hours ago.

It wasn't until the last song of the band's first set that her concentration on them faltered. Almost simultaneously with CrissCross Paul's first lyric, *Yesterday*, Shaun gasped so loudly it brought the *Shhhs!* from those around him, including the teen girl.

"Do you see that?" Shaun said and pointed at the stage.

Phoenix grabbed his arm and pulled it down. "Yes. We all see it."

Shaun reluctantly sat and slowly lowered his arm. "You see Tony?"

"Tony?"

"Yeah. You remember. The monarch butterfly that's been following me around." He giggled and pointed again. "He's flapping around Ringo's head and the drummer doesn't even see it."

"He's not the only one," Phoenix said. "Let me see." She reached out to grab Shaun's CGs but J.J. interjected.

"That won't work. They'll reset once they leave the proximity of his face, but you can do something even cooler." J.J. swiped the CELL screen in Phoenix's hand and pressed **MIXR Control**. "Interface," he said. "The two visors can merge experiences. If there's something he's seeing that you aren't, this will merge both. It's really cool once you get the hang of personalization."

A lot of the owners of many ClearGlasses scrolled up the screen as J.J. continued to manipulate the CELL.

The red text lines were alphabetical and just about all of them had a last and first name except **Winston** near the end of the scroll. J.J. pressed it. "You should have an interface request, Winston," he said. Shaun navigated his CELL to accept the request and asked Phoenix. "How about now?"

"A beautiful, tiger-stripped monarch butterfly, just like the one we saw at Bethany's," she said.

"And in the bus."

"What?"

"You didn't see it? It was sitting on a girl's lap in front of the Carnegie bus and flew out right behind your head."

"Sounds like you had a pair of those CGs on the bus."

"No…really."

J.J. asked Shaun, "Did you personalize?"

"I don't know how."

Phoenix giggled at the antics of the butterfly. It looked like it was teasing Ringo by dipping down between his beating sticks and floating inches in front of his busy eyes. "Kind of lends a new spin to the idea of a Ghost in the Machine."

"Only thing I can think," J.J. said, "is that a third party is interfacing without our knowledge."

"We've been hacked?" Shaun asked. "That wouldn't look very good for a bodyguard."

"Or…" J.J. continued. "Perhaps I introduced a

glitch when I created Winston."

"Can I see?" the teen girl asked.

"Not there anymore," Phoenix said. Moments later, the two Beatles CrissCross band members took a break and left the stage. The MIXRs of George and Ringo also disappeared and a man walked up to the microphone to remind everyone of the fantastic V.41 MIXR-enabled fireworks display that would start in a few minutes.

"We need to get on our way north," J.J. said. "You guys hungry? I know I am. We can see fireworks from anywhere in the city."

"What do you suggest?" Phoenix asked.

"New Pitt extravagant or old school traditional?"

Shaun and Phoenix responded together: "Old School."

"Come on. I know the perfect place."

◎ ◎ ◎ ◎ ◎

Shaun ignored the anxious uncertainty of his own Saturday night fate and it now sat like an unwanted malignity somewhere deeper than he would allow his feelings to go. He was Winston now…and Winston had no fear. He'd proven that much already; standing up to the Three Ties had filled him with found courage. Even the strange appearance of Tony (that Phoenix had also seen), and the FM logo that had replaced the Beatles' drop-T logo on Ringo's bass drum (that Phoenix had not said she'd seen), didn't push any paranoia buttons. There was a reason why he'd been made to see these MIXRs. They were part of Winston's Story, whether one filled with J.J.'s programming glitches or one intentionally created by a third party hack. Winston was his avatar and Shaun now felt quite comfortable playing the part.

J.J. had retrieved his CELL from Phoenix as they'd left the Point, had asked her if she'd like to trade in her V.38 for the new version at a big discount (which she had declined), and had notified their personal Yellow Cab that they would not be returning to the parking garage. It was better that they walk the short distance to the restaurant for security reasons, he'd said, and to experience an unconstrained, agile New Pitt nightlife.

"If it starts raining," J.J. had said, "we can always call the cab to us."

They now stood together beside the Allegheny River bank on what was called the TRHail, renamed from the "Three Rivers Heritage Trail" some time back to reflect the city culture of turning just about everything into an acronym.

Fireworks at the Point exploded behind them and most of the hundreds of pedestrians on the fifty-foot wide, fake-brick-textured river walk stopped to stare, with CGs in place, as did Shaun and the teen girl.

"You want the full-on fireworks MIXR

experience?" J.J. asked Phoenix. "I'll switch you back to my CELL."

"No," Phoenix quickly responded. "I'll take them in naturally."

Shaun's head bobbed with the beat of patriotic music that blared from speakers along the trail that he could not see. "It would be so much better if they didn't drop that BS into it," he said. "I'm digging all of the flags and other red, white and blue MIXRs, but those ads have got to go."

The teen girl's giant smile cracked a bit when she said, "You get used to it. Ads are personalized the more your Story integrates into the City. You'll find yourself wanting stuff you never knew you wanted, and buying it."

"That makes sense," Shaun said. "No wonder I see so much food blasting from the explosions. Sparkler french fries everywhere." Shaun sucked in a deep breath as his stomach rumbled. "How long till we eat?"

"Just a couple of blocks up," J.J. said. "You like Mexican?"

Shaun suddenly saw a couple of burritos explode above the Point. Beans rained down and he giggled. "Yeah. I guess I do…or, at least, Winston does."

The fireworks continued behind them as they walked north along the TRHail. The teen girl led J.J. and Phoenix who walked shoulder-to-shoulder ahead of Shaun. More than once, the three of them had to stop and wait for Shaun to catch up. There was just too much to take in even without the CGs that he had pocketed to avoid anymore personalized, MIXRized food displays.

To his left, the Allegheny sparkled and danced from the combination of near side skyscraper lights and fireworks explosions, and the far side activity in and around multiple sports arenas. Boats and bridges added their reflected personalities to the blue-gray water that, Shaun thought, smelled as mountain fresh as the Greenbrier. Wandering water spray moistened his face and he licked his lips without hesitation. It took him back, only for a moment, to yesterday morning (which seemed like a hundred years ago) when Chris had jumped from the tree-lined river trail to scare him. It had been Shaun's first introduction to the new V.41 and ClearGlass technology, and Chris had given him a glimpse at what was possible: sentries hidden by frequencies that could be revealed by tuning the V.41 just right.

Shaun stopped on the TRHail and stared across the water. A couple of security drones patrolled below the cloudy skies and he wondered. He grabbed his CGs from his windbreaker and set them on his nose but no hidden sentries suddenly appeared. Perhaps a tweak to the V.41 settings could change that but he still didn't know much more about the CELL's settings than how to eliminate all of the floating people bubbles.

"Going our way?" J.J. shouted from within a steady flow of pedestrians that parted around him a dozen yards ahead. "Hey, Winston!"

Shaun didn't immediately respond because the Allegheny had turned into the Greenbrier and he didn't know whether the vision was purely imagination or if the CGs were causing it.

"Winston!"

Shaun removed the glasses and the lush, green mountainside and wide, meandering Greenbrier serenity disappeared. He peeked, again, through the CGs but his memory of home was gone. When he realigned his attention to the New Pitt scenery, it seemed as if everyone on the TRHail was staring and smiling at him.

Again, he pocketed the CGs and pulled out the CELL as he walked slowly forward. On the CELL's display were so many clustered **Hello** bubbles, Shaun couldn't see any of the faces except the one on top. He looked around for that face in the crowd but saw no one as beautiful as the redhead whose name was Dantana, according to her bubble. There were lots of other women on the TRHail, though, and he suspected that many of them were within the cluster on the CELL screen. "Hi," he said to several who were giving him the eye as they passed in the opposite direction. Each one responded the same way: they pointed at their own

CELLs or at their CGs and made the thumb-to-pinky finger hand sign to call them.

"Too much?" J.J. asked once Shaun had finally caught up. "I told you you'd be popular."

Women continued to flirt and Shaun thought that Phoenix's scowl revealed how she felt about it. The teen girl, however, smiled as she walked between Phoenix and J.J. and took Shaun's hand.

"Come on," she said with a giddy girl giggle. "I'll protect you." She lifted the corner or her CGs to reveal her left eye, which was accented with blue makeup that matched her eye color, and playfully winked. She skipped a bit as she led him passed women who now looked more jealous than flirtatious. She hugged his arm at the elbow with one hand and pointed at everything curious with the other. "I bet'cha never experienced this before."

◎ ◎ ◎ ◎ ◎

It shouldn't have bothered her but it did, and not for the obvious reason. They were here on a mission that could change the future of the country…and to confront those that had stolen her software. If nothing else, Phoenix had a few million dollars coming her way if she and her only witness, Jackrabbit Johnnie, could prove it.

So, it was his birthday. So, he was a virgin to all

of this New City stuff. So, he had transcended in some small way into manhood. So what! There'd be plenty of time to consort with the locals later. Besides, now that he'd turned the magical eighteen (or twenty-one), the girl clinging to his arm was jailbait.

The TRHail widened as it escaped the craziness of the Point and the west side of downtown became a different kind of busy. The byway overpass to the right of the TRHail continued in parallel with the river and just a few yards farther to the right, Ft. Duquesne Avenue appeared from behind an earthen, tree-lined slope that helped support the byway above. The farther they walked north, the more intense the activity became along the four-lane city street.

Beyond the dozen people in front of her, Shaun followed the teen girl's elbow-clamped lead and turned right onto a sidewalk that crossed under the byway and connected the TRHail to the street.

"Don't worry about her," J.J. said to Phoenix. "She's doing what she's supposed to do."

Phoenix didn't look at J.J. "Not worried about her," she said. "It's Shaun. Don't you think he's buried himself in the part?"

"Yes. Yes I do."

Phoenix slowed her pace and J.J. matched it. She continued to stare at Shaun and the girl who had stopped on the sidewalk under the bypass and were both looking up, with CGs in place, at the bypass's underside. "And that's a good thing, I suppose?"

"It's what will get us to our destination. You see how everyone reacts to him."

"It's a good thing to be so popular in the City?"

"Yes."

"It's a good thing to have women fall all over you?"

"I don't see that. Everyone in the City would love to have their own bodyguard. It's a practical thing more than it is sexual."

"How does that help us find the Pompadour and your 'Movement' buddies?" She nodded at the teen girl who now hugged Shaun tighter as she pointed up at the bottom of the bypass.

"She *is* one of my movement buddies and, perhaps, we should go ask her. I think you'll find that jealousy is not the proper response to her intent."

Phoenix stopped at the intersection of the TRHail and the sidewalk crossing and moved out of pedestrian traffic to pull J.J. to her. "I'm not jealous. I'm concerned. Remember what I'm carrying."

J.J.'s smile was the widest one he'd offered so far. He rubbed his thin-whiskered chin like some aged philosopher. "A lesson to learn around here is not to assume too much about a person's intent. Suspicion is what got us all into this mess in the first place. Do you really want to know how he's feeling? Do you really want to know if he has some hidden desire for her...or for you? Do you really want to throw away humanity's greatest gift that comes with facing the unknown? What fun or challenge is there in knowing a person's feelings before you can experience them, judge them on their merits, and make your own conclusions that aren't based on collated data points? Look at all these people. They all pass each other by, checking each other's personality metrics to see if anyone they meet is not a pure waste of time. What you're carrying will, hopefully, help us all understand what we've become in the New Cities and to prevent others from succumbing to the same trap. I am concerned about that, but also for you. I don't need access, nor want access, to your Story. I know you the way your uncle described you, and from what I've seen since Kennywood, that's good enough for me."

"And how is that? How am I?

"You're a lot like me. Smart, gullible, desirous of things that seem out of reach. A fighter. How does that score?"

Phoenix looked at Shaun and the girl. "Yeah. Good keywords to start with. I can't believe my uncle thought of me that way."

J.J. gently yanked her arm to turn her attention back to him. "We don't always say what we want to say but that doesn't mean we should let the machines do all of the interpreting. Do you trust me?"

Phoenix looked beyond J.J.'s shoulder to the

triple-decker river cruise ship that had anchored off the Point for the fireworks show and now floated along the Allegheny to serve up its fare of glitz, glamor and gambling. Apparently, she took too long to answer as J.J. added, "I see. Well, that's good. I wouldn't trust me either. Who would? Me and the other FMers are trying to disrupt the status quo, trying to keep the quo from leaking out of the cities into the countryside where people, at least, still say Hello to each other."

"I trust you," she said, truly meaning it because she was beginning to believe that the wrong person had been chosen as her bodyguard.

"Hey Js," the teen girl shouted, pointing up. "We've got a graffiti."

Phoenix and J.J. walked over. The girl still held Shaun's left arm and when Phoenix stopped and stood on his right, she looked up. "Where?"

The girl handed her CGs to Phoenix and tapped a few swipes on her CELL. "You should be able to see it now."

Looking through the CGs, Phoenix saw above her, painted in a multitude of neon psychedelic colors with artistic graffiti flair against the overhead structure, the FM logo. "Another hack?" she asked and gave the CGs back to the girl.

"Probably," J.J. replied.

A crowd began to gather and everyone looked up and shared their CGs with those that didn't have them.

"Pretty," one person said.

"Defacing public property," responded another.

"This city is going to hell," said a third.

"Can't scrub that off," J.J. offered. "Son-of-a-bitches."

More gathered, including a couple of officers from the City Law, who looked up before asking the crowd to disperse.

"Are there terrorists here?" an older woman asked the officers. Everyone in the crowd started thumbing through their CELLs, looking for possible suspects.

"Now, let's not start a panic," one officer demanded. "Probably just a bunch of kids."

J.J. used the distraction to lead Phoenix, Shaun and the girl from the frightened mass to the city street. "Doesn't take much to get them riled up," he said to them.

"You did that on purpose," Phoenix said to him.

J.J. looked at the girl and both of them smiled. "The restaurant is over there," he said. "I'm starving."

"You gonna show me how?" Shaun asked J.J.

"Eventually," J.J. said. "But not on an empty stomach, and not until we make further contact."

"In the restaurant," Phoenix suggested.

J.J. just grinned. "You catch on pretty quick."

Phoenix's infant trust in J.J. faltered for a moment before she realized the true purpose of the graffiti. "Diversion," she mumbled.

"Let's go," J.J. responded.

All four lanes of packed traffic that moved methodically in both directions came to a stop when the intersection streetlight turned red. At that moment, like a herd that had been released from a corral, a mass of people left the sidewalk on the opposite side of the street, walked between all of the stationary vehicles, and headed for the commotion that was only getting worse. The four of them quickly walked against the pedestrian flow, between Yellow Cabs, and dodged a few eBike riders that had slowed to gawk. Onlookers that had not crossed the street stood and stared and feverishly swiped the CELLs in their hands or on their wrists, or the invisible displays in front of them. J.J. led them to the restaurant's front door, squeezed through those that rushed out, and stood among empty chairs previously occupied by those that had been waiting to be seated. "Four for dinner," he said to the hostess who slouched forward against a podium, trying to understand what had just happened to all of her guests. J.J. waved his hand in front of her wide eyes. "Four please."

The hostess shook her head. "Ah, yeah. So, what gives?"

"Looks like New Pitt has a Memorial Day surprise. Four…for dinner."

"Do you have a reservation?"

J.J. turned to the empty waiting area. "Really?"

"Yes. You need a reser…"

J.J. interrupted. "Even for a bodyguard who's celebrating his twenty-first birthday and chose your restaurant to do so?"

The hostess took a moment to flick long black bangs from her forehead before thumbing through a CELL sitting atop the podium. Her eyes widened again and the tone of her voice turned apologetic. She looked up at Shaun. "Winston. Yes, of course. We always have room for bodyguar…for those celebrating twenty-one. Happy birthday!"

"Can we get something toward the back?" J.J. asked.

The hostess looked across the numerous, occupied tables. "Looks like one is being set up as we speak. Give us a second?" she said and left the podium.

Traffic outside began to move again and several people entered the waiting area. At that moment, Phoenix's jacket pocket, the one with Skeeter in it, started making a tink-thumping noise that caused Phoenix to unzip the pocket and peek into its darkness. Skeeter was all lit up and feverishly bounced and flew inside the glass jar.

Someone screamed outside, behind her, and she turned to look. Lots of people rushed past the restaurant's storefront glass. Several stood just inside the front door with expressions of distraught. Vehicles on the street sat idle and it seemed to Phoenix like the entire city had frozen in time.

Parked against the curb just beyond the restaurant's storefront was a Yellow Cab with a digital marquee on its roof that read **#22**. Her jacket-pocket tink-thumped with greater aggression, with certain warning, with the answer, she thought, to who was sitting behind the cab's tinted windows.

She jabbed J.J. in the ribs with her elbow. "Isn't that our cab?" she asked.

J.J. pivoted and squinted. "Yes."

"Did you call it for us?"

"Don't have to. It knows where we are, and when it's not doing double duty as a delivery vehicle, personal cabs stay close to its assigned fares."

"It's got new fares," she said.

J.J. squinted harder. "How can you tell?"

Phoenix tapped her jacket pocket with one finger. "Skeeter," she said to him. "I think it knows those three bastards are close and instinct tells me they're in the cab."

"I trust your instincts," J.J. said. "That's unexpected."

Phoenix grabbed his bomber jacket by the Corsair fighter plane patch just above his left elbow. "Unexpected?"

"Winston. Your table is ready." The hostess startled both of them and they turned to her in unison.

The tink-thumping in her jacket pocket stopped and J.J. saw in her eyes what they both already knew. When she looked back, the cab was gone.

◎ ◎ ◎ ◎ ◎

Their table was between the swinging kitchen door and a hallway vestibule to the right of the kitchen where the restaurant's emergency exit and bathrooms were located. In addition to the restaurant's standard decorative pastel choices for the tablecloth and hand-painted wooden chairs, a huge cake with pastel-colored frosting sat in the middle of it. Five of the restaurant's employees stood in a semicircle behind the table and each one of them held an old-fashioned sparkler that Phoenix had not seen since she was a child. They sang a song in a language she did not understand, but it was quite apparent by their celebratory actions, that it was a traditional Mexican *Happy Birthday*. "Las Mañanitas," they harmonized as the hostess lit the single candle centered in the cake.

"Dessert before dinner," the hostess said to Shaun. "But you don't have to eat it right away. You might want to save room for the really good stuff." She pulled out one of the four chairs and prompted Shaun to sit with the wave of one hand. J.J. offered the chair to the left of him to Phoenix in the same way, then he and the teen girl took the two remaining seats.

"Should I blow it out?" Shaun asked the hostess.

"It's your birthday, Winston," the hostess said. "But traditionally, at least in the Oaxaca Restaurant, it remains lit until the meal is done and you take the center slice."

The candle dripped a bit but didn't reduce in size. Shaun reached out and touched it. A tiny drop of hot wax stuck to his finger and he looked at it a moment before flicking it away.

"Perpetual candle," J.J. said to him. "A tiny flame that lasts until you decide otherwise."

Shaun swiped the same finger through a swirl of pastel green frosting and tasted it. "Don't spoil my dinner," he said to everyone listening. "Sweets are the reward for finishing what's on your plate. At least, that's what my dad always said."

"Can't argue with Dad," J.J. said and looked up at the hostess. "We'll have the Grand Comida and four city waters."

The semicircle of employees left and the hostess returned to her podium to handle a waiting room that was now packed. A minute later, one server returned with a big basket of tortilla chips and a festive pink bowl full of salsa. All four of them dove in.

"You know," J.J. said. "What you're eating isn't real."

Phoenix's first chip hovered over the salsa and she pulled it back to inspect it. She blinked twice, sniffed it, bit off one of its triangular points and said, "Tastes real to me."

"Manufactured," J.J. offered. "3D-printable food."

Shaun had also stopped mid-dip and had chomped a tortilla chip corner. "You gotta be kidding me," he said.

"Part of the sustainable city. Printed not with ink or resin or metal but with agricultural dust. Chips are easy. Salsa…well, that's a Oaxaca specialty. Delicacies such as that can't be printed, yet."

Shaun dipped his chip, savored the salsa and said, "Jennifer would love this. I wonder if a bodyguard could get a hold of the recipe? Bodyguards can do anything." He finished his chip and raised his arm. "Waitress!" he yelled. Almost everyone in the restaurant turned to look at him.

"They're not used to that around here," J.J. said.

The teen girl, while looking through her CGs, said, "Here. Let me." She tapped the space in front of her face and almost jabbed Phoenix in the eye as frustration became apparent. "Js. What's the deal?"

"Let's just say we have some buddies who work in the kitchen and know all about Faraday cages. Your CGs won't work back here."

"Oh, well. They still look cool." The girl reached for a chip and chomped as a waiter brought them glasses of water.

"So, what do we do now?" Phoenix asked J.J.

"Eat and enjoy Winston's special day."

"No. I mean…"

"Patience. I'm sure your uncle planned everything out. He always does. Meticulous bastard. For all we know, he's got them captured in cab twenty-two so they'll not bother us again."

"Maybe he'll drive them into the Allegheny."

"Now *that* would be an interesting hack."

Shaun, who had leaned into the teen girl and had engaged her in a shared finger drawing activity on the side of the birthday cake, pulled his finger away and licked it. He'd drawn *W I N* next to the girl's *J A S*. "Hey," he said to J.J. "When are you going to show me how to hack?"

J.J. brought a finger to his lips. "You might want to keep your voice down. You're already supposed to know how."

Shaun lowered his voice. "When are you gonna show me how to steer a cab into the river?"

"Not even I can do that," J.J. said, ate a chip and drank some water. "With the cage around us, I can't show you anything right now."

Three waiters came through the kitchen door and each set a platter full of the complexity that was the Grand Comida. Just about every imaginable tortilla-wrapped menu item sat among the platters along with heaps of shredded lettuce and cheese, diced tomatoes, sour cream and guacamole. Shaun immediately grabbed a taquito and jabbed it into the salsa bowl.

"Can I get you anything else?" one waiter asked and set a short stack of empty plates on the table.

"I really would like to have this recipe," Shaun said. "Could I talk to the owner?"

"Yes. Sure, Winston. I'll get her." The waiter quickly walked to the front waiting area and whispered into the hostess's ear.

"Really?" Phoenix asked him. "Don't we have more important things to be concerned with?"

Shaun scowled for only a second. "It's my twenty-first birthday. I'm concerned with that right now. And this recipe. Jennifer's gonna love me, big time, when I return home with it."

J.J. reached out and tapped Phoenix's forearm. "He's right. Let's enjoy ourselves. The future will be what it will be, and much easier to handle on a full belly."

They all dug in. A few minutes later, a robust and incredibly friendly Mexican woman, who greeted all of them as if they were family, walked up and stood between Phoenix and Shaun. Her accent was thick but understandable.

"Hola," she said with a smile. "How are you doing

tonight? My name is Cerena."

"Awesome," the teen girl said, filling an empty plate with a burrito and a stack of lettuce and sour cream.

"Good to see you again, Johnnie," Cerena said. "An gracias for choosing the Oaxaca to celebrate such a wonderful time in a person's life." She looked down at Shaun. "I hear you like our salsa," she said to him.

Shaun wiped a runner of cheesy beans from the corner of his mouth. "Si," he said. "I was wondering what the recipe is."

"It is a Oaxacan secret," she said.

"You wouldn't sell it would you?"

J.J. shook his head and waved one hand. Phoenix couldn't believe he'd just asked her such a thing.

"Mi amigo. You would be surprised how many people have asked me that."

"Not really," Shaun said. "It's delicious. Would ten thousand do the trick?"

Phoenix couldn't hold in a gasp. J.J. rolled his eyes.

"Oh no, Señor."

"Not even for a bodyguard who is celebrating his twenty-first birthday?"

Cerena's welcoming smile faded quickly. She looked at J.J. for support.

"Winston," J.J. said. "I think your money can be

spent in much better ways."

"No problem," Shaun said. "We can always hack…"

J.J. brought a finger to his lips as Cerena's expression turned worrisome. "Pardon, Mama Cerena. I think Winston has had too much party."

"If you need anything else, please let us know," Cerena said and forced a smile.

After Cerena left the table, Phoenix said to Shaun, "What has gotten into you?"

Shaun continued eating and mumbled through the food in his mouth. "I was just funning. Winston really does have an affect on people, doesn't he?"

"To say the least," Phoenix responded.

J.J. intervened. "Can't we just enjoy this wonderful meal? Salsa is not the reason we came into the city."

The teen girl pushed her chair from the table. "Excuse me, but I gotta run to the bathroom."

Phoenix glared at Shaun who stared at the girl as she walked away. "I think you upset her, too."

Shaun's confident grin turned sour. "I was just…"

A waiter approached the table with a pitcher of water. "Refills?" he asked.

Phoenix looked up to see the heavy aqua-blue sideburns of the teen girl's brother. He began filling J.J.'s water glass, leaned closer, and whispered, "We've got trouble. The lab. They found it. All of it. Everything is gone."

J.J. could not disguise the incredible weight of the revelation. He dropped his fork and it splattered the sour cream and guacamole on his plate.

"I sent you the May Day but I forgot you'd be here. What do we do?"

J.J. swallowed a deep breath. "What about the district? We still good?

"As far as I know. But won't they…"

A commotion at the front of the restaurant caused all of them to turn. The teen boy's expression became one of complete horror. He dropped the pitcher and it bounced across the floor, splattering water everywhere. He slipped in it as he ran.

"Jasmine!" he screamed.

All three of them stood. Outside, at the curb, was the boy's sister. White Tie held one arm and Black Tie held the other. They waited until the boy was at the front door before shoving her into the back of Yellow Cab #22. Black Tie followed her into the back and White Tie got in front. The cab eased away from the curb and vehicles around it parted a path for it to escape.

Phoenix, J.J. and Shaun joined the boy outside. Hands covered his face. Tears streamed between his fingers. When J.J. grabbed his shoulder for comfort and said "Stay calm, Michael," the boy took off, running north along the sidewalk in the direction the cab had gone.

J.J. pulled out his CELL and both Phoenix and

Shaun stared at the white rabbit May Day picture that Michael had sent him. A second later, the rabbit was replaced by a blue bubble with Jasmine's face and two red words:

That's One.

"Shit," J.J. said.

Inside the restaurant, Red Tie exited the bathroom, pocketed his CELL and stepped carefully through spilled water. He grinned at the cake, swiped a finger through the frosting, smeared his moustache as he stuck it between his lips, then reached down and snuffed out the candle.

◎ ◎ ◎ ◎ ◎

The Theatre District was two blocks from the Oaxaca Restaurant but none of them ran. J.J. reminded them to stay calm, even though it was obvious that he was not. He kept mumbling self-reassurance: "He must have seen this coming. He must have known."

The salsa in Shaun's stomach moved up into the back of his throat to remind him of how badly he'd acted. Just about every fear he'd ever imagined while growing up as far from the Net as possible, flooded through him and this made the cilantro tasting acid on the back of his tongue unbearable. He coughed, split and wiped his mouth with the back of his hand. "I'm sorry," he said. "Damn this place."

J.J. stopped in the middle of the sidewalk and pedestrians diverted around the three of them. He pulled Shaun close and said, "Don't lose it now. We need Winston and you've got to be him or it's lost, ya got me? Now shake it off! You're Phoenix Messenger's bodyguard, don't forget, and if that means you have to act like an asshole, so be it."

Just across the street, the 6th Street Bridge glistened with yellow luminescent paint. Digital billboards lined the suspension cables on both sides and one huge projection floated atop the bridge's center tower. It flashed WE WON! as hoards of people swarmed from the baseball game across the bridge and stuffed the already packed intersection that marked the southwest corner of the Theatre District. Apparently, some fantastic MIXR-enabled augmentation had been added to the bridge since just about everyone was staring up with CGs in place and cheering.

Shaun felt no temptation to join them. He thought he might not put a pair of those stupid, lying, CG devices in front of his eyes ever again. But the fact remained (at least as far as *facts* were made available by the New Pitt Net) that he was a bodyguard fresh into his twenty-first year and Winston continued to garner respect, attention and a bit of uncertainty by those who shuffled around him.

J.J. tapped and swiped his CELL feverishly but his search for Jasmine and Michael revealed nothing.

Shaun responded to his frustration.

"We have others, don't we?" he asked.

J.J. looked up, his temper short, and said, "Of course! But they're all purposefully offline. Michael was their single point contact. Our meeting at the restaurant was supposed to help us find the Pompadour. Whether he, or any of them, did or not, I guess we'll…"

Phoenix interjected. "So, we are lost. You have no lab and Skeeter is useless without it. We have no Pompadour and the drive is useless without it."

J.J. ignored her as he put on his CGs and looked around, shaking his head dejectedly as he did so. "Winston," he said the Shaun. "Help me out here. Our graffiti must be here somewhere. Michael wouldn't have forgotten."

The bulge of the CGs in Shaun's pocket seemed to grow enormous, as if they were alive and taunting him. He left them there.

"Come on," J.J. said. "We need your help."

Still, Shaun denied the request and this made J.J. rip off his CGs and shove both them and his CELL into his jacket pocket. "Dammit," he grunted.

At that moment, a woman brushed past Shaun's shoulder. The hourglass shape of her body and the flowing, auburn red hair that fell in wavy lengths all the way down to her tight, black slacks, consumed his attention. Other men on the sidewalk eagerly allowed her passage and just before she turned right onto 6th

Street, she looked back.

It was the woman who had occupied the top-spot bubble in the cluster of Hellos he'd seen on his CELL while walking the TRHail. It was Dantana. "Come on," Shaun said to J.J. and Phoenix who looked at each other, confused.

He led them quickly onto 6th Street where he stopped to look in toward the City but saw no one who even resembled Dantana.

"What is it?" J.J. asked.

"I don't know. A hunch, I guess."

"I saw her," Phoenix said. "The woman with the long red hair. She's your hunch?"

"I think that's all we have right now," Shaun said to Phoenix then asked J.J., "You have any FMers that match that description?"

"Michael had his own contacts. I suppose it's possible."

Across the street, an incredibly bright digital marquee blinked alternating lights that cascaded around its rectangular perimeter. In the center were the words Byham Theater. The retro, twentieth-century box office in front of the theater reminded Shaun of his history class the day they had covered the 1930s depression era streets of New York City when barkers stood outside, promoting the incredible experiences one could have by shelling out a few dimes.

"Come one, come all," he heard someone shouting

across the street. "E.T. in total immersion like you've never seen it before. Next show is in less than an hour."

"Check it with the CGs," Shaun said to J.J. who didn't question the request. He put them on and immediately responded. "It's there. Above the marquee. Our graffiti."

They waited until the Yellow Cab-dominated traffic stopped and the pedestrian street scramble ensued. When they reached the other side, all three of them stood, nodding. They had found the Pompadour.

The theater barker stood on a short soapbox in front of a pair of double glass doors. He had a captured audience for the claims he made, for the MIXR-enabled promo that he offered in the empty space around him, for the silver and gold-suited ducktails with sparkling rhinestones that he wore, and for the outlandish, super tall, black, white and silver streaked pompadour that bobbed above his forehead every time he blurted out another sales pitch. His face was peppered with silver glitter and his lips, probably the most sarcastic of his entire outfit, pursed a big, cherry red grin. There was a lot about him to take in but Shaun was drawn to the lips. They reminded him of a crazy musical he'd seen a long time ago, the name, forgotten.

"You look like a man who's lost his way," the Pompadour said to Shaun, ignoring the rest of the crowd as he, J.J. and Phoenix approached. "Tickets, please."

The request was odd since no one used physical currency in the City, so Shaun assumed that admission had been added to Winston's account just like it had been for the concert. He pulled the CELL from his windbreaker and, as he lifted it, the Pompadour shook his head and said, "No!" He wiped a silver-painted forefinger with cherry red nail polish across his face where his eyebrows should have been then touched the pointy nail to his lips. "Green tickets. Like the ones they used in the olden days."

Shaun had forgotten all about the cash that he had stuffed into his jeans before departing Marlinton. The eighteen dollars in the form of three ones, one five and one ten were the only "green tickets" he possessed. He dropped the CELL back in his windbreaker and snaked a bill from his jean's right pocket. A crumpled one rested in the palm of his hand and a second poked dog-eared from the pocket.

"Three entries, three tickets," the Pompadour said, grinning hungrily and Shaun.

J.J. moved his hand to cover Shaun's. You don't want to make that so obvious around here," he said. "Authorities don't like outside contraband. If anyone else sees it…"

But none of the people around them seemed to care. They were all looking up through CGs at whatever fanciful visions the Pompadour had provided.

Shaun turned his wrist to hide the bill and with

the same hand, snaked out two additional bills from his pocket without looking at them. When he offered them to the Pompadour, the man quickly snatched them away, peeked into his closed fist and said, "Oh yeah. That'll do the trick and then some. You guys are in for a sweeeet surprise. Follow the usher, please."

He pointed to the right set of double glass doors where a woman in a tuxedo and top hat stood. She bowed, opened the door and waited for the three of them to enter before closing it.

"Welcome to the Byham," she said. "This way."

⊙ ⊙ ⊙ ⊙ ⊙

They rushed too quickly for Shaun to take in much of the preserved majesty of the theater's voluminous lobby. From the painted murals of angels spread across the ceiling to the red velvet ropes and curtains, more than a hundred years had seemingly passed it by, untouched.

The usher opened a door at the back of the lobby along the right wall and led them into darkness interspersed with white flashes. The movie was at a slow point so the immersive audio could not be appreciated. A few more steps and they emerged from the aisle tunnel into the main auditorium. A curved, thin digital screen occupied the entire front wall from floor to ceiling. It was the biggest piece of technology

Shaun had ever seen. On it, and Shaun thought that it was more than ironic, the newest rendition of *E.T.*, the last movie he and his father had seen together before the flood took him, was showing at the exact point in the story that Shaun loved most.

E.T.'s finger glowed and, in the nocturnal silence of the theater, it said, "Ouch."

Though the auditorium had two additional tiers above its already expansive ground level, there were no seats—at least none that Shaun thought of as historically traditional. Apparently, the creators of the newest VR immersive attention theater experience had worked out the physical kinks that had challenged it for more than a decade.

Shoulder-to-shoulder seating had been replaced by what Shaun could only think of as viewing areas. Ten-foot-square sections were occupied by furniture you could sit on, stand up against or avoid altogether, depending on the viewer's experience. The areas were large enough for two people to comfortably and safely engage in the VR-enhanced movie world around them. At that moment, just about every one of them, from the dozens that filled the floor space to the dozens that stuffed the tiers, lifted a finger in front of their faces and of those around them.

"Winston." J.J.'s voice sounded hushed and distant. Shaun blinked and looked down at the end of the aisle to his right. J.J. stood another hundred feet away with a door open below a red Exit marker. Shaun walked in that direction as the auditorium filled with one combined "Ahhh!"

A boring hallway full of doors led to a boring staircase and J.J. led Shaun up two flights to join Phoenix and the usher on the third floor. Again, Shaun was greeted by a boring hallway full of doors that stretched in three directions from the stair landing. The right and left hallways had two doors on each side that were spread at least fifty feet apart. The hall in front of him was just as deep but had just one door near the end on the right.

"Have you heard of nickelodeons, sir?" the usher asked Shaun while leading him into the hallway with the single door.

"Little theaters…a long time ago," Shaun said.

"The visuals have changed but the concept is just the same: a personal journey with the use of new technology." The usher opened the door, pushed it inward on hinges that seemed to float, and waved a hand for them to enter. "He'll be with you, shortly," she added and left them. J.J. closed the door.

"This might be one of the most favored destinations for outer-city visitors," J.J. said. "Your own, personal, VR nickelodeon loaded with a plentitude of experiences to last a lifetime. They say you leave them with a whole new perspective of the world."

The room was large enough to host a dozen

nickelodeonites and had twice as many cushy recliners, a couple of loveseats and two standing chairs like the ones in the main auditorium. The standing chairs were more like vertical sofas that had a cage made of padded bars knit closely around it to keep the occupant from hurting themselves. In front of the furniture, a wide space with shiny gray flooring provided ample room for complete, freestanding immersion. In front of the floor, a curved, thin digital screen occupied almost the entire wall.

"As you can imagine," J.J. said, "the experience isn't cheap."

"Come now. That's not true at all." The man with the Pompadour walked from behind the left side of the wall screen. He'd taken off his long coat and now stood in a sleeveless vest that revealed a tattoo on his right shoulder. It sparkled silver and gold under the room's bright lighting. "The three of you cost only sixteen bucks."

"Do I know you?" Shaun asked. "I mean, how did you know I had cash in my pocket?"

"You know me as the Pompadour but you can call me Pomp for short." Pomp grabbed the rhinestone-studded lapels of his vest and yanked. "I guess you might call it a really good guess. But it proves who you really are and that's important." He took two steps closer to Shaun; his heels clicked across the hard floor. "Besides, that sixteen in green is worth a lot more in certain city markets. It was an equitable admission price." He pointed at Shaun's jeans pocket, leaned forward and whispered, "Hold on to the other two. You never know when they might come in handy." He then stood straight up, and offered his tattooed shoulder to the three of them. "It's much better if you use your special peepers."

Shaun blinked a couple of times just to make sure the carousel horsehead tattoo really was there. Its artistic carnival design was a lot like the one that the Grand Carousel operator had sported back at Kennywood, except Pomp's horse looked a lot angrier. Shaun took a moment to stare at Pomp's heavily painted face and lips, at the height of his mass of hair and thought, just perhaps, the two men were the same.

"Come on," Pomp said. "Use the CGs, or better yet, try these on for size." From a small, rhinestone-laden pocket in his vest, Pomp produced an eye lens case. "The newest tech wonder. Perfect for a nickelodeon." He popped off the two lens case caps. "You ever wore an eyes lens before?" he asked Shaun.

"No," Shaun said. "And I don't think I want to."

Pomp stepped within arms-reach of Shaun. "What you want and what is necessary are two different things. Please. I insist." J.J. and Phoenix both stepped forward and stood at Shaun's side.

For the first time since he'd left West Virginia, Shaun thought about putting an end to all of this...

bullshit! They had what they needed. He'd bodyguarded them this far. He could walk out right now, head for the perimeter, get out of the city, go home, and the world would still move in whatever direction these covert operators intended to take it—but not with him, not with Shaun Winston, not anymore.

"You're a bodyguard, Winston," Pomp chided. "Ain't 'cha got no guts?"

"What's necessary?" Shaun asked.

"That you put in your brand new iTacts, a replacement technology for those cumbersome ClearGlasses. Here…let me help." He lifted a red nail over one of the lenses.

Don't let others get you knee deep in their shit, Shaun thought. *Yeah…too late.*

"I'll do it," Shaun said.

"And your CGs?" Pomp said to J.J. and Phoenix.

J.J. placed his pair on his face and, after Shaun finished with what was a surprisingly easy insert of the lenses, gave the CGs that J.J. had given him to Phoenix.

The Pompadour man turned sideways so they could all gaze at what made them, together, gasp.

◉ ◉ ◉ ◉ ◉

One diversion after another, Phoenix thought. Now what? Perhaps the odd fellow had additional information hidden within the ink of his tattoo. She grabbed the CGs from Shaun's hand and put them on. The augmentation was immediately awe-inspiring. She leaned forward for a better look.

A perfect replica of Kennywood's Grand Carousel floated above the tattoo. It was only a few inches wide but its revolving 3D motion made it look real, as if someone had shrunk the actual thing. Horses on the carousel rose and fell as it turned and Phoenix could actually hear the repetitious 1930s Wurlitzer as it timed the horses' gaits. But the most amazing detail was found in the people on the horses and they made Phoenix lean closer. Little tiny bodies with little tiny arms and legs and heads with faces that were so tiny, Phoenix couldn't believe she was one of them, on a little tiny horse that bobbed next to a horse-riding Shaun. J.J.'s dot of a face rode a horse in front of them.

"How is that possible?" Phoenix asked.

"In here," Pomp said, "all is possible." He snapped his fingers and the spinning carousel disappeared. Phoenix stood straight up as did Shaun and J.J. who were also leaning toward the tattoo. "Do you have what we need?" Pomp said to her.

Phoenix looked at J.J. who nodded. "Yes, I do," she said and reached for the jacket pocket that held Skeeter. She gently pinched open the zipper and peeked inside. The microdrone's multi-colored specks were visible in the dark depth of the pocket, but when she removed the jar and held it in the palm of her hand, the room's lighting erased Skeeter's miniscule illumination.

"Go ahead," Pomp said. "Open it."

Again, J.J. nodded. Shaun's expression wasn't as encouraging. Phoenix spun the lid and, as she set the jar on the floor, the lid dropped with a metal clink against its hard surface. Skeeter immediately exited. Its tiny body zipped up and over the center of the stage floor. Phoenix looked at Shaun who had taken out his CELL and was staring at its screen. A blue bubble with Dr. One's face glowed above the word **Hello**. Shaun pressed it.

The room's interior lights blinked off, filling it with complete darkness except for the three-color, twelve-dot body of the hovering microdrone. Below Skeeter, Dr. One appeared and he looked incredibly realistic. His complete 3D-360 moved without translucence. It and the backdrop that formed looked as solid as the room he'd actually stood in while making the recording.

Behind him was the empty, high-backed swivel chair they'd seen him sitting in on the video at J.J.'s now-compromised lab. Behind the chair, a bookcase was filled with spines of many colors. The rest of the projected backdrop looked anything but studious. Clapboard walls with peeling white paint made the chair-bookcase arrangement look staged. Equipment that they'd found in J.J.'s lab sat on makeshift tables, a few of which had cobwebs attached to their undersides near the legs.

"Hello, Johnnie," Dr. One said and stood next to one of the tables. "A lot of this must look familiar."

"Stuff built for my lab," J.J. said. "But that's not my lab."

"No. It's not your lab, it's mine."

"Anticipatory questions?" Phoenix asked J.J.

"He's not real…of course."

"And I anticipate your next questions," Dr. One continued, "will involve answers to why and where and how et cetera. That's why you're here. Plus, this theater makes for a great, secure location. Very controllable, even from outside eyes." The image walked over to stand next to a vertical, black storage cabinet like the one J.J. had used to store his microdrones. "The future," he said and tapped the top of the cabinet with three fingers. "It's going to be ours or theirs." He looked directly at J.J. and stroked his frosty white beard. "You know how I believe in redundancy, Johnnie. This is me being redundant. The Kennywood operation was bound to go under eventually. The pressure to find you had gotten much too great, but all is not lost. Problem is, you have my mosquito and you have my schematic algorithms, and I have my own lab and I'll show you the way, but first, answers to your questions.

"The *why*, I just told you. The *where*…well, let's keep that a secret for obvious reasons. As for the *how*, that's where my brilliant niece comes in." Dr. One looked at her, which magnified his realism.

"The way that you understand binary is nothing less than machinelike. You see the code as if it was a living thing, a symbiotic creature made whole by the sum of its parts, each code block a vital organ in the life of the program. It just needed tweaking so that it could live in a microscopic world much smaller than frequency bands of electromagnetism. Your code, with my revisions, is what makes MIXRs possible."

"V.41 software," Phoenix mumbled.

"I had to give something to get something, a way to continue using the foundation of the Phoenix code to program a completely different set of parameters. It wasn't easy, mind you. Time at the observatory pretending to help a young scientist who needed no help, time with Johnnie to fine tune my drone tech knowledge, time to build and furnish this second lab, time to learn what the Feds knew about microdrones and how they were going to use them, and time to develop my own kind of microdrone to help the Movement prevent it. It took a few years, but here we all are."

"To prevent what?" Shaun asked.

"There is much unrest across all of North America," Dr. One continued, "much more than most people know. Canada wants the Great Lakes, Mexicans are filling into a southwest already decimated by the water crisis and in the south, they're just downright pissed off. Rural America, there, has been left behind and they have every right to feel that way. The new tech is in the New Cities. The largest fresh water resources are near the New Cities. All they have is mountain rivers and lakes and they will do anything to protect them. Fear is an incredible driver of human behavior and most of the time, it doesn't even matter if the fear is real or not. Masses convinced of a truth don't consider how the truth became, particularly if it reveals what they believe is their only survival. If they found out what mobile MIXRs could do, just the knowledge of their potential use would be confirmation enough to stage coordinated acts of aggression. Here, let me show you."

⊙ ⊙ ⊙ ⊙ ⊙

The entire nickelodeon transformed from a stage-front view of an intricate MIXR-enabled reality to total immersive attention. Smaller screens built into all of the walls around them came to life and screens in the ceiling stitched everything together.

Shaun now stood on the Greenbrier River Trail across from one of the green-camouflaged, metal sheds. Air rushed into the room but Shaun sensed it as a cool mountain breeze. He stood there, fascinated, to think that he was back home. An eagle, like the one back at the concert, dove across rippling water but found no meal worth its effort. It swung up and over to land on top of the shed. At that moment, hundreds of men in green-camouflaged tactical gear emerged from the tree line and stepped into the river. One-by-one they emerged to form a solid green line along the opposite river bank for as far as Shaun could see in both directions.

Dr. One appeared right in front of them. It actually looked like he was walking across the Greenbrier. "There's not as many as you might think," he said. "Probably just a dozen or two from where you stand. And that's the glorious misuse of an evolutionary technology. A game of make-pretent. With a few hundred mosquito microdrones providing webbed triangulation, you could *create* any number of mobile MIXRs that are realistic even without the aid of eyewear. You could even create an army with soldiers that may or may not be real."

Dr. One sank into the Greenbrier and the nickelodeon transformed again but this time, the visions were anything but serene. Shaun was still on the river trail but the skies now filled with thick smoke, and the bodies of soldiers and Marlinton townspeople lay in scattered disarray along both sides of the river.

A mangled body at his feet lay face down. One of its shoulders was gone but Shaun knew who it was. He was too afraid to even attempt to touch the MIXR at his feet. What if he really did grab what really wasn't there and turned it over to see some horrible remnant of his father's face. Across the river, more soldiers pushed forward. A hundred guns pointed right at Shaun.

Shaun plucked out his left iTact and closed his right eye to be removed from the experience. J.J. and Phoenix had already removed their CGs. Total immersion ended and the 360 screen images were replaced by soft lighting. Dr. One sat in his high-backed chair with the lonely bookcase set up against a paint-peeling wall behind him.

"That's what we don't want," Dr. One said, gently rocking. "And if the southern aggression understands that the New Cities do not possess this technology, they'll be less likely to react in such historically bad fashion. They have the right to protect themselves and bear arms even if those arms have evolved into ones and zeros. The Faraday Movement will help protect them by possessing the mobile MIXR tech."

"So you can use it against the Cities," Shaun said.

"And not so we can use it against the Cities. So that we maintain a stalemate. Neither side gets it except the side of Science. There's much to be discovered and the positive applications are potentially immense. We wouldn't want war on the brink of higher understanding. We wouldn't want the Suspicious Society to win."

◎ ◎ ◎ ◎ ◎

Phoenix put her CGs back on, walked over to Dr. One, reached out to touch the chair, and felt a spongy barrier against the energy of which it was made. When she pushed, her fingers went through it and it really did look like she'd poked a hole in the fabric. When she pulled her hand back, the hole vanished.

Dr. One looked up at her. He smiled enough that his lips appeared from behind the white beard and mustache. "Bring me the drone and the drive. My friends will show the way. We're up in the Mill District where all of the real people are."

The eyes were always the hardest virtual elements to precisely emulate, Phoenix thought, but Dr. One's looked about as real as you could get. "Are you dead?" she asked him.

Dr. One lost the big smile but he still grinned. "Does it really matter?" he said and the virtual experience ended.

It took a full minute for their eyes to adjust to the nickelodeon's sudden brightness.

"Wait," J.J. shouted. "What about Jasmine? What about the assholes that destroyed my lab?"

"An unfortunate sacrifice," Pomp said and slipped on his long coat.

"They'll use her," J.J. said.

"At some point, perhaps. But we can't worry about that now. All we have to do is get you from point A to point B. What'cha brung can be delivered and disappear into the hands of the Movement forever."

"And the people who took her could take us," J.J. added.

"Sure. But they're not gonna. One, because they can't access anything without the code and two, no one knows what the code is. The doctor is sly that way, don't you think?"

"I could think of a few more words for him," J.J. said.

Shaun fumbled the other iTact out of his right eye, sealed them both inside the lens case, and offered them to Pomp. "My gift," the Pomp said to Shaun and walked behind the left side of the wall screen. "This way."

Skeeter had flown inside the small jar and now sat inside, motionless. Phoenix walked over to it, knelt, capped the jar and stuck it in her jacket pocket. Shaun came up behind her.

"What did he say?" he asked, looking down. "I saw his lips move but I couldn't hear anything."

"What did who say?"

"You asked him if he was dead."

Phoenix stood from the nickelodeon floor and gazed at all of its gadgetry, enthralled and terrified by the memory of the visions she'd just seen. The Green Bank Observatory, decimated. Bodies of scientists scattered on the ground. The Great Big Thing on fire.

Just one possible future where everything dies.

"He said that it doesn't really matter."

⊙ ⊙ ⊙ ⊙ ⊙

Shaun got used to the loss of control of his eBike pretty quickly. Autoride gave him greater opportunity to consume the city life around him without worrying about traffic and pedestrians and street corner signs. And with the designated eBike lane, they all traveled north on Penn Avenue without stopping for several miles. He could pedal but he didn't have to, and he could turn auto off, but their three eBike escorts had asked him not to. All of the bikes were equipped with an illegal, thirty-minute EMR deflector, the lead escort had told them when they'd exited the back of the theater, and riding in a cohesive, autoride group would help keep all of them hidden.

Traffic remained packed and it moved like thick capillaries full of eclectic city rhythm that undulated within the flesh of mighty buildings, high-flying transport drones and busy sidewalks. Yellow Cabs crawled a few miles an hour by him on the left, but none were designated as #22. In front of him, the three escorts wore full-faced helmets (though they'd offered none to him, J.J. or Phoenix) which had caused suspicion from the time they'd met. Only the lead escort had said anything and all of their faces had remained hidden.

At the corner of 17th Street, the lead escort stopped, even though the street signals glowed green. The five eBikes behind him also stopped and Shaun set his foot on the pavement to hold his up. This caused a momentary bubble of congestion as the smart street adjusted traffic to allow other eBikes a path into the parallel vehicle lane. The escort leaned his bike onto a kickstand, got off, and walked back to stand next to Shaun.

"This is where we part," the escort yelled so that his helmet-muffled voice could be heard by Phoenix, who was parked behind Shaun, and J.J., who took up the rear. "You have about twenty minutes left on the deflectors. It'll take us that much time to secure the meeting. Turn off the autoride and head down 17th and through the Strip District. Meet us in twenty in Arsenal Park." The escort didn't wait for an answer as he immediately walked back to his bike and led the other two escorts straight through the intersection.

Shaun looked over his shoulder as J.J. rode forward to stop next to Phoenix. "It's always something, isn't it?" he said. "We can't just get there. And the longer it takes, the more uncomfortable I become."

"I'm already there with you," Phoenix said. "Particularly since I've got the goods."

When the street signaled red, Shaun rode into the

intersection and slowly maneuvered through a wave of pedestrians. He steered into the eBike lane then rode two blocks to the corner of the Strip's main drag and stopped. The brash city lighting had fallen off quite a bit and though there were lampposts along every sidewalk and alleyway, there were a lot more shadows than Shaun had encountered since departing the Carnegie Science tour bus.

"We have a few minutes, don't we?" Shaun said to J.J. when he and Phoenix stopped next to him. "I want to take a look at the water mill."

"Our bike friends said to go through the Strip," J.J. offered.

"We will. I just want to see it. Might be my last opportunity."

"They were pretty specific," J.J. urged.

"I insist," Shaun said and rode straight toward the river that was outlined by white marker lights along both banks. When he looked back, both J.J. and Phoenix remained standing at the Strip District intersection.

He was a little surprised they hadn't followed but, as he rode, he began to feel peace of solitude and an empowerment from choosing what *he* wanted to do. Since traffic and people and buildings became less of a nuisance the farther he rode, he started weaving his eBike from its designated lane across the two, empty vehicle lanes. Handling it manually proved a bit more challenging than he'd presumed but he quickly adjusted. He tried a big Crazy 8 but found he couldn't lean into the turns enough to prevent loss of balance. The bike almost toppled so he stopped to regain his bearings and to calm his heart, which had jumped a beat. The north end of the TRHail ended at the river's edge another hundred yards ahead and a few people walked in his direction, checked their CELLs, stared at him through CGs and gave him a wide berth.

Mill Street paralleled the Allegheny in both directions. To his left, the road seemed more a part of the City than it did to his right. Well-lit sidewalks snaked south between what looked like warehouses, and several hundred yards farther, they connected to the TRHail.

In an odd way, Shaun was reminded of leaving Marlinton on his mountain bike just a day-and-a-half ago, how, as he'd traveled from the center of town, the old way of living still sat untouched by progress. It reminded him of old man Smith and the many conversations they'd shared while sitting on his makeshift front porch. It reminded him that he missed home and it fueled him with anticipation for return.

There were no sidewalks from the intersection to the right and street lighting was half as bright. Just a few short buildings sat along the right side, but the wide space between Mill Street and the river to the left was the property of the **Allegheny River Mill (ARM)**. This was made apparent by the digital signage mounted on a chain link fence that set its property perimeter for as far as Shaun could see. Large, round water storage tanks, like the ones they still used for fossil fuels, stretched in a long line, two-by-two, near the river. All were well lit and all had small security drones hovering in a grid pattern above them.

At the northern horizon and breaking through the dense cloud layer above a bright halo of light that marked the ARM's location, was a huge tanker drone. Its sudden appearance in the sky and its blimp-like size made its descent seem extraterrestrial. It slowly fell and parked in the sky above the water mill lighting near two other floating tanker drones.

Pedestrians continued to avoid him and Shaun returned a stare from a couple of twenty-something guys in a way that made them increase their matched strides toward the Strip. Shaun crossed his eyes and stuck his tongue out just to feel juvenile and this brought laughter from a pair of twenty-something girls who stumbled and pointed at him a dozen yards behind the frightened guys. Shaun smiled and waved and wished that he had access to the Net just long enough to find out more about them. He considered parking the bike and leaving its EMR-guarded perimeter—the two girls were that cute. He was beyond needy for attention. His altered persona hungered for it. Winston hungered.

Beyond the two girls, Shaun saw lines of people filter onto and off the Strip but both Phoenix and J.J. were gone.

⊙ ⊙ ⊙ ⊙ ⊙

J.J. told Phoenix that Shaun would be fine as long as he remained on or near his bike. He suggested that they do a little people watching while they waited for him. They wouldn't be able to use any CG enhancement inside the eBike's EMR deflection field, but he promised her she'd still witness things she'd never seen before.

They leaned against their parked bikes in a designated, red-glowing rectangle across from a nightclub that had been converted from a centuries-old produce warehouse.

"My glasses shouldn't have shown me such MIXR-enabled detail back at the nickelodeon," Phoenix said to J.J. as a steady crowd flowed in and out of the club. "V.38's don't do that."

J.J. shook his head. "In that controlled space, the interface to the CGs comes from the theater not your CELL."

"I don't know about you, but I saw some pretty worrisome stuff. I'll never get the burning GBT out of my head and my heart. It was that real."

"I saw Kennywood destroyed—just scattered

remains and bodies everywhere, as if all of the rides had simultaneously broken and riders had fallen from the skies still strapped to their seats. Horrors with similar themes but personalized to fill our own darkest closets. The important thing to remember is that it wasn't real anymore than was the extraterrestrial showing in the main auditorium. You have to exercise your mind in a whole new way, to separate it in your head, which isn't easy to do. It's another reason why so many hesitate the New Nickelodeon experience even though they may be financially able."

Selected fashions along the Strip revealed an eclectic mix from simple jeans and jackets to extravagant outfits that rivaled the Pompadour's attire for oddity. Phoenix focused her attention on a woman who passed directly in front of them.

"Do you know her?" Phoenix asked. The woman flicked long, auburn red hair from her face and adjusted a black scarf around her neck.

"No, but I saw her back at the theater. She's the one that led us there."

"Not one of yours?"

"Not unless Michael recruited her."

They watched the woman walk back in the direction they'd come, cross to the opposite side of the street, pass another nightclub that was surrounded by people only scantily clothed, and enter the next building through swinging wooden doors, just like those seen in old westerns. Above the doors was and etched, wooden sign that read: Strip Poker Saloon.

◎ ◎ ◎ ◎ ◎

Though Shaun saw J.J. and Phoenix standing near their bikes a block up the road as he pushed his bike through the crowd, his attention diverted to the red-haired woman named Dantana. For a full minute, it seemed as if she was walking right to him, dividing the crowd as she approached, dressed from head to toe in black high heels, slacks, blouse, coat and scarf. Her eyes never left him and her sly smile never faded until she abruptly changed direction and entered a place called the Strip Poker Saloon.

He knew not to wander from his bike, but Shaun couldn't help it. He had to find out more about her. What was her connection and why was she following him? Maybe it was all a part of the plan. But there was something else…an allure, a magnetism, a desire. And if her body language wasn't an invitation to pursue, then Shaun thought he knew nothing about women. That was, of course, partially true. Shaun really didn't know a lot about women but Winston did.

He decided to use only one of the iTacts, which seemed advantageous to the CGs; he could close either eye to change perspectives. He parked his bike in a designated red rectangle, slipped an iTact into his right eye and entered the saloon.

Of course, he expected to see a piano player and a long bar with a huge mirror and rowdy people gathered around round tables full of cards, booze and naked women, but that's not what greeted him as the doors creaked back-and-forth behind him. There was just a long, black wall that sported an etched wooden sign that read "Strippin" with an arrow pointing left, and "Peein" with an arrow pointing right. Boisterous activity could be heard beyond the doorway at the end of the left side of the entry hall. Dimly lit darkness turned ninety degrees another dozen yards to his right.

Shaun thought about easing himself into the saloon, maybe poking his head in to take a first look, but Winston wouldn't do that. Winston was confident and felt comfortable anywhere.

He took two steps to the left and saw four women, naked from the waist up, sitting at the nearest table, except…they really weren't naked. He closed his left eye and the right iTact erased their clothes. He blinked to the left eye and their clothes popped back in place.

"Shaun."

The voice was behind him and he quickly turned.

"I just wanted you to know how much I really do care. We've had a long journey in a short time."

The voice remained hidden in the dark hallway that led to the bathrooms. "Dantana?" Shaun asked.

"How do you know me?"

"You're in the New City, Shaun. Everyone knows everyone."

"I don't know you."

"Of course you do." The woman stepped into the entry hall and Shaun had to blink several times to fully grasp what he saw. It was Phoenix and it was Dantana, both. "iTacts work much better when you have both in," the woman said, "or else you might not know which vision is real and which vision is more real." She walked over to stand in front of him and Shaun, with both eyes open, saw two different people split straight down the bridge of the nose. Lips half painted in pink pursed forward and Shaun let the Dantana side of her face kiss him on the cheek. She pulled back then leaned forward again. This time, both Dantana and Phoenix kissed him on the lips. Through his right eye, he saw Phoenix's hazel-veined, brown iris and light-twinkling pupil. Through his left eye, he saw Dantana's solid gray iris and bottomless black pupil.

The woman stepped back into the shadows. "She is very pretty," she said. "There's nothing wrong with having the hots for her. Besides, she loves dolphins, and what's more endearing than a woman who loves something that will soon be extinct? Look, there she is now."

Above the swinging doors, Shaun saw Phoenix and J.J. moving through the crowd in his direction. He made left-eye contact with Phoenix then turned around to find the woman gone. He walked to the turn in the right side of the hallway to see that it extended another hundred feet. Closed doors were on either side near the end.

"Shaun," Phoenix said, standing outside. "I mean, Winston. We gotta go."

Shaun came through the double doors, blinking at Phoenix and J.J. just to make sure there weren't four of them.

◉ ◉ ◉ ◉ ◉

J.J. led them north of the Strip to a streetlight-lit residential area. Traffic remained consistently congested but the eBikes, in their own lane, moved with much greater freedom until they came to a split in the road and stopped.

"The park is straight ahead," J.J. said. "I guess it doesn't matter which fork we take."

"Left toward the mill," Shaun said.

Phoenix guessed they had about three minutes before the EMR deflectors died, and she guessed that the protection didn't matter since Shaun might have wandered a bit too far outside his bike's range. Phoenix also guessed that, by the look on Shaun's face when he'd come through the saloon doors, the young man had witnessed strip poker for the first time. He'd looked at her in a way that she'd not seen from him, as if he'd been checking her out, perhaps even casting the images he'd seen inside onto her. She'd touched him and he'd jerked backward and had snapped out of whatever had taken hold then he'd hastily removed and stored one right iTact.

"Why did you say Dolphin to me back on the Strip?" Phoenix asked Shaun who straddled his bike in front of her.

"That's what you told me," he said and took off behind J.J. who angled down the left fork.

From the back of the pack, Phoenix realized how much the New City of Pittsburgh still had to go. Though the homes that surrounded Arsenal Park to her right looked sustainably modern in all respects, and though the street sides were well lit for surveillance, there was a vivid sense of separation from the Strip but, more so, from the inner city. This was the Mill District and the fingers of the immersive society had yet to find firm grip. Residents, here, worked almost exclusively at the ARM and salaries there did not afford many the luxury of V-technology or CGs. Everyone had tech because it was required, but what most of the residents of the Mill District carried were cheap decaders that had been refurbished with location and resource tracking.

The road they traveled continued for several blocks ahead where it ended at the perimeter fence around the ARM's huge, domed central building that stood between two smaller replicas. The entire riverbank, as it turned sharply east, blazed with light. Two tanker drones sat on each side of the domed-building cluster and three more hovered overhead. A rhythmic sound of sloshing water created a trancelike aura, like ocean waves crashing on the beach.

Phoenix followed Shaun into a parking area in front of a three-story building that was totally covered in vined foliage. All three of them stepped off their bikes and stood together. No other vehicles were parked in the lot.

"You see any of our biker escorts?" J.J. asked.

"He said, in the park," Phoenix reminded them and took the lead around the right side of the building. Shaun was behind her and she whispered to him, "You saw me in the saloon?"

"Yeah," Shaun said, brushing a meandering vine from his face. "Sort of. She…you mentioned your love of dolphins, that's all."

"Who's she? You mean the redhead?"

"Her name is Dantana."

"And she knows about my love of dolphins?"

"Seemed to."

"She must be our link then…to the dolphin password. She didn't say anything else…no code-word-sounding stuff?"

"She mentioned that dolphins are almost extinct. Is that code for anything?"

Phoenix had no answer as they emerged from the side of the building's shadows into a well-lit, hundred-yard-long landscaped courtyard with three-story buildings on its four sides. There were lots of trees and lots of benches and a couple of picnic tables and an earthen, solar oven-grill and a playground with swings and monkey bars. In the middle of the park, four sidewalks from four perpendicular directions joined in a circular hub that had a gazebo built around it. A couple of dozen adults and children played or sat on benches or lay on green, healthy grass. One person, wearing a full-faced bike helmet, sat on a bench under the gazebo.

No one paid them much attention as she, Shaun and J.J. emerged from shadow onto the sidewalk. As all three of them approached the gazebo, they looked down to avoid detection from the park's surveillance system. The person sitting inside stood up.

"Follow me," the helmeted woman mumbled and walked off along the sidewalk that forked to the left.

Phoenix and J.J. followed her for a few yards before Phoenix stopped and turned around. Shaun still stood inside the gazebo, giggling. He waved one hand in the air in front of him then stared in the direction of the children's playground for a moment before leaving the gazebo to join them.

"It must be real," Shaun said.

"What's that?" Phoenix asked.

"Tony. You mean you didn't see him?"

"Are you talking about that butterfly again?"

"Did you see him, J.J.?" Shaun asked and J.J. just shook his head.

◎ ◎ ◎ ◎ ◎

Whether anyone had seen Tony really didn't matter anymore. Whether it was the same butterfly that he'd met on the Greenbrier River Trail or had greeted him at Bethany's house or had hitched a ride on a tour bus to New Pitt or had flown with Ringo as he beat his drums didn't matter either. What mattered is that the butterfly had become his own, personal angel, one that reminded him where he was and from where he came. Tony represented a connection across the miles to a more serene, free-spirited life where nature, not man, controlled the course of fate.

The ivy-covered building along the north side of the courtyard provided a wide, ground-level tunnel through the middle of it; the woman in the helmet led them through it and out onto the adjoining street, which they crossed as soon as the traffic stopped.

Residential homes occupied all of the property from the park to the ARM's perimeter fence and they walked deep into it. Street lighting remained surveillance-bright but the homes felt darker the closer they moved toward the ARM. Houses that looked as if they hadn't been renovated in decades replaced modernity.

They stopped for a moment at the back end of the residential area where a road, mostly barren of traffic, paralleled the ARM's perimeter fence in both directions. Three blocks to the left, men guarded an opening in the fence. Towers on either side of the opening provided additional security from the sharpshooters that stood inside. Their escort led them away from it, walked two more blocks to the right, and stood in front of a two-story house with a small porch and peeling white paint that reminded Shaun of the backdrop behind Dr. One's alternate lab he'd seen in the nickelodeon. No lights were on inside. The escort led them onto the front porch, opened an unlocked front door and entered.

Though the house had two floors, and light through the windows erased most shadows, it was hard to find a staircase anywhere. A living room, dining room and kitchen were all furnished but nothing about the rooms seemed lived in. Near the kitchen was a closed door that Shaun assumed was a bathroom until the escort placed the palm of her hand against it and it opened to reveal a set of ascending steps. Up they went without stealth since each step was accompanied by creaking wood. At the top of the steps, the escort opened a second door with the palm of her hand and pushed it inward.

It should not have surprised any of them to see Dr. One, sitting in his high-backed swivel chair behind a desk in a windowless room illuminated by two, flat ceiling lights. But the real shocker was that all three Ties stood behind him. They immediately walked over to surround J.J., and Shaun and Phoenix stepped away from them.

"What's going on, Doc?" J.J. asked. "These aren't our kind of friends."

"It's all a matter of perspective," Dr. One said, gently rocking.

"Double-crosser," J.J. responded. The anger in his voice caused Red Tie to grab his right arm.

"There's only one double-crosser around here, Johnnie, and that's you," Dr. One said. "Double-crossing the system. Double-crossing the country. It's turds like you that are going to destroy what we've worked so hard to prevent."

"You want it for control," J.J. said to Red Tie and jerked his arm from the man's grasp. "We want it to prevent it." He scowled at Dr. One. "Isn't that right, doctor? Isn't that the lie you told me and Bethany and all of the Movement that has counted on us?"

Dr. One continued rocking. "A lie is only as good as the truth it's based upon. I really do care what happens to this country. The water crisis has us on the brink of civil unrest. Western states are becoming deserts. Canada is threatening an invasion of the Great Lakes. These are our truths."

"And to protect our freedoms from the most likely

aggressors," Red Tie added. "Your work will prove most helpful."

"You used Phoenix to develop the foundation of mobile MIXR software and you gave it to these cretins, and you used me so that you could steal my designs and build your own lab," J.J. said to Dr. One, ignoring Red Tie who had, again, grabbed his arm.

"And we used Shaun," Dr. One said, "You are our proof of how effective mobile MIXRs can be. Without the aid of any technology, you were led here by visions outside the City that only looked real. When you arrived, Winston was born and *he* became real to you, too. After living as Winston for just one day, I just can't imagine you spending your life mowing grass and fixing bicycles in a nowhere place like Marlinton, can you? Not with all the opportunities the New City provides." Dr. One nodded at the helmeted escort who stood by the door. "Like women." The escort removed her helmet and a snarl of auburn red hair fell from within. "You and Dantana have something in common. She is my bodyguard just like Winston is Phoenix's. You want to really learn how to hack the Net then she's the one you want. Johnnie is best with drones."

Dr. One got up and stepped around the desk to stand between Phoenix and Shaun. "Give her the jacket," he told Phoenix.

Phoenix looked helplessly around the room before sliding it from her shoulders and reluctantly handing the jacket to Dantana who slipped off her own black jacket and put it on.

Dr. One leaned forward and stroked his white beard. "As much as I've worked with these tie-wearing assholes, I don't trust them any more than you do. That's why I separated the pieces that will give us access to the encrypted microdrone schematics on the drive. Even if they had taken you before your arrival here, they wouldn't have been able to figure it out and you wouldn't have been able to tell them otherwise. Phoenix carried one of the pieces on her back and Shaun picked up the means to see it at the theater, but nothing will work unless Dantana is wearing the jacket." Dr. One smiled at his own clever plotting and told Shaun to put in his iTacts.

Dantana flipped her long hair so that it fell across the front of Phoenix's jacket and turned around to reveal the extravagantly embroidered dolphin on the back. Shaun stood in silence, put in both iTacts and stared.

It was just a simple augmentation—nothing so spectacular as the Grand Carousel that the Pompadour had sported. Floating over the embroidered dolphin, Shaun saw the key to the encryption. "Is that all?" he said. "A bulldog?"

◎ ◎ ◎ ◎ ◎

The Three Ties took J.J. away.

"What are they going to do with him?" Phoenix asked Dr. One.

"Do…nothing…as long as their questions are answered. There's got to be a bunch of his Movement that we don't yet know about."

"You mean *your* Movement?"

"We both know that's not true."

"So, how *did* you know?"

"About the bulldog?" Dr. One walked back to his big chair and sat. "You don't remember that I visited your parents the night you had the stray. I walked into your bedroom and you were sitting with the little guy on your bed. You had a notebook that you were scribbling in. One of the things you'd scribbled was Bulldog Sallie, but written like an early code-writing prodigy."

"You created the drive and Skeeter. You could have just given 'em to them. Why put us through all of this?"

"They wanted Johnnie's lab and they forced me give it to them. Plus, I promised them that the two of you might be convinced to stick around and help us build our own mobile MIXR lab."

"Not in a million years," Phoenix said.

"And you, Winston? A bodyguard with a limited Storyline would help a great deal."

"Same goes."

"Are you sure? You know how convincing we can be. Bethany was convinced. Those two stupid Kennywood kids are being convinced as we speak. And Johnnie? He's in for a real convincing."

Phoenix glared at the back of Dantana's head and said, "Torture, you mean."

"Again, it's all a matter of your perception of the vibrations of interconnectivity. You've seen what immersive attention can provide. It doesn't have to be all fire and death."

Dantana lightly snatched Shaun's arm and he didn't fight the grip. "I want to show you something," she said to him. "Phoenix and the doctor have more to discuss in private. Don't worry. You'll see her again, shortly. I promise."

Shaun reluctantly followed Dantana's lead out of the room and she closed the door behind him. As soon as the creaking stairs outside quieted, Dr. One set his icy stare on Phoenix.

"So, let's talk about you."

© © © © ©

The smell of sweet citrus woke him and Shaun rolled under the bed sheets. He'd forgotten to take the iTacts out and they blurred his vision as he looked at the old-fashioned wind-up clock sitting on an end table next to the bed. It read: 9:10.

He wasn't quite sure if it had been a dream, but Phoenix had been in bed with him during the night and they'd made love. He sniffed the empty pillow beside him, hoping that it had been real.

He sat up from the bed in a spotlight of sunshine that entered the room through windows on three sides. One of the windows was open and a cool breeze caused him to grab his bare shoulders. He stood in his underwear and walked to the open window but, though cold, didn't close it because Tony was sitting and flapping on the sill, and because his attention was consumed by what he saw outside: the Greenbrier River. He immediately reached up and massaged one eye as the bedroom door opened and in walked his father. Shaun gasped.

"Just checking to see if my young man is doing okay." His father hadn't aged a day since the last time he saw him twelve years ago. "Your girl. She's a beauty."

"Dad?" Shaun said. "How can it be? You died."

His father was a grown up, splitting image of Shaun. "Did I? I went missing. I disappeared. But now, I'm back and we've got a whole lot of catching up to do."

"But they said…"

"*They*…were wrong. Now, go ahead and tidy up a bit and I'll be back for you. I've got a couple of kayaks from Jenn's lined up along the Greenbrier just waitin' for us."

Shaun couldn't find his breath. He wobbled over to the bed and dropped into a sitting position as his father left and Phoenix entered. The room filled with the swell of oranges and lemons.

"Shaun," Phoenix said. "Take the tacts out." She walked over, shook his shoulder and clapped her hands. "Shaun!"

Shaun looked up to see Phoenix pointing at her eye. He plucked his left iTact out and closed his right eye. The entire room transformed from a riverfront bedroom to a peeling, whitewashed room with one window, a bed and an end table. Phoenix's attire also changed from a cloth robe to the jeans and shirt she'd worn since Green Bank. She held her dolphin jacket in one hand and sat beside him.

"Listen to me," she said. "We've got to get out of here before that woman comes back. She's got you all…convinced. They wanted to do it to me but my uncle stopped them. He really isn't their double agent. He's ours."

Shaun felt too woozy to completely comprehend. Blinking didn't help much either but he couldn't help it. He was sitting in two separate realities and wasn't quite sure which one was real. He closed his left eye because he preferred looking at Phoenix in a robe.

"Shaun!" Phoenix shook him again. "We've gotta go."

"Why?" Shaun mumbled and smiled. "Didn't you like last night?"

"That wasn't me, Shaun. That was Winston's girl."

"Yeah…Shaun Winston's girl…his guarded body." Phoenix tried to pull him up from the bed but he resisted. "What? Where we going?"

"Dr. One's secret lab."

"He said he didn't have any."

"He planned all of this just like J.J. said. Unfortunately, J.J. and many of his connections in the City were sacrificed to hide his real intent. My uncle used all of us to deceive the Feds for the sake of the Movement. He wants us to flee with him and all of the evidence to a secret lab that he really does have."

Shaun laughed, loudly. "Right! He's such a liar!"

"Shh!" Phoenix hushed. "Get your clothes on and meet me in the park."

"Don't you want to stay here with me?"

"Hurry," she said and rushed from the room.

Shaun yawned and looked at Tony that still sat on the open windowsill, gently flapping. He blinked and Tony remained as the only other thing in the room that was as real as he was. Phoenix returned and sat beside him. Oranges and lemons consumed him. She stroked his lips and kissed his cheek.

"Your father said he'll be ready in about thirty minutes which gives us a little time for…"

Shaun turned from the window, thinking that Dantana looked a lot more like Phoenix when both iTacts were in. In his periphery, he saw the tiger-striped monarch butterfly from Marlinton take flight. Tony flapped for a few seconds as if waiting for him to choose then dipped down and flew out the window.

⊙ ⊙ ⊙ ⊙ ⊙

Two new residents moved into Marlinton the day after the Memorial Day weekend rush departed. This was not uncommon. After spending a few days in the rural West Virginia climate, city folk often sold out their busy, controlled lives to plant new roots in the untamed.

Rumor was that they were a grandfather-granddaughter couple from New Pitt who had moved into a secluded house up on the hillside across the Greenbrier. The grandfather owned land up there. It was said he had some kind of family history in the area.

A full month passed before either of them ventured into town. Jenn had just opened her café for Wednesday morning breakfast when the granddaughter asked to be seated.

"Are you Jennifer?" the young woman asked. When Jennifer nodded, the woman added, "Does

Shaun Winston work here?"

"He does…well, he did up until a month ago. You a friend?"

"Yes," the woman said. "For a short time, he was a really good friend."

"He's a good worker, too. He must have gotten sick of the country life and did what all of our young men do. His mother says he's up in the New City with a good job in computers of all things." Jennifer stepped back. "Do I know you? Did you go to school here? You look a little familiar."

"I've heard that I look like a lot of people." The woman picked up a menu and continued without reading it. "Do you think he'll ever come back?"

"Honey," Jennifer said. "That's an easy one. Eventually, they all come back."

"No matter what you look at, if you look at it closely enough, you are involved in the entire universe."
— Michael Faraday

Become a Part of the Author's STORY

Share your thoughts on the NET

www.ingramcontent.com/pod-product-compliance
Lightning Source LLC
Chambersburg PA
CBHW072200130726
47910CB00011B/1719